Foreign

Foreign

a novel

SONORA JHA

4891

RANDOM HOUSE INDIA

Published by Random House India in 2013

1

Copyright © Sonora Jha 2013

Random House Publishers India Private Limited
Windsor IT Park, 7th Floor
Tower-B, A-1, Sector 125
Noida 201301, UP

Random House Group Limited
20 Vauxhall Bridge Road
London SW1V 2SA
United Kingdom

978 81 8400 282 9

Typeset in Minion by R. Ajith Kumar

Printed and bound in India by Replika Press Private Limited

For sale in the Indian Subcontinent only

For Sahir

Contents

Contents

1

'Indian Children Don't . . .'

IN A ROOM with perfect acoustics, she doesn't hear her smart phone ring. Sixteen missed calls, and then one more—from someone whose heart is pounding at the other end—assemble themselves urgently under the machine's command of silence.

Meanwhile, the smart phone's owner says into the auditorium's microphone, 'And that is why, my friends, you must join me in hoping that tomorrow, President Obama slips on a banana peel.'

The rumble of laughter tells her she has just added around twenty more people to the line that will form in the auditorium's foyer for the sale and signing of her book. In her years here, she has concluded that Americans like nothing more than laughter. They especially like it when foreigners can touch the American funny bone. In Seattle, thank goodness, you can be more satirical than slapstick.

As she answers questions, she looks over at the one vacant spot in the audience. They could have filled that seat too, but she wanted to keep it open, so she could imagine Kabir there. What would he have thought of this evening if he were here instead of visiting her parents in Mumbai? He would have kept his face frozen, his eyes sardonic. People laugh too easily, he would say. And you, Mom, go for the low-hanging fruit of their ill-developed humour.

In the seat next to Kabir's, though, is a smiling face. It belongs to a man named Alec Rauland, who is grinning because he loves her and because this is her big moment. He may not agree with a single word in Dr Katya Misra's *It's Racist Not to Laugh at Obama: Why Caricaturing the President is Important to Politics*, but he's the one who cooked delicious meals for her and took Kabir skiing while she wrote. He's the one driving her home after tonight's wine reception.

Sixty-seven books sold tonight, and she's a hundred steps closer to tenure. The dean is here and so are the key members of the rank and tenure committee. The book should undo some of the damage of the letters that lie screaming in her tenure file. Two of these letters declared that Dr Katya Misra is 'not a team player'. One went so far as to use that most damning of all words in American academia, that single adjective of intangible yet fatal potency that had seen many an otherwise tenurable head roll: Uncollegial. Nobody quite knows what the word means except that it means 'no tenure'.

The other thing she knows is that the word came up a few times during the proceedings of the Ethics Committee that she set into motion against the department chair, whom she had accused of sexually harassing a female student. It turned out that her accusations were proven false, by everyone including the student involved and by the campus newspaper. Dr Katya Misra offered a written apology to the department chair for the distress caused; Dr Katya Misra was generously let off the hook with no more than a written word in her file: Uncollegial.

So, she's now done the collegial thing and invited all these disenchanted people to this event with a personal, hand-written, hand-delivered note on 100 lb recycled white smooth matte cardstock ivory-coloured paper. None of the people on the tenure committee has actually bought her book, but that's only to be expected because she has a signed copy waiting for them in their campus mailboxes. The department chair's copy is wrapped in luxurious 60 lb white textured litho paper with an embossed image of dragonflies working together—as a team—to lift up a daisy.

Katya walks around the foyer, generously receiving all nods and smiles thrown her way. People are dressed rather well tonight, for a city as badly dressed as Seattle. Men are in suits and women in dresses. The aging hippies are here too, thanks to some keywords in the book title.

She swims in and out of conversation over her glass of merlot and her favourite hors d'oeuvre—apple-wood-smoked Anjou pear wedges wrapped with prosciuotto and gorgonzola. She can't eat gorgonzola at home, because Kabir is lactose-intolerant. But if he were here, he would have eaten these anyway, because he is fourteen years old and doesn't care about this thing called 'consequence'.

She looks across the room and sees Alec rapt in conversation with someone. Is that Dr Elaine Steinberg? No, it's Alicia McKinsey, the department's administrative assistant. So, even Katya's fabulous book will not have her faculty friends engage her blue-collar fiancé in conversation. They still wonder what Katya could possibly have in common with a cop from the Seattle Police Department.

Katya knows that the word on the street is that the only thing she has in common with Alec Rauland is that he, too, has a bit of a bad rap. Well, maybe more than just a bit. Six years ago, Alec Rauland shot a Native American man in the shin, on the suspicion that the visibly agitated man was wielding a gun and planning to aim it at a barista in a coffee shop when the barista declined to give the man some money. Turns out the man was asking for coffee. The barista was, yes, turning him away, but the man was only reaching into his pocket for a recyclable coffee mug, not a gun. The trigger-happy Alec Rauland was placed on administrative duties until authorities completed their investigation and reported their findings to the King County Prosecutor's Office. The police chief stuck his neck out for Alec Rauland, who had an otherwise stellar record. The Native American man was paid a large compensation and his medical expenses and subsequent care were taken care of. Alec Rauland apologized and was reinstated. But there was a report in his file.

Katya has also heard that some of the discerning intellectual minds around her believe that Alec Rauland is with this Indian woman as a form of atonement, albeit with the wrong kind of Indian. If she believed that for a day, she would at least get a good laugh out of it. But, no, Katya knows that Alec and she have something that goes deeper, so deep that she can't reach all the way in and turn it into words that she may then say out loud to explain herself to Dr Elaine Steinberg.

Explaining herself, picking an identity and playing into it, would make it all so much easier. But she knows better than to fall into the trap of 'belonging'. Just when you think you do, someone shows you that you don't, or lets you go, or, worst of all, tells you you are free to leave. If rugs are so easy to pull from under your feet, it's best not to stand on rugs at all.

Katya moves closer to the dean, who has looked over at her a few times with a congratulatory grin. On her way, Alec reaches out his hand towards her, but it's too far away for her to squeeze, not if she wants to get a word in with the dean before he leaves. She throws Alec a grin instead. She can hear what he's talking about. That same story, about the first time they met, because that's always the question most people ask him at Katya's university events.

'She was jaywalking, crossing the street right in front of my car. I turn on my police lights and she looks right at me with those gorgeous brown eyes of hers. She doesn't miss a step and goes right on walking. I'm sitting there, shocked at this woman's nerve. I get out of my car, and as I approach, she starts saying all these things in gibberish. Later, I find out it's Hindi, right? But there I am in the street, looking at this woman in her figure-hugging skirt-suit and her high-heeled boots, yanking my chain, trying to make like she's fresh off the boat and doesn't know American pedestrian laws. Or how to speak English.'

Alicia's laughing and she claps her hands. It's a good thing Kabir isn't here. He hates when people do that. It's overkill, he says.

But Alec seems to feel encouraged. 'And then, even though there are all these people watching, I just stand there and ask for her name and I let her go. No ticket. A week later, I still can't get this beautiful woman out of my mind. It was the way she walked, you know, like she owned the street she walked on. So, I find out she's a professor here at the University of Seattle and I call her and ask her out to coffee. Then I find out she actually thinks she owns the whole world. That's enough for me in a woman.'

'Did you run a background check on her through your police department?' Alicia is asking, but Katya doesn't linger to listen. She is now almost by the dean. Someone steps in to shake his hand. She can't just stand here, looking unoccupied. She fidgets for a moment with the buttons on her white cashmere cardigan and irons out an imaginary crease in her black pencil skirt. She reaches into her purse for a discreet glance at her phone.

Seventeen missed calls.

She scrolls quickly through the list of numbers. Each one sends her heartbeat right into her ears. 91-98202-745 . . . her mother's cell phone in Mumbai. No voicemail. Something's happened. Something that can't be said in a voice message.

She's in the corner of the foyer now, has made it here to this quieter spot somehow on the legs she cannot feel. As her call lurches into space, Alec is bounding over and she can see on his face what her own must look like.

Her mother answers on the first ring. 'Hello? Beti . . . he's gone. He's run away.'

'Who?' she asks, dumbly, even though she knows exactly who her mother is talking about.

'Kabir.' Her mother's voice breaks. She has been crying. How long has she been crying?

'How long ago?'

Her father takes the phone now. 'We woke up this morning and found his letter. It says, "Please don't try to find me. I will be fine. I love you all. Tell my mom not to come after me."'

Kabir's handwriting flashes into Katya's head. He needs to work on his handwriting.

'We have alerted the police,' her father is saying. 'They came and took down a report but they . . . they said Kabir will probably just get scared and come back. I am not waiting for that. I am phoning all the higher-ups. Any idea where he could have gone?'

Does she have any idea where Kabir could have gone? How could she? She cannot even picture him in India, in the neighbourhood she grew up in. She cannot even imagine the shape of her child in the streets of her hometown. If he had gone missing in Seattle, she would know exactly where to look.

Why had she let him go? Why did she let him convince her that he should re-connect with India and spend more time with his grandparents? Why didn't she just say, 'No, let's sit down and watch the BBC documentary on India. No, let's just continue to Skype with your grandparents once a month'?

Her father clears his throat on the other end of the line, drawing her back to his question. 'I have no *fucking* idea where he could have gone,' she says. Some people are looking over now.

Alec is taking down notes. What on earth could he be getting from this conversation?

Her father is silent on the phone. He's probably offended by her use of the F-word. Christ. Is this the time to be offended by her *manners*? And isn't it too late to be disapproving of her ways? Besides, where had she learned these ways, anyway? In that home from where her son was now missing. In that home, where her father threw blows at her mother and sometimes at Katya, blows and scalding words. Katya was just using similar words in another language.

'Daddy?' she says.

'Yes?'

'Did anyone . . . did you or Mummy say anything to him? Did anyone scold him or something?'

As soon as she's said it aloud, she realizes it sounds ludicrous. Of course they didn't scold him. They adore that boy. They were thrilled that he was visiting them, for the first time since he had left India as a baby. And even if they did scold him, Kabir is sardonic, not sensitive.

'No. We had a fine dinner at the club last night. He enjoyed playing Tambola. He ate fish fingers and biryani and ice cream. This morning he was gone. He's taken all his things. He took the local cell phone we got for him but he is not answering it. It's switched off.'

'How much money does he have? He can't go too far with what I gave him.' She can't believe that her brain's frontal lobe is still in charge when her body has turned cold.

A pause. 'Your mother and I . . . we gave him . . . he said he found out someone was selling Schwinn bicycles in Mumbai . . . we gave him the money.'

'Great. Good job. So my son has run away and he has money to go God knows where and do God knows what. Please! Why aren't you on the streets, looking for him?'

Alec is gesturing at her. He asks a question. Katya nods and repeats it into her phone.

'Daddy? Did he make any friends in Mumbai? Was he hanging around with anyone?'

'No,' her father says. 'In fact, we introduced him to Brigadier Mehra's grandson who is also visiting from America and the two of them went bowling one day but that was one week back. Kabir said he was bored and didn't like that boy and called him a suburban jerk . . .'

Her father was rambling. He did this when he felt inadequate.

'Daddy, listen. Please call the sheriff's office . . . I mean . . . the commissioner of Mumbai police . . . who is it these days? No, wait. I will make the phone calls from here. I'll call journalists. You call whomever you can. Give them his photograph and detailed descriptions. Oh God! Daddy, he doesn't know anyone there. Kabir doesn't even know the language. Not even Hindi. All he has to do is open his mouth and they will know he's American. He's a sitting duck for all kinds of . . . *where could he be?*'

Her mother is back on the phone. 'Beti, we will find him. We are driving to every place that he knows. We have sent all the servants out and our friends are also driving around. But . . . please tell me one thing . . . was he angry with you or something? He mentioned you got engaged to this Alec fellow? Is there any reason Kabir would want to run away from home?'

'What? No! He *loves* Alec.' And then, 'He ran away from *your* home, not mine.' She regrets this immediately. She can't alienate her parents now. She needs them. She needs to be a dragonfly lifting a daisy.

'That is nonsense,' her mother is saying. 'He was perfectly happy here. He *wanted* to come and visit us, you remember? God knows why you took him to America in the first place. Now this. This would have never happened if he had grown up here. Indian children don't . . .'

A tap on the touchscreen, and her mother's voice is no longer in her ear. But now she's here, facing a roomful of faces, almost all white-skinned, looking over with solicitous expressions, Alec holding her arm, and the dean walking over because Alicia seems to have alerted him, and all that she can think of is that single empty seat in the auditorium, which should have been filled with a brown-skinned boy with big eyes and electric-blue braces and long fingers and shaggy hair that he wore almost down to his shoulders.

In the hours between driving home to get her passport, throwing her things into a bag, and getting her to the airport, Alec has already asked her a million questions, filed a police report for the missing Seattle boy, and made a number of phone calls to people who can make phone calls to the police in Mumbai. He has scoured through the strangest things in Kabir's room, taken pictures, and taken the boy's desktop computer to have it raked and hacked for clues to Kabir's plans. He has Kabir's school telephone directory to make calls to every classmate and their parents. In the middle of the night, he has already talked to Will and Owen and Matt and Madeline, and each one has said they don't have a clue about where their friend might have wanted to go. There's nothing unusual on his Facebook page. The last entry, they say, was twenty-three days ago: 'Landed in Mumbai. Frickin' awesome.'

'Are you sure I can't go with you?' Alec asks Katya for the nth time.

'Yes. I am sure,' she says, throwing pants and shirts and toiletries into a carry-on bag. 'I don't want it to get complicated by taking you along. I haven't been there in almost fourteen years. I don't know what to expect.' She pauses and looks at him. She sees a man, her fiancé, his face open and loving and vulnerable, aching to be for her what she needs him to be. Yet, this fills her with a dreaded loneliness, as if his being here for her in this way is itself a harbinger of abandonment.

Her legs are suddenly filled with a swirl of blood pumping in them, pushing into her limbs an aching desire to bolt. 'If I need you, I will call. I promise,' she says. It's as if her words have been programmed into her and are playing on command.

They manage to book her on a red-eye to Newark airport but getting on the flight from Newark to Mumbai will be difficult. She will wait at the airport, sleep there if she needs to.

Her flight out of Seattle isn't for another four hours, but she can't bear to sit at home, where Kabir's room and all his things are threatening to pull her under, into that whirlpool of despair that tears can sometimes whip up around her.

Alec offers to drive her around the city. It helps him think too, he says.

Katya finds her eyes squinting against the rightness of the rain on the windshield and the passenger window, searching the streets of Seattle, as if by some strange warp in time and space Kabir will walk out of Dick's Drive-In, stuffing his face with a cheeseburger, or wave out at her from the crowd at the #2 bus stop in Lower Queen Anne, or duck out of her view to hide among a group of buddies heading to a forbidden music concert at the Vera Project.

He's nowhere. The windshield wipers function with precision. They leave no room for doubt, no shape or shadow uncertain. She wants to rip them out of the car.

She turns her face away from Alec's line of vision and trains her eye on this city in which she has taught herself the joys of invincibility. The greyness of Seattle has never bothered her. The clouds, no matter how low they hang and hover on your shoulder, have always been reassuringly dense, impenetrable. Tonight, they seem to creep closer and reach in with their icy fingernails of thin rain, tapping on the tops of people's heads and on the cracks on the city's sidewalks, as if to ask with shivering urgency, 'Where is Kabir? Where is Kabir?'

The car is halted in a traffic jam. They are on State Route 99, on the Aurora Bridge. Traffic is usually smooth here, even though people love to look out at the spectacular views of Lake Union under and around them. Often, when she has driven over this bridge at night, Katya has imagined that the swooshing echo of traffic is really the sound of a raging ocean. Tonight, though, the sounds are more guttural, of engines idling as drivers stick their heads out of their windows to look for the reason for the traffic jam. The air and the asphalt before them are awash in an eerie red, from the rear lights of stalled vehicles. Alec turns on his police radio and makes enquiries. A minute later, the tired voice of an operator tells him that a few cars ahead have stopped or slowed down to look at a display of some sort on the side of the bridge.

Alec frowns. Katya wants the car to move, but she would rather not have it move towards something disturbing. When their car draws closer to what every passing vehicle is slowing down to look at, on the passenger side's view, the display at first looks unremarkable. On the grilled iron barrier at the side of the bridge is a bunch of silver-coloured balloons rising into the air, helium against rain. Underneath it, pinned against the grill, is a bright-orange down jacket. It looks like it would fit a teenage boy or girl. Next to it is a sign on bright-yellow construction paper, covered in plastic to shield it against the rain: 'Joey, we loved you, but we never understood.'

'Don't look,' Alec says, just before Katya pieces together what she is looking at. It's a tribute to a dead boy.

Facts assemble themselves in her head. Aurora Bridge is the deadliest bridge in this country after the Golden Gate Bridge in San Francisco. This is where the people of Seattle come when they want to throw themselves to their deaths with a steep fall into the freezing lake. Numbers begin to come to her head, from a news report from a former student of hers who is now a crime reporter for the *Seattle Times*: more than 200 suicides from this bridge. More than five million dollars spent to create the grill barrier around the bridge to prevent the suicides.

When did Joey die? That barrier was built to be insurmountable, so it must have been a few years ago. Was today his death anniversary?

The car picks up a 40 mph speed again, but her thoughts don't turn the corner with it. The bridge has turned from beautiful to bleak. They are now driving by the cheap strip motels. Marco Polo Motel. Blue Video. These are the places you would walk by on your way to death. These are the neon-lit, unsettled, business-only, cash-transactions-preferred milestones of alienation that would mark your tread towards the best spot for your plunge.

Alec is trying to talk to her, but her thoughts are louder than his voice. This city has a high rate of depression suicide among its teenagers. Oh God. Was Kabir depressed? Would she have known if he was? Would she have seen the signs? Was she so busy with her life—so busy not being a team-player—that she wouldn't see the signs? Had he grown more silent recently? Yes, hadn't he withdrawn to his room, lost himself in his reading and his video games? Hadn't his friends' visits grown few and far between? Were these just normal things for a teenage boy or were they signs of melancholy?

Where might she have gone wrong? What might she have denied him? Was she so far away from his inner world that he would not know if he could speak to her? In their outer world, they laughed a lot, went to the movies, had his friends over, paid the fees for his drama classes on time and upgraded his snowboarding gear with regularity. Did they have an inner world together? Did he feel he could halt his mother with a tug on her elbow and say, 'Mama, could we please stop laughing? I am sad.'?

Katya's breath starts to get shorter. She has felt panic before, even this particular strain of panic that is a mother's curse, but she has always had the object of her fear, her child, at hand or close enough to coax and correct her way out of panic. Now, he's gone. *Where could he be trying to go?* A thought starts to come to her, a thin line of thought, a speck that hints at taking her not merely towards her child's journey but maybe to his possible destination. In the next instant, her hand has reached out and turned on the radio. Bill Moyers is speaking about the lowered expectations of the American electorate. Or some such thing. It's all quite comforting to her.

Yet, Alec seems to sense the tightening of her skin. 'Tell me what you're thinking. Keep talking to me, Katya,' he says now, loud enough to seem like a shout.

She shakes her head. Then, because her head feels like it is still shaking after she's stopped, she speaks. 'Do you think Kabir was sad about something? You know? Depressed?'

Alec looks over at her. 'No,' he says, plainly. 'Kabir is the most well-adjusted kid I've ever known.'

'I don't know if that's true. How do we know?' she says, wanly.

'He's always been straightforward about what he wants. Remember the time he started at the new place for middle school and was worried that his classmates would be better than him at snowboarding? What'd your kid do?'

'He asked for snowboarding lessons,' she says softly.

'And remember what he did when some of the boys teased him about being so interested in the theatre?'

'He told them to quit the drama and get a life.'

'Yes. And don't go blaming yourself. You are his rock. He is a brick.' And then, a thought seems to come to him, for he swerves the car into a side street and drives determinedly towards an address in his head. Katya knows she should just wait.

Alec pulls over in a few minutes and stops the car. He is pointing at something. She looks in the direction of his finger. They are outside Kabir's elementary school. She is confused. Why has Alec brought her here?

He opens the door on her side of the car, takes her by the hand and leads her in the drizzle towards the front of the school building. He points to the ground. There's a brick in the ground with Kabir's name on it. A few years ago, the school had a fundraising drive and asked parents to buy a brick and engrave their family name on it. Although this wasn't the kind of thing that attracted contributions from her limited disposable income, something about having a brick in Seattle with the words 'Kabir Misra' inscribed on it had found Katya reaching for her chequebook.

Now, watching the rain wash her son's name cleaner by the second, Katya knows what she wants more than anything. 'I'll bring him back. I will find him and bring him back. He will stand right here on this brick.' The etch and groove of this engraved brick, and all its dirt within, is his home.

As Alec and she wait in line for her to check in for the flight to Newark, Alec scrolls through the missed calls on her phone, noting down the exact time of each incoming call.

'What's this?' he says.

Katya's brain snaps away from the image of Kabir trapped by pimps in Kamathipura. 'What?'

'This number. There are seventeen missed calls from this number. It has the same code as your mother's number. But it's a different one.'

Katya snatches the phone from Alec. 'Oh my God. It's Kabir's. It's the cell phone they gave him. He tried to call! I didn't notice it here. He tried to call me! Oh my God, three hours ago . . . he tried . . . while I was up on stage, soaking up all that glory.'

Alec is already calling the number. It goes into the automatic voice message system.

Katya shuts her eyes and looks away from the phone, her body starting to quake now. Alec tugs at her arm. 'Leave a message,' he says quietly. 'But don't tell him you're on your way.'

She gasps for air. 'Kabir! It's your Mama. Please, baby, it's me. Please call me back. I love you. I am going out of my mind, my son.'

The sobs have reached her throat and are crashing against her head now. Her voice turns unrecognizable. 'I don't know what you are doing, but, my love, please let me in. Please tell me what is wrong and why you ran . . . why you left. I am on your side. I am yours. I am no one's but yours. I . . . I have nothing but you.'

'Please, my baby. Please come home. We'll go to Red Mill Burgers. We'll go to Blue C Sushi. We'll go skiing on new skis. You can ask that girl Amy out to the movies. I mean, you can ask Amy out to the movies. I'll give you money to take her out. I'll . . . I don't know what else. I don't know what you want. I don't know what is going on in your mind. But I'm your mother and I want to know.'

She knows she is rambling. 'Please . . . okay, you don't have to tell me anything. At least call me and tell me you're okay. I will not force you to . . . you can do this all on your terms. Just, please, call me and tell me you are safe. You called me three hours ago. I'm sorry I wasn't there. I am so, so, sorry. Why were you calling, my baby? Did you want to come home? Please . . . call.'

The phone is now a vital organ of her body. When she reaches security check, she must rip it from her to place it in the bin. She will not switch it off for takeoff and landing, and she will count every minute of the hours she is up in the air and unavailable to receive her child's call. And she will definitely not take the Ambien that Alec has given her to get some sleep on the flight.

Kabir. Where are you?

As she gets in line for boarding and Alec pulls her close in an embrace, she says, 'That country . . . it has a way of swallowing you whole . . . if it's not spitting you out. Has it eaten my child? Is he alive? Oh God, Alec. Why was he trying to call me? Was he afraid? Had something happened?'

'You can't let your thoughts go there. Stay focused,' Alec says.

'Why didn't he leave a message? No message. That means it wasn't him. It was someone who has him and his cell phone. Maybe they asked him for my number and tried to call me for . . . ransom? To tell me he was . . . dead?'

Alec shakes his head. He squeezes her hands and kisses her. She knows he will watch her walk all the way out of sight and onto the plane.

In the six hours of the flight, she pictures, again, the streets of Mumbai. It would be daylight there now, and she hopes that the daylight in the visions in her head will lead to clarity. But her thoughts crash into one another and all the scenarios that she turns in her head begin and end on the doorstep of her childhood home. If she doesn't know what her son's quest is, how could she know his journey?

As soon as her plane touches down in Newark, she sees a message waiting on her phone. She is barely able to hold the phone in her hand as she listens to her voicemail. It's not from Kabir. It's Alec. Call me back, he says.

'Did they find him?' she asks before he can even say 'hello'. The flight attendant is frowning at her from across the aisle.

Alec says, 'No. But, listen. It's a good thing it's daytime in Mumbai. We put a call out for the whereabouts of his cell phone. Turns out they found the phone tossed in a garbage heap at Mumbai Central Railway Station.'

'What does that mean? Someone took him and tossed his phone away?' Words a mother should never have to say.

'No. It would have been unlikely that they would have found it so quickly or even bothered with our request from here. But thank God for coincidences. Listen. Someone called it in. Someone at the railway station called the local police in Mumbai because the cell phone caused a terrorism scare. They mistook it for a bomb device. But the same guy actually saw a teenage boy toss it in there. They sure don't take terrorism scares lightly there these days. So when we called the Mumbai police about that phone number, they already had it on their agenda.'

'Dear God. What?'

'Listen carefully and give me as much information as you can before you board the next plane. The guy told the police he saw the boy getting on a train that goes to . . . N-A-G-P-U-R. Does that mean anything to you?'

'Nagpur? They saw Kabir taking a train to Nagpur? Wait . . . they *saw* Kabir? Did he look okay? Was he on his own or was he in someone's custody? Tell me more!'

'He was alone. Apparently, he was seen tossing the phone

in a deliberate manner and getting on the train. This was just minutes after he called you.'

'Dear God. What's going on? Why is he going to Nagpur? No, no. That doesn't make any sense. Somebody has him. Somebody's taking him there. *Nagpur*? What the *fuck*!'

'Calm down, honey. Think harder. I have nothing from this end. No clues on Kabir's computer. That kid has deliberately wiped it clean. He knew what he was doing. He knew I would try and find leads on it. He's been working on this for a while, Katya. He probably tossed his cell phone away because he thought we might be able to track his whereabouts through its reception. He's trying to go to a place where he doesn't want to be found and brought back from. Think hard.'

'Nagpur. Why would my child . . . Oh God. Wait a minute. Nagpur is how you get to . . .'

'Get to where? Katya? Where is your son going?'

People are leaving the plane now, but she has to sit back down. She realizes now what it was, the thread of thought that had begun to form in her head a few hours ago when they were driving around Seattle. With the blood pounding in her head, she still can let the thread of thought now unspool itself fully, neatly. 'Alec. Kabir is trying to go meet a man he has never met before. He is trying to find his father.'

'His father? I don't get it. He's never . . . he doesn't ever mention him, does he?'

Katya is the last one left on the plane. The flight attendant is beckoning at her impatiently, pointing at the door, as if Katya didn't quite know where to disembark. With heavy steps down the aisle and with a voice that refuses to stay at a single pitch, Katya continues to speak. 'No. We haven't talked about him in years. That's why it didn't even strike me as a possibility. But that's the only explanation I can think of. I read somewhere a few years ago that Ammar is an activist in the villages of Vidarbha. Nagpur is the biggest town in Vidarbha.'

A pause. Then, 'Okay, so at least we know his plan,' Alec says.

The fear that had loosened its grip on her for a moment takes hold again. 'But a hundred things could have happened to him on the way. He could have been kidnapped. Assaulted. Raped. He doesn't speak Hindi or Marathi. He doesn't know his way around. He's foreign there.'

Alec says, 'He's fourteen. Also, don't panic, the police should be trying to find him now. He's probably moved higher on their list of priorities now that they think he is a terrorist. They have to rule out that he is a threat, right? I'll bet you they find him before you land in Mumbai. My guys are in touch with the police there and with your parents. I will swamp those folks with documentation from here, from his school and the police and every possible place of authority to show he has no terrorist links. By the way, does he?'

'This is not the time to try and make me smile,' Katya says, although a smile does threaten to mix with the adrenalin.

'He will be fine. The police are after him,' Alec continues.

'The *Indian* police,' she says quickly. 'You have high expectations of them. I doubt they're doing all the things you think they are. Their involvement is of no comfort to me. But if you hear anything, if they do find him, tell them I will pay whatever they want to let him be. No. Tell them I will pay double if they bring him back to Mumbai.'

'Pay? I don't understand.'

'This is the Indian police. You have to bribe them for everything. Oh God, I hope they don't beat him. Or worse. My baby.'

'His father. Won't he protect Kabir?'

'Who? Ammar? We will not refer to him as "his father". If we ever must refer to him, we will use his name—Ammar Chaudhry. He doesn't have a fatherly bone in his body. You know I don't like to talk about him. He rejected the very idea of Kabir fourteen years ago. Why would he help him now? This makes me sick. Right now, if my son isn't already dead, he is probably having his bones broken by the police. Or his heart, by Ammar Chaudhry.'

Alec grunts. 'Can you do me a favour?'

'What?'

'You must leave these thoughts behind on the plane when you land in Mumbai. You have a long and hard road ahead. You don't know what to expect.'

She needs those sobs now, but she is at a crowded airport, a really bad place to cry, yet often a place where you most want to.

'That country. It makes me feel weak. It turns me from Katya to Katyayini. How will I be strong there? I don't want to think about anything but Kabir's face. His hand. I need to find his hand . . . wherever it is . . . I need to hold it and bring him back. Oh God, Alec, please pray that I find him and bring him back.'

'You will.'

'That country has a way of shrinking you, snuffing out your spirit. Please pray that he and I . . . pray that we find our way back.'

'I will.'

'That country. That man . . . oh God, I don't know.'

'That man? Ammar?'

'Yeah. I don't know. It's just . . . he . . . he had a hold on me. All those years ago when he abandoned me and my baby. He has a way of . . . holding on. Even when he abandons you.'

'You think . . . you think he will have a hold on Kabir? On you?'

'No, no. NO! Oh God, please don't think . . . please don't. I am with *you*. I . . . am with you.'

Silence.

'Alec? You believe me, don't you?'

'You are *with* me?' Alec says.

'I mean . . . oh, come on.' *Why is he doing this now?*

'I don't see why you have to go. Kabir is going to meet his . . . the man who would have been his father if . . . '

'If he hadn't abandoned me and my unborn baby for his lofty and pretentious ideals of being an activist for some wretched people. *That* is why I have to go,' Katya says.

'Then let me go with you,' Alec says.

'Alec. Please. Don't make this about you and me. I have to find my child and bring him home.'

She can hear Alec take in a deep breath at the other end of the line. Then, he says, 'You're right. I'm sorry, Katya. This is not the time to reassure me. This is the time to focus. Be Katya. Be Kabir's mother. Be strong. Go find your boy. Bring him home. Bring him to us.'

Oh, the relief.

'I will,' Katya says. She had hoped to only have to deal with one human being there, her son. But now, the game has changed. His father has been thrown into the mix.

Could she do this? Yes, she could. Dealing with just two people among one billion in that miserable country couldn't possibly put this crippling fear in her step? She takes a deep breath and readies herself for pleading with airline officials to get on the next flight to India.

2

Father or Guardian of Meera Andhale

BAJIRAO KNEW GAYATRI was giving him her wordless approval.
All she had to do was brush her fingers over her nose ring and
clear her throat. How many years had it been since she first
thought of this way of nudging him down the right path? And
she did it now, almost imperceptibly, to indicate her excitement
over the possibility of finding a groom for their daughter here,
in the pages of a book at the taluka post office.

This was unusual, they knew. Finding grooms for their
two older daughters had been harder and had required more
favours, more travel and more money than he could ever make
again in his lifetime. More money than he could ever repay to
the moneylenders.

The back of the room of this post office wasn't the way
he remembered it. It was still stuffy and dusty and the walls
were still stained with paan spittle. But now, someone had
put a marigold garland on the postmaster's big desk and thus
this room had been turned into an informal marriage bureau,
and a handful of government log books had been converted

into registers thick with profiles of brides and grooms in the taluka who would participate in the mass wedding. The postal employee who offered this service in his after-hours was sitting there at his table, flipping pages at the rate of two minutes per profile. The people in line had two minutes to identify the groom or bride they were interested in and then they could meet the parents.

Bajirao had to struggle to use his wiry frame to create a few inches of space within which Gayatri, too, could stand with him in this long line. He strained each muscle in his body to maintain his footing among the huddle of other parents. The room grew more and more crowded and the lines were moving slowly. The electricity had been gone for hours and the summer heat wrung sweat out of everyone in the room. If breathing hadn't been so hard, someone would have fainted from the stench of the farmers' perspiration.

'Surname?' the man asked Bajirao when they finally made it to the front of the line.

'Andhale,' Bajirao said, almost breathless.

The man with the register looked up slowly and his lips curled outward like a bow with an unseen arrow. Bajirao understood the mistake he had made instantly.

'You bloody fool!' the man said. 'What are you doing in this line? This is for Brahmins only. You want a Brahmin groom for your daughter? You need a beating to be reminded of your caste?'

The people around them shouted and pushed. The kinder ones laughed and mocked with only their words.

Bajirao held his wife's shoulders and pushed her away from the slaps and blows raining upon him. He was used to this. But she should not have to see her man being beaten this way.

When he finally got away, he avoided Gayatri's gaze. How

could he have been so stupid? Now his carelessness had tainted her memory of this auspicious day. He removed her enquiring hand from his arm and ushered her to the other line. It was much longer. They would have to start their wait all over again, and this time it would be a few hours. But, at the end of it, they would find a young man who would take their lovely daughter away from the hell that was their life.

They spent the hours standing in silence among people of their own caste. The line was longer, the stench more intense, but at least they could stand easier.

And now it was their turn. Another man with another register beckoned them.

The man flipped the pages of profiles of grooms. Bajirao exhaled in relief when he saw Gayatri's fingers on her nose ring even in this crowded room. She had spotted the picture and profile of the young man that seemed a suitable match for their daughter. He heard the faint but decisive vibration in the cough in her throat. He could never miss it or mistake it, not even under the loud dance beat of the song playing on the postal official's transistor radio: zaraa zaraa touch me, touch me, touch me, zaraa zaraa kiss me, kiss me, kiss me . . . zaraa zaraa hold me, hold me, hold me . . . bin tere sanam iss jahaan mein . . .

'Father or guardian of Dinesh Deshmukh!' the postal employee called out in a monotone, in response to the feeble tap-tap-tap of Bajirao's finger over the black-and-white photograph that Gayatri had indicated as her choice. A stocky man with a well-groomed moustache, dressed in a clean kurta and dhoti and cap, stepped out from the crowd.

'Please meet the father or guardian of Meera Andhale!' the postal official shouted, pointing at Bajirao. Gayatri fumbled in her cloth bag and hurriedly handed Bajirao his topi, his cap. The postal employee pointed his chin at the couple of stools behind him, indicating to the men that they may sit down and conduct their conversation there.

❦

The river draws closer to the man and woman sitting on her northern bank, the spot where she exhales her coolest breath. The man is speaking softly, as if aware that, given the way the wind is today, voices could carry over the water. Voices, or smells . . . for his breath is heavy with alcohol.

The river knows this man and woman. The man has grown up on this shore and the woman first visited here as a girl. Her thin, dark legs had waded in and the water had met her at the knee. Unlike most children, this one stood quite still until someone shouted to her—Gayatri, it is time to leave.

Then, a few years later, the child had returned as a bride to live here, married to this man from this shore. They came here on their wedding day, strangers to each other, a boy and a girl throwing flowers and colours into the water on the instructions of a pundit chanting prayers. From then on, the woman came to the river every few days, to pray with other women or to wash clothes.

Each year, the river would help her clean four white cotton kurtas, four white dhotis and three cotton saris—green, yellow and pink. Every few months, there would be a white polyester shirt, brown pants and a red silk sari, and these the woman would not beat with a stick like the women did with their cotton clothes.

The year after her wedding, the woman started to bring the clothes of a baby and then of three others. For some years, she brought four school uniforms, one of a boy and three of girls— white shirts and blue shorts, and white blouses and blue tunics. White ribbons. Then one day, the boy's clothes came no more, and instead his ashes were strewn into the river—ashes with none of the smells that the river remembered on the boy's collars. The woman returned a few days later and for years brought her girls' clothes until they turned into saris and the woman was joined at the wash by her three grown daughters. The woman's hair greyed quickly, especially around her face, which grew browner in the sun of three successive droughts.

The river has helped this woman clean her family's hard work out of their clothes, readying the garments for more toil. The woman used very little soap. Sometimes, the woman came here, the way she had done as a child, to stand in the river, never deeper than her knees, always more still than the water itself.

So, today, the river draws closer, to listen. The man is drawing lines into the wet earth, finger-strokes on the river's head. The woman is smiling, looking only at the man, not at the lines or the numbers he is writing into the riverbank. The man sometimes joins her in her smile and slows down his explanations. But his smile never lingers, for he is telling her about a loan and a mortgage and the expenses for a daughter's wedding, and the low price offered for their cotton crop in the market. He is telling her about a man from the government and a loan officer at the bank and another man who is a moneylender who doesn't work at a bank and has rules of his own.

His voice falls when talking about these things but it rises again as he talks about a man he trusts, an activist. The woman, too, speaks about this wise, educated man who is going to get the farmers together and make the world listen to the stories of deaths in these parts.

The woman laughs every now and then and the man begins to almost sing between his puffs on his beedi. He speaks about how the world would raise its voice, the government would listen, and the farmers would get subsidies. They would be pardoned their crushing loans. And then this family could buy back its lost land. They would once again grow food from their seeds. He would have his woman grow old like a queen, the man says.

At this, the woman laughs a little louder, and her laugh turns into a cough, through which she says something about these days of the haldi-kunku being a good time for the arrival of fortune in the guise of a kindly stranger.

Neither the river nor its beloved woman hear the storm of thoughts in the man's head. The father of Dinesh Deshmukh had approved of Meera's photograph and nodded with deep interest at Bajirao's quick listing of Meera's accomplishments during her nine years of schooling and her subsequent years of housework. He had joined in Bajirao's excitement over the government's benevolence in organizing the mass wedding.

And then, the father of Dinesh Deshmukh had asked for a dowry. A very small dowry, he said. It should come as a relief to you, he said to Bajirao. You must have been setting money aside for years, to pave the way for your daughter's path to matrimonial bliss. The mass wedding was a wonderful thing, but age-old customs should not be tampered with. Tradition is tradition, especially in these troubled times.

The father of Dinesh Deshmukh had offered to be a kind man and wait as long as the morning of the wedding for the payment of the very reasonable dowry of fifty thousand rupees. Of course, the father of Meera Andhale was free to refuse the alliance and look elsewhere. And, of course, the father of such a fine girl would not shame the two families by talking about this delicate matter, this revered tradition, to anyone.

So, the river hears no such thing. And neither does the mother of Meera Andhale, who is the most beautiful thing in this man's life. This woman shouldn't know any of this as long as he lives. And he hopes with all his heart that she wouldn't have to find out in the event he is forced to die.

The father of Meera Andhale reaches into the damp cloth bag that he carries around with him. Among the mundane things in the bag—his beedis, a cloth to wipe the sweat from his face, and a small transistor radio on which to listen to broadcasts of the market price of cotton—is the sachet of pesticide that he had begun to keep close to him. It isn't merely for the purpose of keeping his crop alive. It is also for keeping the promise of death alive. It is meant for use in the event that he has to pour it down his throat, shut his eyes, and lie down on a stretch of land, land he still owned, anticipating the peaceful sensation of life oozing out of his pores, freeing his soul from the indignity of debt.

His wife asks him something, coyly, and he forces his attention back to her. What did you say, he asks her.

She repeats her question, 'Will we have shrikhand and poori at Meera's wedding?'

He laughs softly. 'Yes, we will,' he says. 'I know it has been a long time since you enjoyed your favourite sweet delights. You just wait and see how delicious that shrikhand will be—it will be made from the thickest curd and it will be rich with saffron and cardamom, maybe even pista. You can eat my share and I will watch you eat. You can get fat. I have always wanted a fat wife.'

She pushes him and he pretends to fall, his hands steadying himself upon the river's shoulder as they laugh together. Something shifts on the far corner of the river's shore, an acre away from the woman's cough. The river rushes her waters closer, gathering up her skirts to take a look as the woman rises and then the man.

A strange step falls upon the river's head. Not just strange but also foreign. He moves in a different way. He walks from his knees and his stride is uncertain. The woman quickens her step, urging her man to follow. And so they come upon a boy who stands before them and asks, in the strangest lilt of voice that has ever carried itself upon the air of this river, 'Ammar Chaudhry?'

3

'There's No Getting Around Death in Vidarbha'

PEOPLE JUMP OFF the many mouths of the train before it approaches to halt. Coolies begin to jump on. Startled by this and slowed in her reflexes by her years of living in unhurried worlds, Katya loses her footing and almost falls headlong onto the tracks beneath the train. But a large, greasy man who had until then disgusted her on this train journey, instantly grasps her upper arm in a vice-like grip and doesn't let go until her feet have scrambled their way back onto the floor of the train. The moment she is safe and gasping in relief, everyone around her goes back to what they were doing. The large man is gone. Saving a life, to him, seemed to have been nothing to pause over; it was all in a day's leisure.

It was a miracle that Kabir hadn't fallen off this same train two days ago. That boy had waltzed into this part of the world on the wings of a dozen miracles. From the information she had through the police on two continents, Kabir had arrived safely in Nagpur and had jumped onto a bus to Yavatmal and then a smaller bus to Pandharkawada town and then hitched a ride on a bullock cart and then walked around asking for his father by name. No one had abducted him or molested him or even robbed him of his Schwinn bike money. Her child had wandered in here and found Ammar Chaudhry in a village named Dhanpur.

And, unlike Alec's expectations, no police had been sent for him. A couple of phone calls, a battery of questions and a flood of paperwork from Seattle, all earned Kabir the stamp of 'Not a terrorist'. Katya was relieved, of course, but wondered what this said for the global war on terror. An American teenager named Kabir going missing and throwing cell phones into garbage heaps in railway stations, to her mind, ought to sound very, very suspicious.

So Ammar had not turned the boy away.

What must that meeting have been like? A reunion? No, a reunion implies that there had once been a union. But Ammar had refused to look at the baby, even when she had offered to bring Kabir to whichever village Ammar had fled to, claiming that the poor needed him. *I am meant to serve these people. I cannot stray from that path, and the moh maya of you and the baby will only make me weak. Your presence in my life will make us all vulnerable to attack in unfriendly places. Don't take me away from the people.*

Moh maya. 'An attachment to worldly illusion' is how he thought of their flesh-and-blood baby. And, for a Muslim man, Ammar Chaudhry sure could spew out Sanskrit. Well, the moh maya had found its way to his doorstep now, that is, if there *is* a door and a step to whatever hovel he is living in here.

The moh has no idea his mother is on the way . . . as soon as she can fight off coolies and little children who swoop down on her to beg for money, in competition with an old man with no arms or legs. She is glad she remembered to take off all her jewellery, even her engagement ring, and put it away in her purse.

She is glad to get off the train so she can breathe again, free herself from the scent of rust soaked in the vapours of urine. She is glad she hasn't brought any luggage. Her backpack, with her few light clothes, sandals and some knick-knacks, will do perfectly for this short trip. Her parents had bought her a return train ticket. And a one-way ticket for Kabir: Nagpur to Mumbai. They had tried to come along. She had nipped that swiftly in the bud. This whole thing had to be as free of drama as possible.

Everything that is industrialized around Nagpur looks so different from what she remembers from those years she had travelled in these parts as a reporter. But the outskirts, even in this drought they are reported to be having, are all earth, still all earth, at least from this distance. She looks up at the June sky. It is colourless in the blaze of the sun. She finds herself thinking of what it will feel like when the rain comes and human faces turn up to the first drops, like in all those years of her childhood, when she knew that the rain was set to fulfil its promise of khush haali, abundance to people across her country—farmers and children, stock-brokers and lovers.

Dodging people on the railway platform and hailing a taxi outside, Katya thinks of the line from her childhood English poetry books— '*Into each life some rain must fall.*' For years, not knowing the origins and contexts of the quote or of Longfellow's poem, she had believed that this spoke of good tidings—into every life must come an outpouring of joy. It wasn't until she had used this line in America—in her attempt to offer hope to a friend awaiting news of a long-overdue promotion—that her world turned inside out. In Seattle, where it rains nine months in a year, her Indian understanding of this Western proverb had been particularly hilarious.

But now, she is here, and she must leave before these misunderstood idioms reclaim her.

The taxi driver outside the railway station laughs at her demand that he drive her all the way from Nagpur to Dhanpur village. He drives her, instead, to a private rental car service. In their poky, air-conditioned office, sealed shut in its thick smoke of incense and decorated with pictures of locales of Venice and Switzerland (as if one could rent a private car to drive there from this very lane in Nagpur), she offers to pay them double if they will leave right away and make no stops on the way. She ignores the leers and the lingering looks of the men haggling with her.

The drive to Pandharkawada, the smallest town near Dhanpur, is a moving mass of dust. For most of the five-hour drive, the car is caught between a bus and a truck. The sound from the socket of wind between the bus and a truck turns up the pitch of her headache. Every now and then, she sees glitz on the highway—shiny, chauffeur-cleaned, Korean-built cars with laughing young people, mostly young women, dressed in short sundresses and huge movie-star sunglasses, hobo bags swung over their arms like the stars of *Sex and the City*. They pull over and take pictures of the gaiety of their road trips. Smooth, waxed arms and legs wrap around BFFs; lip-glossed smiles await tagging on Facebook. The cars don't detour from the highway.

Katya has forgotten how humid it can be in this part of monsoon-starved Maharashtra. The trucks on the highway raise a tornado of dhool-mitti. But at least this dust is clean, unlike the sooty polluted particles that rose into a thick mist in Mumbai when she landed last night. This, here, is the skin of the earth settling upon the skin of the sons and daughters of the land, even those daughters that this earth drove out with taunts of being an unwed mother. This earth kept her sons close, drew them deeper into her womb, bequeathing to them her inheritances. No son of hers would be ensnared by this earth. The landscape grows less concrete. Trees blazing with bright orange gulmohar flowers start to zip in and out of her sleepy gaze. Even as they drive deeper into the rural heartland, here and there, she sees ramshackle houses holding up towering television satellites. *So fucked up.* She nods off.

When she startles awake a half hour later, the paths are narrower and the crunch of dirt under the wheels of the car is loud. The roads are gone and the dirt tracks have no buses, only creaking trucks with men and women packed in them. Katya throws another thousand rupees into the bargain with her driver at the sight of a herd of goats that blocks the bumpy path ahead. The driver takes the money and then asks Katya to vacate the car.

Asking for directions in the village, Marathi comes back to her, startling her with its comfortable claim on her tongue. Ammar Chaudhry kuthay aahe? Where is Ammar Chaudhry, she asks the men and women upon each mile of walking. She reminds herself that her son has done this with fewer words and an unsure step.

They are at the cremation grounds, she is told. Ammar Chaudhry and his son are at a funeral. It's been years since she said his name out loud, and she has said it so many times in the past few days. It still comes as a shock now that she says it in a local tongue with its intimate lilt and hears it come back at her with such matter-of-factness.

A funeral? They know Kabir is Ammar's son? Which one of these pieces of information is making her palms clammy? A crowd gathers around her, which tells her she is getting closer to Ammar's stomping grounds. More people look interested, more people are staring at her openly. She knows she sticks out like a sore thumb, probably far more than her son had, with her cargo pants and white T-shirt and backpack, not to mention the salon highlights in her hair. But there's nothing she can do about it now. Sorry, dear people, for causing this stir in your universe, but I'll be in and out before you know it.

She follows the adolescent boy who has been dispatched to lead her to the cremation grounds. She tries to keep up with him on the stony, uneven ground and almost stumbles on the gravelly dips. *And Alec had said she looked like a woman who owned the street she walked on.*

Then, without a warning, the boy stops and points to a group of men standing before a raging fire. He puts his hand out to stop her in her tracks.

Right. Yes. Women are not allowed in the cremation grounds.

But the grounds have nothing but a suggested boundary, tacitly understood by those who belong here. She is standing but a few feet from a funeral pyre, looking right into the faces of a grieving family.

And there, with his back to her, is her son. She would know that head of hair and that stance anywhere, and it's just as well, because little else on him distinguishes the boy from the other males standing there.

But there he is, her son. Not missing. Not lost. Not kidnapped. Not raped. And not dead.

He is standing with his hands in his pockets, his shoulders holding themselves in a constant shrug. He is wearing a white kurta. He hates wearing kurtas or anything Indian. And now he's wearing a white kurta and standing there at a stranger's funeral? With Ammar Chaudhry?

With his father.

Kabir is standing there with a man he has clearly taken as his father. Her child's body and the back of his head have a . . .

relaxed . . . stance to them. He is nodding deeply and listening with intent to the man.

Katya realizes now how unprepared she has been for the sight of Ammar Chaudhry. Fourteen years have fallen upon this man and yet, apart from a slight stoop to his shoulders and a lot of grey in his hair, his body and the parts of his face she can see belong to that very man whose poetry and passion had made her world fall apart fifteen years ago.

She stands there, watching her boy and his father as they watch a dead man burning. With no wind to carry the flames, the blaze rises up in a vertical dance, aimed straight at the sky, as if pointing an accusatory finger at the heavens.

She wants to snatch Kabir away, but her sudden appearance is sure to cause a commotion and this is someone's father or husband on the pyre. She can hear a woman wailing on the other side of the grounds. Somewhere on the other side of Katya, the unwed mother, is a widow. The snatching can wait.

Under the midday sun, the heat from the flames is almost too much to bear. She can see Kabir flinch every now and then and she knows his skin must feel hot to the touch. Maybe if she stepped up gently . . .

'I have brought you here because *this* is what I do,' she hears Ammar say to Kabir. She almost stumbles back in her surprise at how far his voice carries itself. Of course. These are silent places. It is also startling how his voice hits her. It's the same voice in which she had first heard the verses of Mirza Ghalib.

'There's no getting around death in Vidarbha, and the sooner you see it, the less miserable you will be,' Ammar says to her boy.

Kabir nods deeply and then sits down in a squat on the ground.

'When you have seen these suicides and funerals long enough, you learn from the expressions on the faces of the bereaved how they are related to the man who has died,' Ammar says.

He points at a man standing at the front of the crowd. 'You will notice there are no women here, because women are not allowed at cremations. But you see that old man holding his turban in his hands and drying his tears? He's the father. The pain on his face, the way he is looking as if even crying is not worth anything—it is characteristic of a man who has outlived his son.'

Son? Katya's skin starts to turn cold before the fire. Does he have any sense of what he is saying? All this pain, all this sensitivity for strange people, and no sensitivity towards his own son? What is the purpose of this ridiculous lesson he is giving to Kabir?

Ammar speaks again. 'You see the other younger man, with the tears running down his cheeks but holding his face expressionless? He's the brother of the dead farmer. His thoughts are probably focused on how he will have to find ways to help out his dead brother's family. And the toddler he is holding tight to his chest? The child is struggling, because the man holding him is not his father. The boy doesn't know that his father's body is melting under flames and that the people around him are waiting to hear the skull crack. The child is crying with a full throat because all he knows is that this is not a good place to be in. And that something has changed about his mother at home. You need to know these things, my son. There is a lot of pain in this part of the world. And most of this pain is in these nuances that could escape an insensitive eye.'

'Why are they waiting to hear the skull crack?' Kabir's voice sounds strange, heavily American and almost deferential in this atmosphere of clear hierarchy.

Ammar throws a glance at him. Then, he says, 'It's the Hindu belief that it is upon the cracking of the skull that the soul leaves the body.'

She has had enough. Her boy doesn't need to listen to this.

Clearly, this is Ammar's way of preparing the boy for a soulless 'goodbye'.

Kabir says, 'Does it ever happen that the skull doesn't crack?'

Ammar starts to reply and then pauses. He squats down now and shuffles an inch closer to Kabir.

'I don't know if you are old enough for this, Kabir,' he says. Kabir looks like he is about to respond, but Ammar continues, 'But, in Vidarbha, as you can see from the cries of that orphaned child, you can age a decade in a minute. So, here's the answer to your very astute question: if the skull doesn't crack, the son of the deceased—or another male relative—must take a club, step up to the pyre, and beat down on the head until it splits open.'

Then, just like that, Ammar puts his arm around the boy's shoulder. His arm falls there with ease, as if it were familiar with this terrain, as if it had held these shoulders over the years as they grew out of their chubby roundedness into today's angularity.

'All right. That is *fucking* enough!'

Katya's voice rips out of her so hard that even the unseen widow stops wailing. Kabir jumps up from his squat and runs towards her and then slows his step as if his mind is reaching out to halt his reflexes. Ammar draws himself up slowly, but Katya's hand shoots out, palm raised, as if to say: Halt. Right. There.

'Mom!' Kabir says, 'What . . . what are you *doing* here? Why did you . . .'

She throws herself upon him and hugs him close. 'How could I not come?' she says.

'I'm sorry. I really am. I was going to call Nana and Nani and then I thought it would be a bad idea. I thought they would know somehow that I'm safe and you would . . .'

She holds him at arm's length now, gripping his elbows, like she always does, like they always do. Yes, just as she thought, his body is hot from being close to the fire of someone else's life and death.

'I would *what*?' she says. 'I would just go get a Starbucks latte and go on with my life?'

'No, no. That's not what I meant. I thought you would . . . understand.'

'Understand? I don't believe this. Understand what? That, without a word to me, you suddenly want to meet the man who . . . who . . .'

'Can't this wait?' Ammar's voice breaks into hers. 'Katyayini . . . this is someone's funeral.'

Katya turns her gaze to the man who began it all, the man who had, quite literally, thrown her all over the map, the man who brought upheavals. Behind him, a skull cracks and a soul finds its way to its gods.

☙❧

They ride in silence in Ammar's jeep. Nothing but silence is possible when you're being tossed around in the backseat while your boy and the man who sired him take the front. It's taken Kabir just two days of being here to slip into the skin of chauvinism. The child who had looked to her for every social cue now jumps right into the front passenger seat and she is now the watchful one, waiting for the right moment.

Thirty minutes go by and she's still staring at the back of two male heads. Kabir's she would recognize anywhere. But this man in the driver's seat, his curls are now looser, his neck wider. He catches her eye in the rear-view mirror. Her stomach falls, but that could just be the jeep going over a nasty bump in the road. No, she's wiser than that. That lurch is familiar. Those eyebrows in the mirror are frowning at first and they grow easy as she glares back. Nothing has changed. Katyayini's discomfort was always Ammar's release.

'Stop,' she says.

The word flies right back into her throat. No one hears her over the roar of a passing truck.

'Stop!' she says again.

'We're almost there,' Ammar says, looking straight ahead at the road.

'We're almost *where*? We'd better be heading to fetch Kabir's bag.'

Silence.

'Excuse me? Did anyone hear what I said? Stop the fucking car.'

Ammar slows the vehicle down but doesn't stop. They're in the heart of the village now, and people turn curious eyes upon their approach. Every now and then a man here and there bows and holds a single hand up to touch the middle of his forehead to greet Ammar.

'What is that? Some sort of Jedi salute that you have taught your beneficiaries?' Katya says. Ammar stays silent. Kabir says, 'Mom, why do you make *Star Wars* references when you haven't seen a single one of those films?'

The laughter of two males mingles together as if they had laughed together before. At her? Yesterday? What had Kabir told Ammar about his mother's present life? What had Ammar told the boy about her past?

This is ridiculous. This is not the way she had expected things to turn out here. This isn't some cosy family reunion. She starts to ask for the car to be halted once again, but Ammar is now already stepping on the brakes.

In the nearing twilight, they step out of the jeep and she grabs hold of Kabir's hand and pulls him behind her. She has spotted the perfect venue in which to show this young man where exactly he has arrived.

A group of women and girls is gathered around a water pump. At their feet are urns in steel and copper, lined up in two groups, one filled with water and the other empty. The women look over at Katya and Kabir. They nudge each other to be silent. Some of the girls giggle at the sight of Kabir, but not the girl who is working the pump with both her skinny arms. She stays focused and intent on her task, gathering the trickle of water, aiming it right into the neck of the urn so nothing is spilled. The sound of the pump going down in a thunk and up in a metallic whine makes Katya's pores pucker up on her skin.

But Katya is grateful for the sweat on the girl's face. She's tempted to fish out her iPhone and take just one photograph on its dying battery. But she's not here to take pictures. She's here to take her son home.

'Watch,' Katya says to Kabir.

'What am I watching?' Kabir says.

Katya taps the side of Kabir's head. 'Watch what she's doing. She isn't doing shoulder presses at the gym. She's sweating to get water for her family.'

'I see that. She's not pumping iron, she's pumping water,' Kabir says. He turns around to look for Ammar, who waves at him and walks away towards a group of brick houses. He walks into what looks like an office with a board outside saying, 'Vidarbha Bachao Samiti'. The Save Vidarbha Trust.

'This is where you are, Kabir. In a place where a boy or girl your age can take nothing for granted. This is not a vacation. You have run away from home to come to a place you think you can hang out in for a few days?'

'At least a few weeks,' Kabir says.

Katya takes a deep breath. 'Pack your bags. We are going home now.'

'No.'

'I beg your pardon? Did I hear you right? So, wait a minute. *This* is your rebellion? This . . . escape to the Third World? You couldn't just smoke some marijuana in Seattle? Flunk a class or two?'

'Maybe get a girl pregnant?' Kabir says.

Katya blinks her eyes. 'What did you say?'

'Oh, hell. No, God no. I didn't mean it that way . . . I was just going along with your stereotypical examples of . . . Mom, please.' He looks around him as the women gather closer.

'You think it's all so funny. Has that man told you what happened between us all those years ago? Has he told you how he seduced me with his poetry and his passionate activist crap and wooed me all over the streets of Mumbai and then got me pregnant and left me? Hunh? Is that what you laughed about with him?'

'What? Mom, nobody laughed at anything. I . . . I cried.'

Katya stares into his face. He doesn't look like he has been crying. He is lying.

'I tried to call you, Mom. I called you from the railway station in Mumbai because I was confused. I was scared. I didn't know where I was going and I didn't know how Baba would deal with me suddenly showing up here in his life.'

She feels something shift hard in her chest, as if someone has reached in and casually broken a piece out of her heart like rotting fruit from its tree. A flicker of a recent memory claims a frontal space in the lines of thoughts running through her head. It's the memory of her resolve from a couple of days ago, on those rain-soaked streets of Seattle, that she would *listen* to

Kabir, hear of his sadness, partake of any pain in *his* chest.

But, no, no, this is not where she must listen. This is not that place. They would stand by that brick with his name on it, on 7th Ave. W., Seattle, Washington, 98119. There, she would listen. This spot of rutted land here was just making her son say loopy things.

'Who the fuck is Baba?' she says.

Kabir sighs. 'Ammar. My father. He said I should call him Baba.'

'Well, you can say "bye-bye" to Baba in the next ten minutes. Get your bag.'

'I am not leaving. I want to stay. He wants me to stay. He said he didn't abandon you or me. All those years ago. He says he just didn't want to get married. He wanted us to live in Mumbai and he would visit and he wanted to play a role in my life. He didn't want you to take me and move to America.'

'Oh, he said that, did he? And did he say how he expected an unwed mother to keep face in India? Did he say how a Hindu unwed mother with a baby sired by a Muslim man should have asked her parents to understand?'

'Mom. He regrets it all. He . . . he wants me.'

She doesn't want to hear it, but it comes nonetheless, 'I want him. I want my dad.'

The sensation in her head is of her brain turning over, in a slow somersault, not dissimilar to the way her womb had felt when Kabir turned over in it. She knows it's just jetlag, but it's gripping her quickly. Her eyes start to shut everything down and she feels like she will fall to the ground right here, in a heap, by the water pump of an Indian village whose name she doesn't even remember.

Kabir reaches out to steady her arm. He says, 'Mom, I love you. But I must stay. My father needs me here. There are men dying. There's a frickin' suicide every eight hours. Look around you. This is Dhanpur, a village of widows and a few men standing. Baba is doing cool stuff here. He's *helping*, you know?'

Katya inhales sharply. Hearing Kabir say the word 'suicide', so soon after that night on Aurora Bridge, feels like she is standing pinned against that grill barrier and it's coming loose against her weight, threatening to take her down into those waters. She feels suddenly displaced, neither on this ground nor on that bridge.

She must focus on what he is saying. She must respond to this rapidly escalating situation in which Kabir was finding a hero in the man she really should have raised him to hate. 'He's helping, is he? Where was his help when I almost lost you to those overzealous doctors when you were a baby? Where was his help when they misdiagnosed your sleep tremors as fits and insisted upon brain surgery? If I hadn't taken you to America then, your brain would have been mutilated so that some greedy surgeon could make money. Where was this man's help then?'

The women are hovering too close now. Some of them are whispering. One of these whispers carries itself into Katya's ear: Mulaa laa hyaa vayaat baapaachi garaz aste. A boy needs his father at this age.

Katya feels naked before these women and their sickening comments. How do they know her secrets? How do these eggs of shame travel so swiftly here and incubate in these dank spaces to hatch into gossip? She steps closer to Kabir and grips his elbows. He flaps his wings to shake her hands off as if they are water.

Katya stumbles. Behind her, the water pump stops mid-whine. Katya reaches out, grabs his arm and squeezes down on it. 'Listen, young man. He is not worthy of being called your "dad". He will break your heart. This . . . this hellhole of a village will make you sick. These people are damned. Ammar hasn't been able to change anything. These people haven't been able to change anything. They live and die like animals in a disease of their own creation. And they will pass that disease on to you. It's in their water, the water that the girl is pumping. They'll offer it to you with a smile and kill you.'

'Baba's bought me bottled Bisleri mineral water,' Kabir says. He's smiling, no, laughing, at her. But it's not his Seattle smile, not her son's laughter. His lips have the curl of a stray dog's.

Before she knows it, her hand has flown up and Kabir's face is reeling from her slap. And then another one.

A woman steps between them. The woman puts one hand on Kabir's face and pushes him gently away while with her other hand, she clasps Katya's flying, slapping hand. The woman's palm and fingers engulf Katya's like a dry, chapped leather glove.

This woman's face commands the concentration of all of Katya's senses. There's her nose ring. And the gaunt face, almost masculine but for its frailty. She has a countenance that could have been beautiful on another continent.

Her face is framed by grey hair, a few tendrils of which escape the bun drawn from a tight tug of symmetry between the centre parting down the woman's head. More than anything else, Katya's eyes are riveted by the streak of vermillion thick down the parting in the woman's hair, thicker than you have ever seen. It is rare in these parts. Maharashtrian women identify their marital status with the mangalsutra around their necks, not the vermilion in their hair. This woman seems to want to proclaim it. My husband lives. I am not a widow.

As her eyes meet Katya's, it's as if the woman's world splits itself wide open to view. Katya can see her sitting in the cotton field. Every day, she sits in a clearing and prays. When the rains don't come, she sits longer. Even the storms that rage in this woman's world are simple. She loves the cotton around her, she hates the cotton around her, just like she loves and hates prayer, for prayer holds expectation and disappointment in the inhaling and exhaling of the same breath. Prayers carry with them a sense of dread for the possibility of going unanswered, or, worse, mocked. Still, this is a woman who prays.

'This is Gayatribai.' Kabir's voice is shaking.

Katya looks over at him. His eyes are red, from fighting back hurt and shame. He is glancing at the girls in the crowd of women. He's just a teenaged boy whose mother slapped him in front of teenage girls. It's the same world.

Katya looks back at the woman who is standing between Kabir and her. The woman's hands are now over her mouth, covering a gasp as she realizes that her reflexes made her leap up and physically restrain this upper-class, English-speaking woman.

Kabir says, 'Gayatribai is the one who brought me to Baba two days ago. I met her and her husband by the river. I didn't know whom to trust, but I thought I could trust them. They were just sitting by the river, you know? They understood what I was saying. They brought me to Baba.'

Katya wants to say something to this woman who is now shrinking away from her, tugging on her earlobes in apology. Words in Marathi rise and collapse on Katya's tongue. She says nothing.

And then, the woman's gone. She's picked up her two urns, still empty, and hurried away.

Gayatribai. The boy should know that her name is Gayatri, because they know someone by that name in Seattle. But he has been here long enough to know that you add a 'bai' in these parts to show a woman respect.

Katya turns to Kabir. 'We leave tomorrow. Say your goodbyes.'

Kabir's mouth falls open. He tries to say something but it comes out in a high pitch and he stops. These are the months of his life when his voice teeters between a boy's and man's. He clears his throat and tries again. 'Please. Mom. Give me some time. Please. Give me . . . give me ten days.'

'And what will you do in these ten days?' Katya says. The thunk-and-whine picks itself up behind her.

'I will find . . . I will find my footing.'

Staring into the boy's face, Katya knows he has chosen his words with care. But she has no fucking idea what he means.

4

'Kids and Cows and Strangers,
All Come Home . . .'

AMMAR CHAUDHRY'S OFFICE is cluttered. But that is not the first thing Katya notices when she walks in. It's the man himself. He is doing nothing but standing there, leaning against his desk, watching her walk towards him, waiting, as if he has been waiting fourteen years in that very spot.

'Ten days,' she says, looking past him at a map on the wall, sprawled from end to end, ceiling to floor. The map has red drawing pins pierced all over it, in no clear pattern. 'We're staying for ten days,' she tells Ammar without looking at him.

'You are staying, Katyayini?' Ammar says.

'No, I . . . *we are leaving.* But we will be here for ten days. My son needs some sort of closure and I'll stick it out to give him that.'

'Closure?' Ammar says. He is biting the side of his lip, reining in a smile. 'It's such an American term. Life offers no closures.'

She doesn't want to take his bait. She will not try to answer for America. Not here, in this part of India. Not to him. This is the thing with people who stay back in this country. They develop this resentment towards those who got away. They tell you that you have become 'so American'. Tum to bilkul American ho gayi ho. And it's never intended as a compliment.

'Look,' Katya says. 'I . . . '

'I'm looking,' Ammar says. He takes a step towards her, running his eyes over her.

For just one moment, she is back there, in the Mumbai brothel where they first met. It was the summer of 1992. Ammar Chaudhry was holding a condom in his hand. She was a cub reporter sent by her newspaper editor to interview the idealistic young man who was working to raise awareness of AIDS in Mumbai's red light district, Kamathipura.

Sitting there, among the giggling prostitutes Ammar had managed to round up for a talk, he was demonstrating how a condom should be used. A sullen woman, who looked like she might be the madam of the brothel, was holding a banana onto which Ammar was unrolling the condom. Katyayini couldn't take her wide-open eyes off the spectacle—she had never seen a condom before. And bananas were her favourite fruit.

She had walked into this scene in the madam's humid living room. The madam hadn't allowed Katyayini to bring a photographer along, and her trepidation nearly made her turn around. She tried not to think of how she might easily be trapped here and forced into prostitution. No one would ever find her. She hadn't told her parents she was going to the red light area—why worry them? And the newspaper—would they send the police to rescue her?

Seeing this young man then, she had felt reassured. He was from *her* world, the urban world of writers and university graduates and English-speakers, people with clean beds that they didn't need to share with anyone they didn't want.

She often wondered if Ammar had always seemed more handsome to her because of the filth in which she had first seen him. In the midst of prostitutes who masked themselves with cheap make-up so they may look at least a little like the sexy Hindi movie stars on the posters lining the walls around them, Ammar looked like a film star himself, an inaccessible object of desire. Katyayini first saw his face in profile—angular, strong, his black hair long and tousled, ending just below his ears.

And then, he turned to look at her. The frontal view of his face was gentler. He smiled, and his eyes skipped quickly over her. Katyayini bit her lip, unsure of whether this might be her chance to speak.

'Salaam! You must be Katyayini Misra,' Ammar said.

Katyayini nodded at him, and then at the women in the room.

'Well, Katyayini I doubt that you could grant these young women the husband of their dreams, no matter how much they pray to you. So, I must teach them how to insist that their non-husbands use a condom.'

Ammar started to laugh by the end of his sentence and Katyayini joined in. His laughter, his laughing face, distracted her from getting his reference right away. It was only later that it clicked—the Hindu goddess Katyayini granted suitable grooms to women who turned to her in prayer. For these prostitutes, neither the goddess nor the journalist could do that. Condoms were the best things on offer.

She had spent the afternoon following Ammar around the brothel, watching him work, asking him questions and writing on her notepad so she wouldn't have to look into the yellowed eyes of the women around her. She had wondered how she must look to them, with her fairer skin and her simple make-up of lip gloss and eye pencil, her crisp white kurta filled with the highest grade of chikankari embroidery, delicate, intricate, meant to be worn in places where it would be assured of immaculate housekeeping, clean air, and spotless reputations.

But Katya today wasn't going to follow him around now, not in this land that would never take her as seriously as they took him. She wouldn't defer to decisions, not when she had known him to be a megalomaniac, always setting about rescuing this population or that. Yesterday it was prostitutes. Today it is widows. There never was any room for a wife.

'May I use your computer to book our plane tickets back to Seattle?' Katya asks.

Ammar hesitates and then steps aside so Katya can walk to his desk and sit down at his computer. Right there, next to his computer, is a framed picture she recognizes instantly. It's Kabir, dressed as Feste, from last summer's production of *Twelfth Night*, at the Young Shakespearean Theater Company in Seattle. The picture looks so out of place in this shabby office of musty files that Katya stares at it, confused for a moment. Did Kabir bring this here to give to Ammar? She looks closer. It's not a photograph, it's a coloured printout.

'What the fuck is this?' she says, pointing at the picture.

'Katyayini, you wouldn't let me stay in touch with Kabir. You wouldn't even send me a photo all these years. So I started looking for his name on the Internet. I found this in a review in the Seattle newspapers last year. It's the first and only picture I had of him. So, he is interested in theatre? In acting?'

His words are falling on the back of her head. By the time they get to the front, they have turned into questions. *Did he try to write to Kabir? Did he ask him to come here, to run away from home and meet him in this village?*

Ammar is still talking. 'He looks mostly like you, but he has my hair, my tastes and my manner. Na?'

Katya is still staring at the photograph, trying to find enough saliva in her mouth so she can swallow the scream that is forming in her throat. Nothing here belongs to her nor does anything of hers belong here.

Ammar fills in the silence. 'I wish you wouldn't use such bad language,' he says. 'Does that set a good example for our son?'

Those last two words hit the back of her head like a whip. Katya reels around, takes a deep breath, and speaks with as steady a voice as she can. 'You. Will never. Refer to my son as *our* son. And you certainly do not have the faintest right to tell me how to raise him. He is your seed. But he is in no way your son.'

For a second, she thinks Ammar is about to respond. But instead, he searches her face, and she is struck by how much anguish he is wearing in his expression. Just moments ago, she saw the same look on her son's face. But if she slips now, on the dark, downhill tracks of their despair, which lonely ditch would she land in?

She sits down at the computer, waits until it dials up to connect to the Internet, and then she counts to ten days later and buys two one-way tickets from Mumbai to Seattle.

She can sense Ammar watching her every click. She is quick to send her airline itinerary to Alec's email. She doesn't have the time to write Alec in any detail, but she knows he will understand.

Ammar is probably wondering if he can will her into turning around and looking to him for some sign of what she should do, like in those days long ago. As she prints out the e-tickets, he says, almost to himself:

Koyi mere dil se poochche
Tere teer-e-neemkash ko . . .

'Stop,' she says. 'Bringing Ghalib into this place and these times is tawdry, to say the least. It might have helped you get laid all those years ago. Now, and here, it's like masturbation.'

On her way out, she does not look over to see how Ammar has taken her comment. But her eye falls on the wall with its map and its unruly web of drawing pins, growing a bloodier red in the failing light. She does not have the time to find out what that whole thing with the red pins means.

Kabir is waiting outside like she'd asked him to. His feet are covered in cow dung. 'I stepped in cow crap,' he says. 'And I'm hungry. Where are we going?'

'I don't know. We'll find a hotel or a government rest house or something.'

Ammar's voice follows them. 'There's no such thing here. The town has a small motel, but it's a few miles away. And it has all kinds of unsavoury elements staying there. Things have turned dangerous around here. Low-brass government officials who try to find local prostit . . .' He stops, looking over at Kabir.

'I know what a prostitute is,' Kabir says, smiling. 'I'm not a kid, Baba.'

Katya looks away from them. This is the first time she has heard the boy address Ammar.

'I have sent a messenger over to ask the villagers to gather for a meeting. We will find you a family to stay with,' Ammar says.

◦◦◦

In the centre of the village, a crowd is huddled under the peepal tree. More and more people are arriving, despite the swiftly sweeping darkness of dusk. Ammar has asked Katya and Kabir to sit on the concrete platform that hugs and circles the peepal tree.

Kabir whispers to her, 'Architecturally, this place is a work of genius.'

Katya frowns. 'There's nothing architectural about this place. I don't know what claims of genius you might be projecting here.

53

Everything is random.'

'Exactly. But look at this platform. It's a bench that goes all around and uses the tree as a natural canopy. Look at that house there. It has the same kind of platform squared up all around the house. Kids hang out there and play. People stop and sit. They watch the kids. The kids watch them. A cow puts its front legs up on the platform and pokes its head into the window. See? Genius.'

'I don't see the genius in any of it,' Katya says.

'Exactly,' Kabir says. He sounds earnest, not cocky. 'Nothing seems to be quite by design, and so just about anything goes. Kids and cows and strangers, all come home.'

Ammar is waving everyone into silence, so Katya does not get a chance to respond to Kabir, which is just as well because she doesn't know what to say. The boy seems to be reading too much into his new surroundings, giving it a due that isn't this devil's to have. How long before the novelty is gone and the reality of failing electric supply and the stench of public excrement claim his youthful cheer? Three days? Four? The airlines might even let them advance their tickets to get out earlier. Meanwhile, these mosquitoes can only be helping.

Ammar says to them, quietly, 'I will introduce you both to the village. Then I will ask if one of the families here can host you. I will ask the woman of the family, not the man. There is also no better way to ask a woman for her assistance than to do it in front of her entire village, in the presence of her man, her neighbours and her elders. There is no better way to honour her and to free them all of any suspicion of force or favour.'

They like him, Katya can tell. They all fall silent as he raises his hand, even the children. They pull themselves up into attention.

Ammar speaks in Marathi. 'My brothers and sisters, I am touched that you are all here. As you know, some stories from my past have found their way into my present.'

Kabir nudges Katya. She translates Ammar's words for him in a whisper and then adds, 'If he says much more about these stories from the past . . .'

'Shhhh,' Kabir says.

Katya turns to strain against the disuse of a once-familiar tongue as Ammar goes on. 'This boy is my son and this woman his mother. Please allow us the dignity of not asking us to explain any more. They are here to . . . to . . . they are here because the boy wants to learn about his father, his father's work. I have said to him that to do this, he has only to look at this village. You are my life. You are my work. You have been my family for two years now. Today, I am asking you for something. It would not be right for the boy's mother to stay in my home. I do not want to insult our Indian culture by doing that. I would like her and my son to stay with one of you.'

A murmur goes up in the crowd. Katya tries to catch some of the words but they are not sitting close enough to the villagers.

Ammar continues, 'We will pay for all expenses. They will adjust to your home. The boy is well behaved and will not cause any trouble.'

Katya looks over at the crowd before them. Even in the deepening shadows, she can see faces rapt in attention, brows furrowed, lines falling into lines on weathered skins. A sweep of black-haired heads and a sprout of faces the colour of mud. She's peering into a human landscape from the past.

As if reading her thoughts, Ammar tells the people a little about her past. 'This lady's name is Dr Katyayini Misra. She doesn't look Indian any more, but I guarantee you she is Indian.'

For some reason, the crowd seems to find this funny. People join in Ammar's quiet laugh.

He goes on. 'She is from here, from the city, from Mumbai.

Some years ago, she was a journalist and she wrote about the problems of the poor in India, people like you. Even though she comes from an upper-class family, her heart is with those who struggle. She travelled with me to villages like this one and she got government policies changed with the power of her reporting.'

'Why did she leave?' a voice says from the crowd.

Kabir listens to Katya's translation of the man's question and then leans closer to her and whispers, 'Yeah, why *did* she?'

Ammar says to the crowd, 'Maybe she will tell you when she is a guest in your home.'

Again, a little laughter. Almost like the laughter in the auditorium in Seattle two days ago. But dissimilar. The laughter doesn't move outward but inward, into itself, as if the laugh was on the laugher.

'This is ridiculous,' Katya whispers loudly so Ammar can hear her. 'I can't believe we are sitting here waiting for someone's ...'

The crowd murmurs again. A man has stood up, far back in the gathering.

The man doesn't address her or Ammar, but the crowd. He says his wife believes that the boy and his mother will light up their home. If the guests approve of their hovel, he says, his family would be honoured to have them.

Katya feels Kabir's arm around her shoulder. 'I know that man,' he says. 'He is Bajirao. You met his wife a little while ago. They're the ones who ...'

'... took you to Ammar, okay, okay, I know,' Katya says, squinting into the crowd to get a better view of the standing man.

If a man could be said to have receded into himself, it could be said of this man, Bajirao. It's not that his body is frail or slight. It's just that he seems to ... take up less space than most men. On his head he wears the white topi that is customary in these parts. His jaw is wide and could have been considered strong if the rest of his features didn't belie it. If he had much flesh on his face, he would have jowls. Without those, his face seems to be just skin struggling to find a hold on its bones. His eyes are sunken into dark caverns carved out over sleepless nights. Yet, when he grins beneath his thick moustache, as he does now, looking down at the upturned face of the woman sitting by him, his face springs into fearlessness, even hope.

Kabir is looking at him, too, and now looks back at his mother and whispers, 'Let's not ask to see their home or inspect it or anything. Let's just say "yes", right here and now. Please.'

Katya turns to look at her son. She nods at him and then at Ammar. She looks at the man in the crowd and, instinctively, she folds her hands and bobs her head from side to side in a combination of assent and gratitude.

The man looks down again at his wife, who seems to be doing nothing more than adjusting her nose ring. He looks up from her face and speaks to Ammar and the villagers. He tells them he will not accept a rent. Things are bad in this village, but they haven't forgotten how to be hospitable. His ancestors would never forgive him. Taking money for giving the guests a roof over their heads would be more shameful than sending his daughter off to her wedding in tattered clothes.

A hum of consent has gone up in the gathering. Katya knows better than to protest. Oh, well. She would just have to find some other way of repaying this family for the couple of days of shelter. A gift for their home, perhaps, or a couple of saris for the woman of the house.

The same question comes at them from several people in the crowd: Will the boy and his mother stay for the big wedding?

Ammar turns to Katya. 'There's a mass wedding of hundreds of brides and grooms in the region. Two weeks away. What shall I tell them?'

'Tell them we are leaving in ten days or less,' Katya says. Ammar turns back to the crowd and tells them what she said. More murmurs. Then, Ammar starts to talk to them about something else. A silence falls over the crowd.

'Earlier today, I took my son to the funeral of Ganpatrao Kodolkar. We could hear his widow wailing and his infant crying just because his mother was crying. Apart from this crying, you and I . . . we are voiceless. The government can't hear our cries for help from deep within this well of poverty in which we are lying, almost dead, keeping our feeble eyes on whatever light we can find. As we crawl our way out of this well, we must find a way to tell our story. You know we have had small protests here and there, some rallies, some petitions to the government. These have convinced me that we must now find a stronger, louder voice, and shout and tell the world that we are rising, that we want to stay alive and make our crops strong again. Those of us that can, must sing a harvest song for those who can't sing any more.'

Apart from Katya's hurried whispers of translation to Kabir, there is not a sound in the crowd. Are they suspicious of him? Are they wary? A dog howls in the distance, but stops abruptly, as if startled by its own pitch amidst the quiet.

'So, my brothers and sisters, we will protest in a bigger way than ever before. In one week from today, on the day the chief minister of Maharashtra drives on that eight-lane highway outside our village, the highway that mocks the dirt roads of this village called Dhanpur, we will march in a rally of thousands and we will make the chief minister listen. Dhanpur can change the world. *Who is with me?*'

One by one, every single man in the village rises to stand.

They have to struggle to follow Ammar in the dark on the long walk to the home of their hosts. Ammar is carrying Kabir's backpack. Katya insists on carrying her own. After several quiet steps into the first mile of their walk, she nods at Kabir and he bounds over to Ammar to walk alongside him.

Katya finds herself straining to keep her eye on Bajirao and Gayatribai instead. If she strains harder, she can also hear a few words between them as their voices are carried into the night. She watches as Bajirao reaches into a tree, breaks off a twig thick with peepal leaves and nudges Gayatribai with it. The woman reaches out absently to take it from his hands into her own.

'This is for your prayer tomorrow,' Bajirao seems to say, his voice low. 'You forgot to pluck it from the tree.'

Gayatribai looks up from the twig and into her husband's face. She smiles and looks back down. Katya imagines the woman carrying in her eyes the image of her husband's mouth widened in that grin. Gayatribai caresses the leaves of the ancient peepal, which, Katya knows, is steeped in a hundred legends. The woman wipes the dust from the surface, tracing her fingertips along the rim of each leaf, shaped like a perfect, unbroken heart.

Around them, other people walk towards their own homes. Children squeal and chase each other, running in the darkness from one group of adults to another, all within the map of a community that seems so sure of its step in these harsh parts. Warm dirt rises in puffs along the trail on which they walk or run. People slow down or stop for passing bulls and bullock carts. Couples and families fall away from the larger nucleus as they break smaller paths towards their own huts. Scents and sounds of frugal cooking float over from homes, and the children now run urgently towards these.

Farewells arise here and there. Punha bhetuya. See you tomorrow.

'Will we be able?' Katya hears Gayatribai ask her husband, so quietly that even he doesn't seem to hear it the first time. Her voice is ragged, almost masculine but for its tone. As if sensing an eavesdropper, Gayatribai glances around her, assessing how far her voice might carry on a night as still and sultry as this one. 'Will we?' she asks into her husband's silence.

'Yes,' Bajirao says to her, no hesitation in his voice. 'You believe that it is God who comes to our homes in the guise of guests. Do your gods dare walk away from your home? Dare I turn your gods away?'

Gayatribai leans into his arm and laughs. Her laugh turns into a cough. Bajirao puts his hand on her head. When her coughing has subsided, the man and wife walk quietly for several steps. The call of a koel in the trees punctuates their silence.

Katya is startled as Ammar slows his step suddenly and moves closer to her. Kabir runs up ahead and walks alongside Bajirao and Gayatribai, who smile at him together.

In the dark, she can hardly see Ammar's face, yet she can sense he is looking at her with questions. Are these questions about today or tomorrow . . . or are they about years ago? He takes in a breath, as if about to say something, but Katya is distracted by Gayatribai's voice and squints into the dark to follow the woman's shape. Gayatribai is talking about nothing important, just the quotidian preparations for the visitors and about her absence from the fields. She would wake earlier, clean and feed the bullocks, fetch water . . .

'No, not so much work. Meera will help. Inside the house.' Bajirao says. 'At least until her wedding.'

They are at the house now. It is more hut than house, even though it's made of bricks and clay and cement. It has that bench-like structure on the outside, the kind that calls out to kid and cow and stranger. But it's the outer walls of the house that catch Katya's eye. Even in the dark, the house stands out in its ultramarine blue, the colour of deep, still water.

The house has no shape. The run of the bricks seem to lead its walls into awkward lines and unsure corners. The roof of the house has beams laden with coloured tarp and thatch in no particular order. This is the kind of asymmetry of architecture that seemed to have fascinated Kabir earlier. Well, they would see how long the fascination lasted.

Gayatribai and Bajirao hurry inside to clear the path for their guests as a young woman arrives quickly at the doorstep with a lantern.

'Meera?' Gayatribai calls out with urgency. 'The house is clean?'

Meera's eyes widen at the sight of the strangers but she nods and instantly joins her mother as they duck inside. The darkness doesn't conceal either the smallness or the paucity of the home. Everything smells musty but has a veneer of some sort of vigorous effort at cleaning without the means to cleanliness. Katya looks around for the bathroom. She is unable to stop a grimace at the sight of the broken-down latrine. She isn't sure, but she thinks Bajirao might have caught the look on her face.

Kabir is still outside. Katya realizes this when she sees Gayatribai hurry out with a bowl of water. She follows and watches Gayatribai pour this on the boy's feet and rub them down until the dried dung on his feet is gone. Kabir stands there, looking mortified, groaning and laughing at the same time. He looks to Katya for a cue. She shrugs. He joins his hands in a 'namaste' to Gayatribai. Gratitude. The woman clucks her tongue and ushers him inside her home.

They are quickly served a simple meal of rice and dal on misshapen aluminium plates and bowls. Their hosts are ashamed of this, she can tell. Of course they would be. This is not the meal they would have planned if they had had more time.

Why did Ammar impose on them all of a sudden? Surely the motel would not have been so bad?

Suddenly, she feels the urge to talk to Ammar. She wants to step outside with him and ask him questions and have him ask her questions until every thread of every answer has been tugged at, unravelled and turned smooth as silk. Maybe it is this tautness of questions between them that Kabir is hanging on to. Maybe, if the tension broke, they could all be done and on their way.

But the only one leaving now is Ammar. He says a quiet goodbye to each person. He ruffles the hair on Kabir's head, as if the boy were ten, not fourteen. Kabir, of course, doesn't seem to mind.

As Ammar ducks out the door, he says to Katya, 'In the early years, I often imagined you coming back with Kabir to see me. But I had never imagined . . .'

Then, just like that, mid-sentence, he's gone. She wants to call out and say, 'I didn't. I haven't come back in any way.' But their hosts are looking at her, hovering, wondering what she might need from them next.

Ammar has given them sleeping bags. As Katya lays hers out next to Kabir's, the girl, Meera, brings out a steaming cup of chai. She has a clean, open face. She looks like her mother might have looked at her age. Her hair is long and runs down her back in a neat and tight plait.

'How old are you?' Katya says.

'Twenty,' Meera replies shyly.

'I hear you are getting married.'

The girl smiles and heads back into the kitchen.

There's too little milk in the chai for Katya, but, of course, she won't say anything. She won't say anything either about how the caffeine in tea keeps her up if she drinks it at night, even though the last thing she wants tonight is to toss and turn and think.

The home seems to be settling down a little and Kabir falls asleep. Then, Katya hears the sounds of someone leaving the house. Sitting up, she can see the back of the hut, where another door leads out. Bajirao is readying to head out into the night. She has always resented this: how easily these men stride out into the world in the dark. Katya sees him mumble something to Gayatribai as he puts on his sandals. Gayatribai looks confused and somewhat unwilling to let him go. But she also looks tired, and maybe that's what takes over as she waves a gentle goodbye at the door.

The home soon falls into the kind of silence and darkness that is only possible in a village. Invited by the silence, the caffeine kicks in. Katya is tossing, turning, thinking. She needs something to read. Each of them has been given a lantern of their own, so it wouldn't be difficult to light it and read without waking the others.

She pushes herself up from the floor and lets her eyes adjust to the darkness and to the shapes around her—people, walls, corners, objects. Finally, her silent steps and her groping around the small home yield what she is looking for. Paper. It's a paper bag, stuffed with a paper folder or envelope of some sort. She should let go of it, set it back down on the little stool standing by the bed on which Gayatribai is sleeping. The stool is on the side of the bed that's vacant, Bajirao's side. This is Bajirao's property she is holding. But, surely, it's only some newspapers or something he likes to read? Or it could be personal documents, in which case she will put it right down.

Back on her sleeping bag, by the light of her lantern, she empties out the contents of the folder. She shuffles through them, moving slowly. There's no sound more likely to awaken a light sleeper than the whisper of paper.

Here's a land deed. Red ink runs across some of the pages.

Acre after acre sold. On parts of the document is a smudge of some kind. She squints and holds the pages closer to her eyes. It's a tiny sign of 'Om' scrawled in the same vermilion that she saw earlier today on Gayatribai's head. She holds the paper gently now—the vermilion dust comes off easily from the pages, and she does not want the symbol to look less legible for being handled by her.

She turns her attention to the newspaper clippings instead. Most are in Marathi, but an occasional one is in English—typically bad writing, shoddy phrases, archaic reporting styles. These are clippings from the local newspaper, in Marathi, carrying news of suicides. They are arranged by date, beginning around five years ago. At first, there are long news reports, with bylines of special correspondents. Then, shorter ones, with bylines of staff reporters. And then, as the reports become more frequent and closer in their dates, there are only photos with captions. Why has Bajirao picked these particular reports? Are these the suicides of farmers he knew? She reads the datelines on the reports. Yes, they're all from Dhanpur.

She doesn't let her eyes dwell too long on the images—men hanging limp from ropes; men on funeral beds decked with as many flowers as their families can afford; men—and women—with their eyes turned inward and mouths opened, slack by death. Note to self—this is strictly prohibited viewing for Kabir.

The next moment, Kabir's face is a foot away from hers and he is shaking her awake. Is it time for school already? Or is he late for drama practice? Did Alec sleep over? Why does her condo smell of years of human perspiration? Why the heck is Kabir holding up a lantern?

Probably sensing her disorientation, Kabir shakes her harder. She has to push him off to make him stop.

'Mom. *Look* at this stuff. How can you sleep after reading it?' he whispers urgently.

The papers and clippings are strewn around them. Had she actually fallen asleep right after determining that Kabir shouldn't look at these?

'You shouldn't be looking at these,' she says in a weak whisper. 'They're . . . they're someone's personal property.'

'That didn't stop you. But I'm glad it didn't. Look, Mom, look. There's some weird and scary stuff here.'

'Yes. It's all weird and scary. Which is why I'm saying we need to get the hell out.'

'No. Actually, we need to find out what this is about. Look.'

He's holding up a newspaper clipping. She squints and reads the headlines and the first few lines. These articles don't seem to belong in the category of those she was reading earlier. They carry two pieces of news relevant to this village. On the left, a report on the upcoming mass wedding. By a special correspondent. The government is taking charge, it says. The villagers are pleased. The arrangements have begun. On the right, a report about human organ sales. Photographs. Farmers selling kidneys in illicit trade to corrupt doctors who operate by night. The police has clamped down, but the dealings could have simply shifted location, the report says.

Which one of these reports had caught Kabir's eye despite being in the Marathi script? Which one of these reports is relevant to the owner of these press clippings? Surely, it is the one about the wedding. Yes, of course it is. It carries an address, which she can now see is underlined in pencil. An address of a post office. Strange. But of course.

'Not that one,' Kabir says, watching her face closely. 'The other one. What's Bajirao doing looking at pictures of people selling their organs? That's what's going on in this story, right?'

She peers closely at the report. Under it, a series of numbers is scrawled in Marathi. Katya never did learn the Marathi script too well. But she can tell it's a telephone number.

'Okay. This is disturbing, yes,' she says, gathering all the papers up and putting them back into the folder. 'But it's got nothing to do with us. Bajirao is a grown man. He knows what he is doing with his life. Besides, this may or may not mean anything.'

'Mom, are you sure?' Kabir says.

This question from him and the tone he asks it in always gives her pause. The problem with raising an only child, and a child so hungry to understand the world, is that he has few points of reference among his peers. He is a mini-adult without the years that lead into the answered questions of adulthood. This question from him—Mom, are you sure?—always makes her realize that no, she's not so sure.

'Yes, I'm sure,' she says. 'Bajirao is not crazy to go offering up his organs for sale in the illegal human meat market when his daughter is going to be married off in a couple of weeks.' Something about her words makes her falter and lower her voice. She makes up for this by firmly shutting the folder, standing up and tiptoeing it back to the stool from where she had picked it up. Gayatribai is a heavy sleeper, but probably also an early riser.

Back in their sleeping bags, Katya puts her hand on Kabir's head and pats it the way she used to when he was a little boy. He hasn't allowed her to do this for years, but now he lets her. Even though his back is turned to her, she can sense his large eyes are open, staring out at a piece of sky through the accidental skylight formed above them in a spot in the roof where the tarp didn't quite marry the thatch.

Katya lies awake thinking. The newness of this place has grabbed the boy's heart. The strangeness of these people has gripped his imagination. How deep will he go?

Sleep draws her away from her final coherent thoughts for the night: why isn't Bajirao home yet? Will he return before Gayatribai has risen?

5

To Speak of Sweet Things

HE WANTED TO be home before the visitors were awake, so he could wash the alcohol off his breath. Gayatri would know, and she may look at him with that fallen face of disappointment, but she would understand. Yes, she would rush to him with concern when he told her he had to drink in order to dull the pain from the doctor's stitches on the gash to the side of his stomach.

A mad bull had rushed at him in the dark as he was heading home from his brother's house. Yes, that's what it was. It had been so terrible. A raging, mad bull. It must belong to that stupid Dongre. Hadn't the village asked that man several times to keep an eye on his cattle?

Would she believe his lie?

Yes, she must. She would have questions, a lot of questions. He would answer her questions right away like he always did. The gash isn't too deep, at least not from the way it looks on the surface. Gayatri didn't know about these gashes. She didn't know about kidneys. She would only want to know about what the doctor had said. He would tell her a part of the truth—the doctor had said Bajirao should continue to walk around, keep an eye open for redness around the stitches, and not lift heavy weights. He wouldn't tell her that the doctor had wanted him to lie in bed for at least four days before all that. This doctor, who operated by night, this man who was probably doing this to earn more money for his own family, he had deftness in his hands and kindness in his eyes. It hadn't been hard to call his phone number and schedule the operation in the middle of the night. Only those things that were lawful and governed moved slowly in these parts; illegal transactions were swift. Their contractors understood the delicate exigencies of daughters' dowries and the unexpected visit of Gayatri's gods in disguise.

But what would he do about Gayatri's gaze? She would watch him like she had watched their dying son all those years ago. She would watch like she had watched each of their three daughters survive the many diseases and illnesses of their years. She would watch without blinking, the way she had done when they had almost lost Meera to the outbreak of chikungunya fever in the village two years ago. Deep down, though, he liked this watching of hers.

But, today, she had to watch over others. Maybe she wouldn't notice him.

Bajirao abandoned the notion right away when he saw her rush to the door and stand there, peering at him through the mist of the morning. Gayatri's eyes widened as she saw what wasn't visible—the pain radiating through his innards. Bajirao wanted to rush to her. He wanted to tell her the truth. He wanted to cry into the lines of her neck and tell her that he had sold a piece of her husband last night.

Then he wanted to whisper and tell her that the sale will never make him any less. She fills up the empty space that now lies inside. She keeps him whole.

A shadow came up behind Gayatri. It was the foreign woman.

The woman of anger. The mother of that curious boy. The woman who had shaken Ammar Chaudhry. Would she just leave quietly one of these days, dragging her boy away against his will? Or would she stay to bring storms into their lives? He felt uncertain about this woman, even though he could sense her own uncertainties, more naked in the assertive swagger of her carriage. Still, Gayatri seemed to like her. He could see it now in the way she greeted the woman's arrival, looking away shyly from the woman's expansive namaste, but responding with a nod and smile directed at the floor. With a thrust of her chin, Gayatri indicated to the woman that there was tea awaiting them all.

He slipped in through these cracks of gestures and conversation, slipped into a private corner of his home, to wash and ready himself for his first day as a man with a missing part.

Gayatri must have set the fog of prayer into motion during the dawn hour. And now, the summer air trapped even the thinnest vapours of incense and smothered them into all the fibres through which they could crawl. One of these was his moustache. Here, the incense mixed in with the stench of arrack and beedi still lingering on his breath. It was ungodly, his drinking and smoking. And there was someone in this home who believed in godliness.

'You should lie down.' Gayatri had come up behind him.

'That Dongre's bull . . .'

She looked at the cash he was holding in his hands. He placed it under the pillow of her bed, where he always put their cash, for her to pay for household expenses.

'Did Dongre's bull also give you the money?'

He wanted to say something in a raised voice, but that voice didn't come and neither did the anger.

'Gayatri . . .' he said.

She spoke in a low voice now. 'Is this money for the upkeep

of our guests? Why? They come from a rich land. They can pay for . . .'

'For what? For the food, yes. For the oil and the mosquito coils and soaps. But not for the latrine that we must repair for their use. Not for . . . the moneylender's man . . . who shouldn't come knocking on our door for money while they are here. Not for all the shame of this household.'

She took a step back from him. He could see it on her face—he hadn't spoken this way in years. Was it the pain in his body that made him speak this way? The medicines? The layer of blood drying between his skin and the bandages?

Gayatri left for the kitchen, where Meera was readying to serve poha to the guests. Bajirao followed her and watched as she hurried to throw a handful of roasted groundnuts on the poha just before the bowls were carried out to the guests.

His nostrils quivered from the scents rising up around him. He knew it couldn't be true, but it was as if the scent of the vomit that Meera had splattered all over the hut two years ago in the throes of her chikungunya fever had now erupted out of the mud floor of the home. Could the guests smell these ghastly smells? Were they disgusted? How would his family get it all clean?

Why have they come here during the scent of a drought? Why come to witness our season of sweat?

The foreign woman turned to look at him. Had he said something out aloud? She started to smile at him but, as if then forgetting her initial intent, her face slipped into a frown instead. What did she see? She now looked from him to Gayatri and then back at him. It was as if her mind was racing.

Bajirao was overwhelmed now with longing for Gayatri. He wanted her all to himself. He wanted these people to evaporate into the humidity, leaving no scent behind. He wanted to reclaim the rituals of his morning. He wanted to be awakened by Gayatri stirring beside him before she slipped away to attend to her many chores of dawn.

He wanted to inhale deeply the scent of her sweat, so much thicker than his, as it soaked into her pink cotton sari. Days and nights of her perspiration dwelled on the same cloth before she could take it to the river to wash it. He neither hated nor loved this scent. Sometimes it tortured him, a reminder that he had failed her as a provider. At other times, it filled his morning dreams with the faith that she would always stay with him, beyond him, for she was the healthier, hardier one.

He felt some comfort now. As the sun climbed into the sky, the drier scents would rise and, with no wind to carry them, these scents would gently tease and torment everyone here. Outside his hut, the scent of raw mangoes—diced, salted and seasoned with turmeric, chilli, cumin and coriander—lying on sheets of white muslin cloth to roast to a pickle in the sun. A women's NGO from Nagpur had arrived two years ago and set up a project for the women in this village to make pickles and sweets. This way, the women could bring home some money when the crops faltered or . . . failed.

Oh, but the aroma of cooking, a rich starchy smell of rice and salt boiling away, laughing in iron pots in a row of homes as the glutinous amalgam achieved a higher temperature than the sun. There was also the smell of chickens being slaughtered for the market. Would the guests expect to be fed chicken? Or do they know that just like the mangoes and the sweets, the chickens would rarely be eaten by those who lived and worked with these delicacies? These foods were their livelihood, not their sustenance.

But then, there was the scent from the tent of the lohaar, melting scraps of metal to make nails to sell in the market. This smell could be harsh sometimes; it could sizzle in the nostrils. It was as unwelcome as the tidings from the sale of the nails were welcome.

Today, and twice every week, there would be another scent, when the doctor from the subdivisional hospital fifty-six miles away would arrive in Dhanpur. The doctor would bring with him the smell of bottles of glucose, saline and tetracycline injections, which he would give to anyone who could afford them for thirty rupees, no matter whether or not that person needed this medical bounty.

Thinking about the doctor brought Bajirao back to the raging pain in his body. The pain had sharpened each of his senses. His brain, too, could not cease its questions.

Were they even inhaling, these people from another land? If they were, could they smell the timeless fragrance that had sensually nourished generations of villagers, never discriminating between landowners and the landless, Brahmin or Shudra, Hindu or Muslim, the hungry or the well fed? This classless smell drifted here, there and everywhere: the scent of dung cakes lain out by the steps or plastered over walls in every home, drying quickly in the scorching sun, ready to turn to fuel. Ah, this smell was as sweet as the sheera served at the wedding of a rich man's daughter. It arose thick in the morning while the dung was still wet, and it faded as the dung cakes dried.

Would the guests know that this scent brought the reassurance that the cattle were still alive, that they still found some grass to eat and ruminate on, to expel through the four chambers in their stomach, in that holiest of reminders that life may still go on?

'Have you forgotten?' Gayatri's voice interrupted his thoughts as she walked over to him and handed him a small copper bowl filled with poha. 'Have you forgotten what day it is today?'

His brain struggled against the medication in panic. He started to sit down to eat, playing for time. The pain kicked in again, as if Dongre's mad bull had indeed struck him right now.

He caught his cry in his throat. But Gayatri had already gasped loudly as she saw his lurch, and the foreign woman looked over at them. Her frown reappeared, sharper this time. The boy appeared from the kitchen, looked at his mother, and took in the scene.

Before Bajirao could gather his words, Gayatri spoke calmly, telling the guests about the bull, the doctor, the stitches—the whole unfortunate incident in the night. The story seemed to come as a relief to the foreign woman. The boy had many questions and his mother got busy translating for him.

Lifting his dhoti around his knees, Bajirao lowered himself into the corner of the porch of his hut. At least he didn't have to hurry to the field this morning; it was inauspicious for a farmer to till his land on Naag Panchami. So, he could do now what he did on each of his free days for the past twenty-three years since he had brought home a shy seventeen-year-old as his bride. He would watch Gayatri bustle around their home in this long morning as the approaching day cast its early shadows and then its bright light upon her. He would watch the sun dance in the corner of his hut until the light would fall upon the single millimetre of space on Gayatri's gold nose ring that tipped it into a circle, his circle of existence.

'We are expecting important visitors today,' Gayatri said. Bajirao could tell she was watching him from a corner of her eye.

Oh! How could he have forgotten? The bile rose into his throat and the room started to swim. Gayatri's voice held him upright. 'The parents of the groom we have selected for Meera will soon be here. They are coming to see the girl.'

The boy had a million questions: Doesn't Meera know the

groom? How could this be the first time her in-laws-to-be are seeing her? What do they mean by 'seeing her'? Did Meera get to see her groom? The foreign woman stopped translating his questions after that.

In the next hour, the scent of goddesses rose into the air, the incense overwhelming it all. He could see that Gayatri had spent some of her money from the mango pickle and sweets project on buying a few basic things to offer at today's Naag Panchami festival, for which the in-laws would stay. Bajirao wanted to claim his pain and crawl back into slumber, especially at the thought of their rupees lying before the clay idol of a snake that Gayatri believed had lived in the head of Lord Shiva and was sent to earth this day so the farmers would have a good harvest. The only thing that gave him any pleasure about this festival was the prospect of watching Gayatri as she joined the others at the temple in dance.

A few months ago, for the haldi-kunku festival, Gayatri's group of friends, twelve married women in the village, had fasted for fourteen successive Mondays so that their husbands would have long lives. Bajirao had heard Gayatri humming the prayer greeting under her breath:

Tilgool ghya
gode gode bola

Even that day, Bajirao had wished he could go back to sleep. It had hurt, listening to his wife chant the greeting. On that day, she didn't have the tilgool sweets, the sesame seed laddoos to offer other women and greet them with the chant: 'Eat this sweet offering . . . to speak of sweet things.' And today, she didn't have the milk or the sweets for the serpents. Bajirao now thought of how he never had summoned up the heart to point out to

Gayatri that three of those men for whose long lives their wives had prayed were now dead, by suicide.

He watched now as she signalled the truths of her day. He knew she wanted him to eye the things she was gathering into the little straw basket, all objects of the only opposition she had with him—religious faith. Tiny plastic sachets of camphor, turmeric, blood-red vermilion-dust, a pinch of rice grains, a stick of incense, a brass bell, a yellow flower. All of them wordlessly formed themselves into a jewelled chariot of devotion on which his wife would ride fiercely away from his swamp of realism, his quicksand of evidence that mounted day after day, steadfast as the blazing sun. Today, when Gayatri would join her hands together and look to the heavens, Bajirao would shield his eyes with his hands and look to the sky.

This was the third festival in the last month and there would be many more during these months of phagun, between June and October. Each basket of prayer cost five rupees. Each rupee that they sent up from this hot earth to a cold god took them further away from their chance at reclaiming the four acres of land he had mortgaged for a loan. Each of the past four successive years of failed cotton crops had claimed an acre of the land passed down from his elders. And now, Meera's wedding. If Gayatri's gods rained down just one more misfortune upon them . . .

'I am not buying sweets for today's prayer,' Gayatri muttered under her breath as she cleaned around him. She left quickly, before he could frame a response.

He would never take away the possessions of prayer from Gayatri, but it was the only expense he could dwell upon, like even a rich farmer must dwell upon his wife's glut of gold ornaments. If only it didn't take money . . . if only all it took was his last breath, to keep Gayatri speaking of sweet things.

6

'Bajirao is a Lucky Man'

THE FATHER OF Dinesh Deshmukh did not look pleased with the presence of the strange guests. And there seemed to be no way to take him aside and explain to him that their presence and their casual questions would do him no harm. Bajirao had a silent question for him, too: What harm can come to you, sir? You are the father of the groom.

Still, the man looked slighted. His wife and he sat on bamboo stools on the porch of the hut, which Gayatri had washed down with water and decorated with a floral rangoli pattern. They were sipping tea and eating with suspicion the foreign chocolates that the boy had insisted on laying out on a platter for them.

The whole ridiculous scene made Bajirao want to do the unthinkable—declare this wedding cancelled, the matrimonial alliance withdrawn, the announcement made that Meera Andhale, daughter of Bajirao Andhale, would stay a spinster for life. But even this was a luxury he had no business toying with in his mind. Only the groom's father held the right to declare an alliance annulled.

Bajirao jumped as the foreign woman's voice rang out. Even

in her broken Marathi, the question she asked the father of Dinesh Deshmukh was like the lash of a whip across Bajirao's chest, 'Mr Deshmukh, how did you react when you were told that there would be no dowry transactions for the mass wedding?'

If the father of Dinesh Deshmukh said anything right away, Bajirao would not be able to hear it, so hard was his heart beating into his ears. But the man was simply looking over at Bajirao, his glare stone-cold.

The foreign woman repeated her question, moving her words around a little. She seemed to have assumed that the man was silent because he hadn't understood her the first time.

'I was happy,' the father of Dinesh Deshmukh said, his gaze still on Bajirao.

'Happy? Are you sure?' The foreign woman seemed to think this was funny. There was a mocking laughter in her voice and a playful twitch on her face. Bajirao looked away. Had she really forgotten our ways so completely?

'I am sure,' the father of Dinesh Deshmukh said in a dull voice. 'I was happy.'

'So, you do not like the dowry system?' she asked.

'I do not like the dowry system.'

'That is to be admired,' the foreign woman said, getting a little serious now.

'Yes.'

'Do you have daughters?'

'Two. Both are coming up to marriageable age.'

'So you will not pay dowries for them?'

The man finally looked away from Bajirao and fixed his eyes on the foreign woman. 'If I am a man as lucky as Bajirao, I will not have to pay dowries.'

'You think Bajirao is a lucky man?' The foreign woman pulled her stool a little closer to the father of Dinesh Deshmukh.

He pushed back his own stool, as if repelled by her. She didn't seem to notice.

'Any father of a bride who is not required to pay a dowry is a lucky man,' he said.

'So maybe your daughters will also get married at a mass wedding such as this one?'

The man was silent. Then he said, 'If that is their fate, yes. But . . . '

He seemed to have thought the better of it. Bajirao wanted to say something and end all this right then. But the foreign woman spoke again.

'Their fate? You say that as if it is a bad thing.'

'Every father dreams of giving his daughter a big wedding. But we now have these new ways, all these new things. Let us see how long the new system lasts.'

'So you would prefer to give your daughters a big wedding?'

'It is a matter of prestige. My status. Usually, the dowry that a daughter-in-law brings into her husband's family helps her younger sisters-in-law to get married with prestige. But, in my case . . . the timing is such . . . Bajirao is a lucky man.'

'Your son is a lucky man, too,' the foreign woman said in a flat tone.

Bajirao wanted to sink into his pain. This had to stop. Everything was going bad. Everything was turning to hell.

'See? Your son is a lucky man to find such a lovely bride.' The foreign woman seemed to sound almost sweet now. This was the first time he had heard this in her voice since she had arrived here yesterday. He looked up at her and saw the reason for her comment.

Meera had emerged from inside the hut, with her mother and her mother-in-law-to-be. She was looking . . . like a woman. She was looking like her mother, all those years ago. Her head was lowered, and he saw now how thick and black her hair was, how Gayatri's red silk sari made her look a little fairer-skinned than usual, and how the small studs of gold on her earlobes made two little punctuated points about her father's status: He is alive. He will pay.

Ammar Chaudhry arrived and the morning took a turn for the better. He quickly assessed the situation. He whispered something in English to the foreign woman and the boy. Ammar spoke easily to the father of Dinesh Deshmukh, who at first looked suspicious and then seemed to unstiffen his back as he realized that Ammar Chaudhry's words were not questions but pleasantries, the kind more suited to the stature of the bride's side.

The father of Dinesh Deshmukh nodded curtly at everything and then declared that he had best be going. His wife would stay back for the festival and return home with other ladies who hailed from their village, but he was a busy man who must go back to his urgent matters. Then, as he straightened his kurta, patted down his moustache and strode away, he shot a look to the father of Meera Andhale that said, quite unmistakably, 'You will probably want to make amends for this morning. Let us discuss the new amount soon.'

Ammar Chaudhry had plans for the day. 'Everyone is available today because of Naag Panchami,' he said. 'It's a good day to go tour this village and beyond, for supporters in the protest.'

The boy jumped up and put his sandals on. His mother said something to Ammar, who looked over at Bajirao. Seeing this, Gayatribai said, 'My husband was struck by a bull last night and had to get stitches from a doctor. It is best that he . . .'

'I will go,' Bajirao said. Gayatri had lied all morning for his sake, to keep him from lying out aloud. He knew she believed that a woman of God would be forgiven; a godless man would not know where to seek forgiveness.

But a godless man would find his fate in the company of men. 'I must go. This protest rally is important, no? I must do everything to help.'

Ammar hesitated and then nodded. 'Bajirao will ride in my jeep,' he said to Gayatribai. 'I will not let him be in pain.'

The foreign woman started to say something, as if to join Gayatribai's hesitation about Bajirao's departure. Then, she seemed to check herself. She rolled her eyes with a deliberate air of nonchalance. She said something in English to Ammar and the boy. The boy argued with her for a while. Gayatribai invited the foreign woman to go for the prayers with the women of Dhanpur. This seemed to make up the foreign woman's mind. She would stay close to her boy. She would go with the men.

Ammar walked through the village, greeting the villagers with 'kasa kai!' as if he had grown up among them, a man of this earth, a son of this soil. He came from the world of people who wore suits, but he only wore clothes like Bajirao's own, although the garments were always clean and fresh. He carried in him the bearing that came from being educated in English. Yet, in the two years he had been here, he felt the movement of this village, heard the tenor of its talk and sensed the cruelty of the cloudless skies straight up above this very road.

What, then, was his history with the lost woman who had arrived here? She followed him with a quick but wary step and her son watched them closely. There seemed to be some matter of pain between them, a history that had determined the expanse of space now between their separate tread.

The boy had a camera and he was taking a hundred pictures a minute of Ammar Chaudhry stopping here and there, pointing at this and that.

What did it feel like to have a son? He knew once.

The village elders were already gathered under the peepal

tree. They grew silent as Ammar and his group approached. They greeted the foreign woman, seemed to want to like her, by her association with Ammar Chaudhry and probably because her son looked so much like sons of their own.

Ammar said, 'My biggest question these days, just like yours, is: when will it rain?'

Shouts of approval and agreement went up around them. They talked about the rains that arrived a few weeks ago, played hide-and-seek, and then left. It was as if the heavens spat down on us and then stomped away, someone said.

The boy said something. Ammar translated: 'He says that where he comes from, a village named Seattle, it rains nine months in a year.'

Gasps went up around them. Ammar continued, 'He says that people in Seattle wait for the sun. People celebrate when the sun comes out, just like we celebrate when the rain comes down. Can you imagine that, my brothers?'

Laughter and awe mixed in. The boy asked more questions. Ammar said, 'My son wants to know more about our rain. He wants to know about the history of this village and its seeds. He wants to know why the men in these villages are disappearing.'

The crowd drew into a closer circle. This time, the visitors did not sit on the cemented bench. They sat crouched among the villagers, even the foreign woman, whose frown grew deeper, not from anger so much now. Could it be from being immersed in the stories?

As the day wore on, frugal midday meals emerged from kitchens and children were lain down to nap on the laps of the elders. Still, the villagers spoke, answering questions, asking questions.

Kisna-kaka arrived now, Bajirao's own older brother. The air always shifted for Bajirao when his brother was near; Bajirao felt just a little bit lighter, as if someone had taken a heavy plough from his hands and asked him to sit down and wipe his forehead. Kisna-kaka is what the village called him. Bajirao had grown up calling him bhao, older brother. He was twelve years older than Bajirao. He was the one who had left for the city for an education. When their father died, from a heatstroke, Bajirao was still a boy. His older brother had left his education in the city and returned to take care of his younger brother and tend to his father's fields.

Now, both brothers had slowly lost most of their father's land. They had slowly grown apart. Kisna-kaka had grown detached from the affairs of these villages in recent years, but he arrived, nonetheless, today. Someone must have run to his home to invite him to what was looking now like an important event. He nodded at Bajirao and settled into a corner of the crowd. After another half hour of talking in the blazing sun of the afternoon, Bajirao, Kisna-kaka, a few other small farmers and some farm labourers accompanied Ammar Chaudhry and the visitors in the jeep as they travelled to four different villages, meeting their leaders.

The boy seemed to grow tired but he also seemed to become more and more grounded into this earth as the sun coloured his skin. His mother and he listened to people talk about matters they considered most urgent. Water for irrigation, money for a daughter's wedding, funds for seeds and pesticide, repayment of a loan spent haplessly on alcohol or medicine.

In one of the meetings, the boy suddenly spoke again. 'I don't understand. Please start at the beginning. Why are the farmers killing themselves? Who started it? Was there a time when things weren't so bad?"

So they tell him of the mythology of Kapasi Rishi, the sage who had come to these parts and planted the first cotton seed.

'That is where the crop got its Marathi name, kapas,' Ammar said.

They tell the boy of the 10,000 years of farming in India and of how Vidarbha turned into the Cotton Belt of India. Farmers had found their crops yielding a variety of long cotton. This cotton would be beautiful, they could tell. This beauty needed a charkha, a loom, to draw out its splendour. The charkha was invented and cotton sales flourished. Then, the British came in with machines and exploited this white gold. The British men, the goras, lay railway lines wherever the cotton grew thick and the mills began to spring up in Mumbai, fuelling the city with a cotton economy.

The villagers told him the stories that were carried down from their ancestors, stories of how families from regions far and wide were proud to marry their daughters to the sons of Vidarbha. He listened with interest to each story, down to those of barely a generation ago, in the 1940s, stories of the ladies in England who slept on the soft cotton bedsheets that came from the seeds of Vidarbha.

The more romantic stories gave way to the more pragmatic ones, stories with so many numbers and facts that they didn't sound like stories any more. The villagers told the boy about the glorious times, until the middle of the 1970s, when these villages were thick with flora and fauna and the land yielded a rich two or three quintals of cotton per acre of farmland. The cost of seeds and fertilizers was low and the farmers' standard of living was healthy, with disposable income to cover more than food, clothing and shelter. The farmer would grow his own barley and lentils and his til oil, get milk from a cow he owned and build his own house or hut.

'But it all changed in 1977,' said an elderly farmer in his gravelly voice.

'No, it was in 1980,' Kisna-kaka said.

The old farmer shook his head. 'You are a young fool. It was in 1977. It was the year my daughter-in-law gave birth to our first grandson. The child who died. Would I forget something like that?'

And so it was that everyone agreed—it was 1977 when a hybrid seed from America found its way to Vidarbha. Men from the city roamed the village singing glories of these 'Bt Cotton' seeds on loudspeakers: 'The Indian government is joining the world! The world is our market! Jai Kisaan! Glory to the farmer!'

The farmers had rushed to buy the seeds. They were expensive. The government banks had offered loans. The farmers had taken them. Those who didn't meet the credit standards had taken loans from some other men who had arrived as if on cue—the sahukars, moneylenders, with their oily manner and their frightening rates of interest.

At first, the cotton had grown thick and fluffy, and if a farmer walked down to his field at night, he would see rows of soft moons in it, matching the white light of the moon above. The harvests were so rich and the bales of cotton so mountainous that the farmers would almost die from the way their bodies ached after harvesting. Such was their joy.

Slowly, the yield had fallen. At first, the farmers didn't know why their crops were failing. A single year of a poor monsoon would mean no water, no irrigation, and long periods in the day without electricity. The farmer, his tools, his machines, his seeds, all grew useless. More foreign seeds arrived and so did more moneylenders. The farmers bought the seeds and planted them all over, even where they once grew their lentils and oil for their own subsistence.

'Why did we buy those seeds?' Kisna-kaka said, almost under his breath.

Bajirao wasn't sure if Kisna-kaka wanted an answer to his

question. He did not want to challenge his brother, but this was a time when they were all talking. They were amidst these strangers and they were asked to speak.

So, he said, 'Because when everything else works, the seed works.'

His older brother slowly nodded. Relief washed over Bajirao and, for a moment, the pain in his side seemed to ebb.

He spoke again. 'When everything else works, the cotton from the seed is beautiful. But everything doesn't work. If this year's drought is worse than last year's, the rains might as well not come at all. The seed will fail me. If the market doesn't pay me a good price for whatever I harvest, I will not be able to repay my loans. I will need new loans. For years, the government is setting a price that is too low. And if something else happens, even one little thing . . .'

He didn't have to say any more. Everyone around him murmured and nodded.

'What is "one little thing"?' the boy asked.

His mother spoke this time. 'One little thing . . .,' she said.

Bajirao was surprised to hear her voice after she has stayed silent for so long. The other farmers and he had almost forgotten she was here.

She told her son now about the blow of the many 'one-little-thing' events that happened to people who were poor—an illness in the family, another daughter to be married, a sick bullock . . .

The boy listened, staring at this mother, and then said, 'But why *suicide*? Why not ask the government to invest more or something?'

The woman said nothing. Nobody said anything. How could they explain this? What kind of question was this? Did people not get desperate in the country the boy came from? What did they do when they became desperate? What else was there but suicide?

The foreign woman seemed to grow distant again, as if her thoughts had suddenly travelled to another place. The only thing that indicated that she was still among them was that her hand reached out and ruffled the hair on her son's head.

Ammar Chaudhry covered up the villagers' silence with his words. He told them the story the way it would be told to someone who had such questions. The suicides had begun in 1997, he said, when India's free-trade policies began to pit the 3.2 million cotton farmers of Vidarbha against cotton farmers from all over the world, especially from America. The farmers here didn't have subsidies from their government like American farmers did. The Indian government also gave in to the pressure of foreign powers and took away the tariffs that protected Indian cotton industries from foreign competition. The foreigners came and flooded the market. And then, when the local cotton yield here was poor, the price of local cotton plummeted. The farmers sat stunned.

'By 2010, more than 32,000 farmers had chosen death at their own hands in Vidarbha,' Ammar said. 'And more than 200,000 in India.'

'How many, Baba?' the boy asked.

Ammar repeated the numbers. The boy looked disbelieving. No, he looked like he did not want to believe.

Ammar told him that men, and some women, died by hanging, by drowning themselves in a river, but mostly by swallowing the very pesticide they fed to their crops. And this year, it was said that every eight hours, a farmer chose to kill himself.

'Do you know where I got these statistics from?' Ammar asked the foreign woman, who was looking at him with some disapproval. He didn't wait for her response. 'I got them at the National Crime Records Bureau.'

When she frowned at him, uncomprehendingly, he said,

'That is the only government office keeping statistics of farmers choosing death over misery. They are counting these men among criminals. No Department of Rural Affairs, no district government office, no health official is counting these frightening numbers. These deaths are going down as a crime record against the farmers, not as a record of the failure of the seeds or crimes by the government.'

Ammar Chaudhry looked back at the farmers now: 'We have to change that. We have to throw out those seeds. We have to shout in protest.'

They all gathered back at the meeting area and stood under the peepal tree once again. They stayed silent at that last bit of information from Ammar. Some children ran out of their homes and used the silence of their elders to get closer to the foreign woman, to tug at her fingers and press their grubby noses into her shoulders until she finally had to squat to the ground to manage them. The elders watched, alert to any transgressions in respectfulness on the part of their children or to any suggestion of rejection from the foreign woman. The foreign woman's son, who had grown tired over the hours, now looked with his jaw fallen softly open at the sight of the children from a world strange to him taking hold of his mother.

She rose then, gently but firmly pushing the children away in a manner so close to their custom. The villagers laughed. Could they assume she was one of them? She had been witness to their stories today. Her presence and her son's had opened their words and memories to each other, too, after years of staying bereft of easy conversations around this shared pain.

Ammar Chaudhry spoke again. 'I did not want to roam empty-handed in your villages on Naag Panchami, so I have brought a small thing to share. I also want to offer these humble treats to you to celebrate the arrival of . . . of my son.'

Bajirao saw the foreign woman's back stiffen. The easy smile that had been playing about her face, lingering from her entanglement with the village children, flew right off, like a bird at the crackle of a twig.

Ammar walked over to his jeep and brought back two large cardboard boxes gaily patterned in red and gold. He playfully waved away the children who shrieked and crowded too close to the items he held in his hand. Someone quickly brought out a stool from a nearby hut and Ammar Chaudhry lay these precious things down on it with a flourish.

Over the next half hour, Dhanpur village turned into a carnival as people gathered to pass around golden brown tilgools, purchased from the city market, but manufactured in this very village.

Bajirao looked around for Gayatri, who should have arrived here from the temple visit by now. There she was, standing with Meera's mother-in-law-to-be, among a group of women. She was looking straight into his eyes, smiling so lightly, only he could tell the smile was there. He nodded at her in the same imperceptible manner. He would take a tilgool, she would take a tilgool, and, since tilgools were also being handed out for those who had not left their homes to come to the meeting, Gayatri would take one for Meera. And thus, Gayatri would have at least three tilgools for tonight's late prayer.

He also knew that Gayatri's smile had not actually been a signal to action. It was a message, an affirmation that here, now, was another sign that he should cross over to her side, her world of faith. For, although Ammar Chaudhry had brought the sweets on the pretext of an offering, the tilgools were here, weren't they? Sent by Someone Else?

Children greedily stuffed the tilgools straight into their mouths, struggling to hold them inside. They laughed when the boy from America tried to do the same. As they giggled, their saliva let some of the dissolving sweet ooze out of the sides of their mouths. These emanations were not wiped away, but gathered onto the back of a hand or onto a piece of stick to be licked after the more mealy part of the sweet was gone. Some of the adults nibbled on theirs, savouring each seed of sesame, each lump of jaggery and each fragmented globule of ghee as Ammar Chaudhry talked and talked, allowing them the dignity of silently slaking not merely their hunger but that single sensual pleasure that lay most dispossessed in drought, flood and famine—the sense of taste.

A motorcycle presented itself in the distant dust. At first it seemed to be passing through, but then it began its pacing—an engined tiger on the horizon. Its rider moved the machine with a deliberate thrust every now and then, raising dust despite its low speed, like a smoke signal announcing that somewhere, not very far away, there had been another suicide. The government official on the motorcycle would investigate it, following a scent of his own, all the way to a conclusion of his own, that the farmers' families deserved no government compensation for the loss of the breadwinners. Bajirao knew this man was too far away to see the tilgools dribbling from happy young mouths, but close enough to know that nothing sweet would last too long in these parts.

Then, all of a sudden, for the first time ever, the man started to draw closer. Mr Sachin Patekar. A small man with a big job, on a large motorcycle. In a flash of steel and a cloud of dust, he drew closer and closer in a straight line towards them. All they could do was watch his approach.

Even Ammar Chaudhry looked perplexed. Mr Sachin Patekar, Chief Agriculture Officer, accountant of subsidies and suicides, hereinbefore only seen from a distance and comprehended through the words of his notices in the mail, was sputtering his motorcycle to a halt in the centre of their gathering.

He dismounted and spoke. 'Word has come to my office that some rotten activities are being planned here.' Mr Sachin Patekar was startled for a moment as a low voice behind him started to speak in English. It was the foreign woman, translating to her son automatically. Mr Sachin Patekar stared at her and then spat on the ground. The foreign woman's eyebrows sprang up in shock. The boy stepped closer to her. Ammar Chaudhry gestured to her to be quiet and step back. She put her hands on her hips but nodded, glaring at Mr Sachin Patekar.

The chief agriculture officer spat again. This was more irrigation than this spot of land had received in months. Even in this tense moment, and probably because of the lingering effects of his medication, Bajirao couldn't help but smile invisibly at his thought.

'It is a good thing that you have all gathered here today. I will not have to send you an official notice. So listen to me now as I make one thing clear. Saavdhan. Do not do anything foolish. If you think you will succeed in marching on the road, you are highly mistaken. The police have been informed. If you do any nonsense, you will lie at home with broken legs and your wives will go alone to the fields. Do you want that to happen?'

Ammar took a step towards him and held up a hand to halt his speech. 'Kripaya thamba,' he said. Please stop. 'You are out of line in coming here with your threats.'

Mr Sachin Patekar looked right through him and turned then to look at every gathered man in the eye, one by one. 'Brothers. Who is this man? Who are these people? You are letting religious minorities and NRIs come and teach you A-B-C?' He spat again. 'Throw them out. Don't bite the hand that feeds you. Be grateful for the package of subsidies that the government has given you. Be grateful for the beauty of Bt seeds. And remember—when

90

chief minister sahib's motorcade passes through these villages, you will do nothing but stand on the sides and wave.'

He turned around, mounted his motorcycle, started it up, and drove away.

7

Drought, Desire, and Deceit

SOMETIMES, A SINGLE day is enough. Yesterday was that day. It was enough. Yes, Ammar, you were right. A child and a woman will only get in your way. There's no place for us here. Now, if only Kabir wouldn't be so damn struck by everything.

But he is. The people and events from yesterday have only left him intrigued. Maybe a little shaken, trying to wrap his head around the casual talk of suicide, as if it were just a decision of whether or not to say 'No' to drugs.

Just a few days ago, she had been wondering if he was capable of suicide, of throwing himself off Aurora Bridge like a boy named Joey had. Alec was right about her boy. Kabir wasn't one to find an answer in suicide. He was one to ask questions.

But he is asking questions now on the wrong side of the Pacific. And, by the end of yesterday, he was actually taking notes. What's the boy doing taking notes? Does he think this will make an interesting school project—'What I Did for My Summer Vacation'? Try explaining this crap to your ninth grade class, Kabir.

The Internet connection finally dials up for her. This time,

Ammar isn't peering over her shoulder. He's out, recruiting more farmers. He wanted to go alone today. Good. Maybe he was already getting weary of having Kabir and her along.

She is grateful for these few moments alone before a computer. Kabir has negotiated some time to wander the village. He wanted to roam by himself, but Gayatribai wouldn't let him, so she's taken him along with her to the cotton fields and the marketplace. Bajirao is resting at home. His gash started to bleed last night. That gash . . .

Three emails from Alec. The first one is in response to her airline itinerary: 'I'll see you at Baggage Claim. Glad you guys are coming home.' Two more emails, one just to her and the other to her and Kabir. In the first one, he asks questions—about Ammar, about Katya's health, about the outcome of her apprehensions. In the second one, he outlines plans for a camping trip when everyone's home.

Dear God, no. This time spent here in Dhanpur is like one long camping trip gone wrong. When they are back in Seattle, Kabir and she will want indoor plumbing, fine dining, and Teatro Zinzanni.

Katya writes quick responses to both emails. She won't have much time before the Internet connection is swallowed up by the electrical outage, the one that is actually planned. Load shedding. Kabir had thought the word sounded funny, dirty. The unplanned outages are like a ticking bomb you get used to carrying around in your fanny pack.

She's here to gather news reports to show Kabir. He was right in asking those very astute questions yesterday about the suicides. No one had answers for him, least of all Ammar. Well, there's enough coverage right here about how suicide begets suicide. Here's an article in the *Indian Journal of Psychiatry*, with a psychological autopsy of the Vidarbha suicides. It shows how farmers are killing themselves for the compensation money given to their families. Calculated, pre-meditated suicide. Here's a study by the Indira Gandhi Institute of Development Research, Mumbai. Aha! Just what Kabir needs to read—

> [P]ress reportage on suicides can have both negative and positive impact on suicide contemplators. Sensational reporting with detailed information on the mode of suicide, graphic illustrations of the suicide, repetitive reporting with constant flashing of images related to the suicide, in both print and electronic media have been found to lead to an increase in suicides due to the imitation effect or the 'Werther Effect' (World Health Organization, WHO, 2000). Imitation can take the form of contagion, 'a process by which exposure to the suicide or suicidal behavior of one or more persons influences others to commit or attempt suicide' (Centers for Disease Control and Prevention, CDC, 1994).

The printer in Ammar's office doesn't print front-and-back. She watches as it struggles even with the single-page printing. The ink in the cartridge starts to fade, but she gets her copies printed anyway. And then just as she readies to log off, she clicks on the 'History' in the browser window, a force of habit from raising a boy into his teens.

Kabir's name pops up in the link of a blog—www.immigrant-song.blogspot.com. The blogger's profile has a picture of Kabir, sitting on the bench that skirts Gayatribai's house: a brown-skinned, long-haired boy grinning against ultramarine blue. His expression is serious, except for a half-smile, actually a deliberate widening of a corner of his mouth, showing his braces and heightening the absence of humour on his face. The boy's arms are outstretched, holding his camera to take the picture of himself.

The profile says: 'I'm Kabir. I'm from Seattle, Washington. But I'm here, in Dhanpur village in the Yavatmal district in the Vidarbha region of the state of Maharashtra in India. If all these names haven't sent you running back to Facebook, thanks for caring. Stay a while. Read about a death or two.

'So you thought Seattle had one of the highest rates of suicide in the world? Think again. In Vidarbha, they have a suicide every eight hours. Yes, while you slept last night, another man swallowed pesticide and laid himself dead. Here, I will chronicle some of these suicides. If you want to help, spread the word. Read. Write in. Write out.'

Katya's head slumps into her hands on the desk. She forces herself to read one of his six blog posts.

Few things may lead you to Dhanpur village in the state of Maharashtra, in western India. But if you were to find yourself here, you would be drawn to two men in this village. Both men sit on the precipice of a revolution.

The first man is Bajirao Andhale, a farmer who is today the face of the terrifying crisis that grips rural India. Andhale has lost almost all his land and is hanging on to the little piece he still owns. He has thousands of rupees of loans to pay off to banks and to illegitimate moneylenders. 'Things will be better when I have married off my daughter and reclaimed my land,' says Bajirao. I admire the man's tenacity, but I think he's full of shit, aka False Hopes.

His daughter, Meera Andhale, is to be married in less than two weeks at a mass wedding, which is this government's way of helping farmers with wedding expenses and rescuing them from the vice of dowry. If you haven't any knowledge of the dowry system, have the wherewithal of the Internet. In other words, look it up, dudes.

Meera's father-in-law-to-be, Mukesh Deshmukh, abhors the

idea of dowry and has welcomed the alliance of his son to Meera with no payment of dowry at all. Meera is not a pretty girl, but I have a crush on her. No, seriously, I don't. She's really nice, though. She gives me seconds on food. I would like to post a picture of her here, but I want to respect her privacy. She speaks a little broken English and went to school until tenth grade. Now, she mostly likes to hang around inside her house. She's allowed me to post wedding pictures later. Watch this space.

The sky above this village still looks unhealthy. The monsoon is playing hide-and-seek this year and the Indian prime minister, Manmohan Singh, has declared this a year of drought. By the way, the monsoon here doesn't imply hurricanes and storms. It just means 'rainy season'. I want to see this 'rainy season', yes, even though I'm from Seattle. I hear it's quite intense. And I don't mean 'intense' as in 'Oooh, Adele is intense'. I mean, it's a downpour, and it can make or break people's lives here.

The farmers may see little help from the prime minister, but they see much hope in one man—Ammar Chaudhry, an activist educated in the best universities in India, who has moved from the city to work here. Chaudhry works tirelessly, demanding farmers' rights to better irrigation, better loan rates and to loan waivers. His chief demand is the exit of foreign seed companies that sell genetically modified seeds that have ravaged the lands of Vidarbha. One word—Monsanto. Two words—get them.

As his first attack on the problem, Chaudhry has plans for a massive farmers' rally. Thousands of farmers in the region are expected to come out to start a peaceful protest against the Indian government and against foreign seeds. 'I hope the world will be watching the Indian farmer,' says Chaudhry, who is also the one who brought the news of the mass wedding to this village.

I will stay here for the protest. I will blog it, not 'live', because the Internet connection here doesn't allow for that. But I'll blog it as soon as I can. If all goes well, I'll also stay for the wedding. It's not every day that a girl like Meera gets married.

Four pictures—a billboard advertising Bt cotton seeds, a plate of food from Gayatribai's kitchen, a shot of the back of Ammar's head, addressing the farmers yesterday, and a close-up of a single, shiny, genetically modified seed on the leathery palm of a woman's hand. Gayatribai? Yes, those were her green bangles. That was her leather.

In the menu of links on the blog was a section that said: 'What the Assholes Say'. Among these are the same links as the one Katya was compiling and printing out from, about suicide begetting suicide. Kabir had commented under these—'To those who accuse these farmers of being crazy or of killing themselves out of "greed for the government's compensation money", I ask, "Ever think of how bleak things have to be that you'd be salivating over the prospect of money your kids would get from your death?"'

Thirty-two comments. Twenty-four 'shares' on Facebook, sixteen on Twitter.

Katya throws her printouts into the trash bin. She would have felt some pride at the mature inflection in most of his writing, if the last-but-one line of the blog wasn't swimming before her eyes: '*If all goes well, I'll also stay for the wedding.*'

Clearly, Ammar was instigating this. He was giving the boy hope. In this dreary place of death and dour men who spat at the sight of strong women, her boy was thinking of revolutions and weddings and food.

Oh, Kabir, we must get the hell out of here. But he would resent her forever if she made him go now. He might even run away again. What needed to happen to make him *want* to leave? And if that wasn't likely, what would *make* him leave?

Only one person could make him leave. Ammar Chaudhry. But why would he do it?

Because he did it once before. He could do it again. The last time, Kabir was not even born yet. This time, he was at that perfect-imperfect age of a breakable heart. It would hurt, but the pain would be like a band-aid being ripped off. Better that than a surgical procedure.

Yes, Ammar would have to break Kabir's heart. And the only thing that would make him do that now was the same thing that made him do it the last time—the fear of commitment.

◦≋◦

'I want to see the village by night,' Katya says to Ammar after dinner in Gayatribai's kitchen. Kabir is outside, helping Gayatribai and Meera clean the dishes, ignoring their mortified clucking.

'I can ask Gayatribai to take you, but it's not very safe,' Ammar says.

'I'll be safe if *you* take me, won't I?'

Ammar looks at her closely. She looks back at him, letting a smile tug at her lips.

'Yes. You will.' Ammar's voice is low. 'But it would get tongues wagging.'

He goes outside, where Bajirao is tending to his bullocks. How was she to try and get Ammar to indulge in something bigger if she couldn't even get him to be alone with her for a few minutes?

Then Ammar returns and says, 'Mr and Mrs Andhale would like to take us for a walk.'

Gayatribai enters the house just in time to hear this. Even though Ammar's words are in English and even in the darkness of the hut, Katya can tell that Gayatribai is blushing from his use of the term 'Mr and Mrs Andhale' and the elevated stature of romance that Ammar is conferring on them by mentioning their conjugal bond. Katya lowers her own head and smiles as Ammar watches her.

The walk through the village is more silent than Katya had expected. Bajirao and Gayatribai lead the way, at first too self-conscious to look at or talk to each other. Katya watches them fall in step with each other. With no definite destination, they still seem to lead into the same path. Bajirao may gesture with a slight movement of his chin and Gayatribai with a tug on her sari, this way or that, or with a brush of her face with her hand. Their bodies seem so familiar with each other's sway that they appear to be two halves of the same rhythm.

Katya watches Ammar from the corner of her eye. She is getting used to looking at him this way but is hoping for a chance to sit down face to face, so she may lift and lower her gaze and have that gesture hold some meaning.

Ammar is walking with his hands clasped together behind him. His steps are slow and long, as if the act of walking is also one of deliberation. This is a walk she associates with an older generation, the one of freedom fighters and founding fathers. It isn't a walk, it is a stride—maybe even a prowl. Katya giggles softly, but loud enough for Ammar to hear.

For a moment, Katya thinks he is about to say something. But then, he gives her a quick nod and strides over to Bajirao and begins to talk to him about plans for the next day, when the two men will tour nearby villages to gather support for the farmers' rally. Katya is about to quicken her steps and catch up, but Gayatribai slows her own pace, almost automatically, so she is now walking by Katya. She keeps her face lowered and the two women walk in silence. Katya follows Gayatribai's gaze. She is watching her man walk through pain, and her face flinches with his every few steps. Katya wants to ask if the woman believes her husband's story about the attack from a bull. But she doesn't want to stir up something new. Besides, she must focus on her task for tonight—it's been a little bit derailed, but it can be brought back on track.

The little marketplace in the village is still humming with activity in the night hour. The central stretch of the street is awash in a golden glow of light from lanterns outside each stall, and then punctuated every now and then with brighter light, from fluorescent bulbs in bigger shops. Music plays in this stall or that shop, all of it loud and different, so what arises is a sound like an orchestra gone mad. Steam rises from pots still cooking dinners for those farmers that don't have families awaiting them, or for drivers of trucks that pass through Dhanpur. Men sit in groups sipping chai, poured out of aluminium kettles into small glass tumblers.

Katya slows her steps and stops here and there to look. Maybe Ammar will follow her and she can get him to slip away with her for a while.

These villages have changed since she was last here. Yet, they haven't changed enough. The little grocery store stocks DVDs, and music CDs, cell phones with SIM cards, all varieties of soft drinks, chocolate, Good Day biscuits, and sachets of shampoo for straight, curly, black, brown hair, or hair requiring protein treatments. Katya's eyes fall on the collection of DVDs in the store. She sees Hollywood films among them—*Spiderman II, Star Wars, How to Lose a Man in Ten Days, Avatar* . . . these are stacked together seamlessly with Bollywood DVDs.

Yet the houses, these huts, they all look the same as they had years ago. The same thatched roofs falling apart over mud houses clinging to the occasional brick embedded in them. How did people determine what would change and what would stay the same? Why is it that a cell phone could be seen as more desirable, more life changing than a solid roof over your head?

'Katyayini, our hosts want to show us their favourite place in the village.'

Ammar has come up behind her. She turns around and meets the impact of his searching eyes—close and large and questioning—barely a few inches from hers. After more than two days of the briefest looks, the intimacy is suddenly too much for her to bear. Katya looks away, but nods.

She would have to draw upon sterner stuff. What she was planning to do was for the best. She could not fritter away these moments that would get her closer to taking her son and getting on that plane home, where her child would be safe in his own environment.

Bajirao and Gayatribai walk ahead of Ammar and Katya but stay close enough so that they won't be swallowed by the darkness. Ammar offers Katya his arm—the path is getting stony and unpredictable as it rises and falls.

The feel of Ammar's khadi kurta is just as she remembers, but the muscles under her hand feel taut, restless. Every now and then he sets his hand around her waist, guiding her behind the couple that is leading the way.

A sheet of silver leaps up before them. The river is slim from the drought but still ripples like a silk ribbon under a lush moon.

The four of them stand silently for a while by the water. Then, Katya sees Gayatribai nudge Bajirao and the two of them turn to walk away. Ammar is about to call after them. Quickly, Katya touches his arm and lays a finger on his lips.

She isn't ready to gaze into his face yet, so she keeps her eyes on Bajirao and Gayatribai walking away from the water. Again, she stiffens a little at the way Bajirao is holding his body against pain.

'Do you want to get closer to the water?' Ammar asks, touching her forearm, pointing to a stretch of the riverbank by a tree. The night is warm and humid but her skin has turned suddenly cool under his briefest touch.

His skin has the same scent as years ago. This is a man who perspires all day but smells of nothing more than a hint of salt. His hands are like those of a doctor. Always clean, always soft and firm.

She can do this.

She reaches out for his hand to help her step over the rocks next to the river. She squeezes his arm as she lets herself slip a little. He pulls her up close and puts his one arm around her waist, the other gripping her hand as they walk together to the tree.

Treat this like a job, she tells herself. Her closest friends in America have slept with many men. What would their advice be? Men are easy, they would say. Any woman can walk into a bar and walk out with a man who wants to get laid.

Those conversations about one-night stands seem so far away. Here, Ammar's sudden desire to talk threatens to get in the way of her plans.

'Katyayini . . . despite everything . . . despite the confusion of the decisions of our youth . . . I have always held you and our . . . you and Kabir in my thoughts.'

'And what are you thinking right now, here, with me, Ammar?' She wants to bring him back, to her, right here, the Katya of today, with this skin and this touch and this teasing grip on his arm.

He smiles hesitantly. 'I was thinking . . . I have been thinking, ever since I saw you at the cremation grounds . . . that, for the first time, I feel as if you are easy within your skin, your clothes. It's as if you are finally dressed in . . . yourself.'

Katya looks down at her khaki cargo pants, her navy blue linen shirt, well fitted and drawn in at her waist with a pale blue leather belt.

'I don't understand,' she says. Is he trying to change the subject? She looks closely at Ammar's face. He looks sincere.

'Well, I was thinking that . . . the way you looked all those years ago in Mumbai . . . that wasn't quite *you*. That first day in the brothel, and then every time we met . . . you looked as though those Indian clothes you wore back then . . . the churidaar kurtas and the bangles . . . like you were *forcing* them upon yourself. You could just as easily have been dressed this way back then. But you wore your Indian clothes like a . . . *badge* of some kind.'

Ah. Good. He seems to be getting circumspect about her. He probably doesn't even know it, but he's beginning to want to fault her in some way. Now, if only he would let go of Kabir, too. She'd just have to help him along.

'Am I sounding like a boor?' Ammar says.

'Yes, a little,' she says, laying her hand on his shoulder and pushing him. 'You are a boor.'

Boor. What gems these were, these words she had left behind.

'*My* Katyayini . . . we were barely in our twenties back then. I probably tried too hard to look like a starving poet myself. Na?' He puts his arm around her shoulder.

She shakes her head and then rests it for a brief second on Ammar's shoulder. 'If you don't mind,' she whispers, 'I'd like you to hold me. I have been so scared these past few days. I have been confused for years. I don't want to feel those years between us. No distance between us.'

Ammar is silent.

She puts her hand on his chest and puts her head back on his shoulder. 'Oh, I hope no one can see us. Can they, Ammar?'

He seems not to hear what she has said. His eyes are on her throat and on the opening of her shirt. Katya waits for him to move, but he doesn't.

She stretches her feet out and dips them into the water before them. Letting one hand slide from Ammar's shoulder to his thigh, she leans over towards the water. She reaches down into the river and cups some water in the palm of her hands. Throwing her head back, she slowly pours this water on her throat and sighs as it trickles down her cleavage and soaks her bra.

Ammar continues talking. 'Anyway, the point is . . . you look absolutely lovely now. Self-assured and stylish—*that's* how I should have said it. Instead, I began to critique your sartorial savvy from so many years ago. Typical male?'

She looks at him. He's rambling. That's a really good sign.

He's been staring, she can tell, from the way his eyes dart quickly away. 'Not so typical.' She laughs. 'You are special, Ammar. And you look good yourself—handsome, almost robust. Shame on you!'

Ammar smiles. 'Ghalib would say . . . her gaze upon me puts a glow on my face . . . and she assumes that this ailing man is well.'

And she falls in step with Ammar as his effortless Urdu flows like a stream within the arid landscape on which they tread towards a stretch on which to lie.

Unke dekhe se jo aa jaati hai munh par raunak
Woh samajhte hain ke beemaar ka haal achcha hai

Katya stops. His fingers have found their way into that space they had lost years ago—he has a firm clasp on the bangles that Gayatribai gave her, and the back of his knuckles are brushing against the inside of her wrist. Katya leans against the tree on the shore as Ammar's Urdu breaks its verse and his lips fall quiet upon hers.

His head leans into her hair and she hears him inhale, feels him nuzzle deep into her neck. Alec likes to do that, too. Before she can help it, she has stiffened. Just beneath Ammar's face, her shoulders have shifted from being a place of rest to being the two frames of a guillotine.

Ammar pulls back and searches her face. She shuts her eyes and buries her head into the V-opening of his kurta.

'Please . . . don't stop . . .' she says.

'Katyayini . . .' he says. 'I don't want to hurt you again.'

'You won't. You won't. I am not a twenty-one-year-old any more. I know how not to get . . . how to prevent having a baby. My body is now a woman's, Ammar. Please. Take away those bad memories of the past. Give me new ones. Give me new marks on my body to take away those scars.' She wonders if she is putting him off.

But no, he seems to draw her closer with every word. She says the same things again, this time in a mix of Hindi and Urdu. Just as she had expected, her words strike his body into urgency.

The sounds of the river become louder in her ears. Ammar's lips on her body seem to bring the river upon her, lapping at her wherever his touch goes. After years of Alec's hands, Ammar's feel so wrong upon her but also very real. Ammar moves intuitively, looking closely at her face and almost at the pores on every inch of her skin to look for the ones that open themselves up for pleasure.

Can she distance her mind, her soul, her conscience from the very real presence of this pleasure?

She can. She does. She bucks and writhes and grips and gasps at every sensation that the river shames her into feeling. She feels a man turn hungry within her, hears the man turn into an animal upon her.

Then, in the long minutes in which they lie upon each other, trying to return their breathing to normal, Katya assembles her words in her mind, weighs each one for impact.

When Ammar reaches into her neck to kiss her with the sweetness of a man she never really knew, she says softly, 'The beauty of what just happened . . . I hope it leads to further beauty. I hope it plants a girl in me. She who will bind us together. She who will keep us here with you. I want to stay. Ammar. Oh, Ammar. Please let Kabir and me stay here with you forever!'

He sits bolt upright. Looking away from her, he stands up and pulls on the clothes he had shed.

'Did I say something wrong?' Katya says.

He doesn't answer. He gets up on his feet.

There goes a man haunted by the spectre of responsibilities. There he runs, from the shadows of her neediness.

Those old twinges of the pain of abandonment come upon her, but she shooes them away. They have no place in her heart now. This was an event of her choosing and it was going just as she planned. She lets him go. It will be hard to find her own way back to Gayatribai's home but she will manage. She wants him to be alone now, with his thoughts, and with her recent words echoing in his head.

Katya puts her head back down on the broken, thirsty land. She wants to laugh quietly to herself, to stretch languorously and savour the knowledge that her move will soon pay off. But, instead, she feels uneasy, as if the dirt beneath her body is creeping upon her and parching her thoughts.

What has she done? Is this the way home? How firmly would she hold Kabir's hand now? How closely would she draw Alec into their embrace at Baggage Claim?

Before the tears can roll past her temples, through her hair, and into the cracks in the earth, she pulls herself up, puts on her clothes, and sets about finding her way back to Gayatribai's home in the mounting night.

8

Lost

There's a feeling I get when I look to the west
And my spirit is crying for leaving . . .

KABIR'S IPOD IS cranked up loud and Katya can hear his music through his headphones.

'Really, young man? Are you trying to send me a message of some sort? Your spirit and mine can leave for the West any time, you know,' Katya laughs. She wonders if he can pick up on the tiredness in her laughter. She couldn't sleep at all last night.

Kabir looks at her and starts to hum. She reaches over and takes one of his earplugs out of his ear. It's a rule he seems to have forgotten—one ear must stay open to conversation. Little talk is happening, though, on this mother–son trip to the marketplace. He goes back to kicking stones in his path.

'Not quite downtown Seattle, hanh?' she smiles. She straightens the neon-green backpack on his shoulders. He carries it everywhere. It's probably a good thing—he always has clean drinking water on his back, her young camel.

He peers at her. 'You look odd today. What's up, Mom?'

'Oh, nothing. Just a little jetlagged but so happy to hang out with you.' She wonders if he is old enough to be suspicious about Ammar and her going for a walk last night.

As if he's read her thoughts, he says, 'You hear from Alec at all?'

'A couple of emails,' she replies quickly. 'He has plans for when we go back.'

'We should bring him here. He'd love it. Unless ... you think it might be awkward with Baba? Maybe some day?'

She swallows her rising alarm. She hadn't thought Kabir was dreaming of comings and goings of this sort, leave alone bringing her worlds to such a ridiculous collision.

'Maybe some day. You need a haircut, young man,' she says.

'Oh, cool. Can I go to one of those crazy little barber shops here? They cut your hair with these hideous cool blades. And their shops are filled with pictures of Indian movie stars.'

'Those blades probably carry HIV viruses. We'll wait until we're back in Seattle,' Katya says.

He pauses in front of a cart selling mangoes. He moves his flattened palms slowly, inches above the different varieties of mango. The purpose is to see how motionless he has to be so that the swarms of flies stay undisturbed on the fruit. The man who owns the cart doesn't look pleased with Kabir's little sport.

'Kabir, do you want me to buy you a mango?' Katya asks. This question is really for the benefit of the mango seller.

Kabir gestures at her by sticking his fingers into his mouth and pretending to gag.

'How could you not like mangoes?' she says. She shoots an apologetic glance at the mango seller. Kabir has little idea that his gesture could be construed as rude.

'Because it's the most predictable fruit in these parts. I had my fill of it in my first twenty-four hours in Mumbai. Mango slices, mango pulp, mango milkshake, mango mithai, mangoes whose flesh you suction and scrape off their skin with your teeth, mangoes that you cut down the middle, like an avocado, mangoes that you suck on from a hole in their head, mangoes in vanilla ice cream, mangoes in *mango* ice cream ... everything but mango lassi.'

'That's an American invention. Mango lassi.'

He nods, losing interest. Maybe she's told him that before.

In my thoughts I have seen rings of smoke through the trees
And the voices of those who stand looking ...

'Led Zeppelin?'

He nods again. He seems pleased at her correct guess.

He says, 'It's so cool listening to Zeppelin while looking at a little brown kid taking an open crap on the glorious Maharashtrian landscape.'

She can't help but laugh. 'Wait a minute. I thought you were totally smitten by this place.'

'... *And she's buying a stairway to heaven*,' he sings, throwing her a smile. 'I may like a lot of things. But I'm not smitten. You seem to think I am a giddy Indophile or something. I'm not.'

'What else do you like here?'

'It's easier to tell you what I *don't* like. That will be a finer conversation. At least it will be longer. Okay, so the farmer dude whose house we are living in looks like he's ready to die, but he works his butt off anyway. I don't like that. His daughter blushes when anyone mentions her wedding. I kinda like that. Gayatribai looks like she could have a lot to say, but is holding it all in because no one's ever asked her much. I don't like that. Ammar Chaudhry, the man who *sired* me. I like that. The mosquitoes and the smells and the bad news everywhere ... I don't like that.'

He skips ahead and jumps into the store selling DVDs. He rummages through the collection. The shopkeeper looks hopeful. But then, Kabir is distracted by a beam of light falling in the middle of the floor of the shop.

'Did you notice this light in the store we went to earlier? The newspaper-recycle store?' he says.

Katya shakes her head. She's still thinking about his quick remark about Ammar. She wants to talk to Ammar. Where is he? She hasn't seen him since last night. He didn't come by this morning to pick Kabir up as he had promised. The boy waited all morning. He refused to go to the fields with Bajirao and Gayatribai, just in case Ammar was simply running late. It had been hard to watch. But it was the band-aid being ripped off. How long before Ammar comes and tells them to pack up and leave?

'Mom? Are you listening? This beam of light's been following us from store to store. It's my little patch of thrill. Are you listening?'

She breaks away from her thoughts and looks at her son. He beckons at her and points. 'Look here. It's been spying on us. It seems to come from the sky and also come right out of the jute bags on the floor. It springs out of the chinks in these women's bangles. It jumps up from those steel tumblers in which we are served our tea. At one time, I thought it was shooting right out of the head of this little beggar girl who looked like she had highlights in her hair, but I know her hair was just bleached by the sun. And look here . . .' He positions himself so the light seems to fall right into his wide-open mouth.

The shopkeeper is staring at the boy. Yes, I have a strange child, she says in the look she gives the man.

The boy runs out of the shop now. She hurries to follow him. He runs into the gully behind the shop, his head looking from the sky to the ground until he suddenly stops. He's found what he was chasing. It's his patch of thrill again. The light is falling on the dusty, unpopulated narrow path between the back of two shops. He turns his back to her and before she realizes what he's doing, she sees a trickle of urine fall into the golden light.

'Kabir!'

'Just anointing my motherland with my rich waters. *Kabir was here.*' His shoulders are quaking with laughter.

'That's disgusting!' She is glad he has turned away so he can't see her laughing helplessly, quietly. She is just grateful no one is around to see their little subterfuge.

They walk past stalls selling umbrellas. They walk past sheds that repair bicycles and sweetshops where boys as old as Kabir are frying golden jalebis in iron pots of hot oil.

He seems comfortable in these narrow lanes. She says, 'Have you been here before? Did Gayatribai bring you here? These people seem to be getting used to you.'

'That's a bad sign. Never stay in a foreign land long enough for them to see you as one of them,' Kabir says.

'That's right.' Oh my God, was he getting anxious enough to want to go home? That would be perfect timing. But no, he's being facetious.

'I came here with Gayatribai yesterday. She wouldn't let me out of her sight. But you were fine with it. Strange, how the same mother who won't let me walk alone more than a few blocks in Seattle now lets me roam free in an Indian village. Do you think just because people are busy dying they won't harm a child? How can you be so sure that the fat priest with the conch shell isn't a child molester? Has anyone checked with his . . . whatever the Hindu equivalent of an altar boy is?'

She laughs loudly now. 'So you don't want to roam free?'

These are the seasons of emotion and like the winds they
  rise and fall
This is the wonder of devotion—I see the torch we all must hold.
This is the mystery of the quotient—Upon us all a little rain
  must fall.

He walks up to her now and puts his arm around her waist.
He's growing. He's almost as tall as her.

'I'm doing fine, Mom.'

'All right, all right. What do you want?'

'There's a thing I saw in this shop yesterday.'

'What is it?' She's intrigued. What could he possibly have
seen here that he would like to bring back to Seattle? Not one
of those DVDs, please.

He leads her by the hand to . . . the sari shop. He points at a
sari that has already caught her eye as they walk in, draped on
a hanger. It's silk with a border of gold. The colour is hard to
pin down—a rusty peach? A reddish orange? A yellowish brick?

'Why do you want to buy a sari? Please tell me you're not
like those Americans who drape saris on their walls or use them
as throw blankets or . . .'

'It's for Gayatribai.'

He's avoiding her gaze. He's peering closely at the sari but
not touching it, as if he's afraid to smudge it somehow.

'For Gayatribai? Do you mean for Meera? For her wedding?'

'Gayatribai stopped at this store for just a few moments when
she brought me here. She bought a wedding sari for Meera. And
then she stopped and looked at this sari for just a second, you
know? She held it up to her face and peeked in the mirror and
then quickly put it away before the shopkeeper could see her.
You know? She's . . . like . . . the mother-of-the-bride and all.
She should look nice at the wedding. Right?'

Katya can't remember the last time she's seen the boy so uncomfortable. She looks away from him, beckons at the shopkeeper who is hovering around them, and within minutes they are out of the store. Kabir puts the plastic 'Beauty Sarees' bag into his backpack.

He runs way up ahead of her. It's dusk. She wants him to stay close. But it's still crowded in this busy part of the village, so maybe it's all right. Some children younger than him start running around him in glee. Not too close but near enough for him to hear them giggle. One of them runs really close past him sometimes, and the others shriek, as if the little kid had done something bold—like seize a snake by the neck.

Kabir slows his step, walks with some nonchalance and then suddenly spins around and leaps towards the children. '*Raaaawrrr*,' he growls, contorting his face. The children leap away from him, terrified. They turn around and run without once looking behind.

'Yeah! Go home and tell your moms that the Indian foreigner is really an alien from space!' Kabir shouts at them, trying to keep the laughter out of his voice.

Then he breaks into a run, waving at her to follow. Where is he headed now? She sees him bounding towards a wooded area. This is not the way she recalls coming here. Does he know another way to their hosts' home? The group would soon be gathering for dinner. She can't let him just go his own way and waste time.

She shouts out to him but it's useless. Of course. He has both earphones in his ears now. He's bounded into the woods. This boy! He goes from being a wise old soul to being a two-year-old. She quickens her steps and tries to keep his black T-shirt in sight. The neon-green backpack is a better bet.

She's in the woods now and Kabir's figure comes into view.

Oh, good! He's stopped running. He waves at her again as she catches up. She waves both arms vigorously, trying to express her anger to him through the quickly fading light. That stops him. 'What the hell!' she shouts as she reaches him. She whacks him on the back of his head, not too hard, not too lightly.

'That would be enough for me to call Child Protective Services back home,' he says with a scowl.

'Yeah, well, too bad this isn't "back home". And I have no idea where we are. I hope *you* do.'

'This is the route Gayatribai took when I went to the market with her. This is the way I took on my own later yesterday afternoon. It was nice and shaded so it was cooler. I sat in the woods and read a book yesterday. Except . . . '

'Except?'

'Except it wasn't so dark.'

'You *think*? We don't even have our lanterns. Let's turn around.'

'Wait. Look. I see someone with a lantern up ahead.'

He breaks into a run again. She tries to grab his arm but . . . he's fourteen.

And he's right. There's a light— no, two lights—moving up ahead, and if they keep their eyes on the lights and walk quickly, they might catch up and ask someone for directions. People here would probably even walk them all the way to Gayatribai's home.

'Okay, this is creepy,' the boy says as she catches up.

They have lost sight of the lanterns. The silence that's growing around them is nothing she has heard before.

The boy starts up a chatter, probably to fight his nervousness. 'We don't have cell phones. These trees look nothing like the evergreens back home. And there's the whole business of snakes. Actually, snakes don't seem too bad right now compared to this stupid vision in my head of the ghosts of the dead farmers lurking behind these trees, watching us, closing in on us to throw us onto a burning pyre.'

'Lovely thought.'

'*Damn*, I would give anything for those annoying kids to be following us right now. Or even that priest with his conch shell.'

'Maybe if you shut up, we can listen for some sounds that will help us.'

He ignores the sharpness in her voice. 'Or maybe we can use our instincts, pick a path and just run, straight and narrow,' he says.

Katya thinks she hears a shout. She grips Kabir's hand as he is about to run. She puts her finger on his lips. She hears it again. This time she knows it's not just her, because Kabir cocks his head and listens, too.

'It's coming from behind us. It's not coming from the wooded area,' Kabir says.

They listen again. 'Kabir! Katyayini!' The voice is clear now. It's Ammar, running up behind them.

His shape looms up out of the shadows and they run towards him.

'Where do you think you're going? It's not safe to just . . .' Ammar puts his arms around both of them. Katya recoils a little but wants to keep his arm close. She is shaking—she wants to still herself. Kabir is grinning in relief but he pulls away from Ammar's awkward hug in a teenage boy kind of way.

'Katyayini . . .' Ammar says. He looks at the ground and then away, deep into the wooded area. 'Katyayini. I spent last night and this morning thinking.'

Ah. Here it comes. Should she let him do it in front of the boy? Should she let the boy catch his breath a little before his father breaks his heart?

Ammar doesn't give her much time to think. His words

tumble together. 'Stay. Yes. I love the dreams you talked about last night. The three of us are family. We'll make this family bigger. Thank you for opening my heart up to what I really want. I am mad with joy that you both will stay.'

Katya loses the last few of his words, her blood is ringing so fiercely in her ears. Her hands start shaking again.

Kabir is looking from Ammar to her. His face moves from confusion to shock.

Katya fumbles over her words now. 'Don't . . . I . . . you must . . . Ammar, please, not now. Let's go . . . let's talk later.'

'Why? This is as good a time as any. I ran around looking for you. And watching you both run up to me . . . I have never been so sure . . .' His hands are clasped around his head. He turns around in a circle, laughing, shaking his head at the sky.

'Wait a minute,' Kabir says. Katya lunges at him to put her hand over his mouth but he jumps out of her reach. 'Doesn't Baba know about Alec? Or did you break off the engagement?'

'Who's Alec?' Ammar asks.

The woods turn into a shroud, suffocating all sounds, smothering all air, yet turning shrill with every passing second.

Words put themselves together on Katya's tongue. 'Alec is my fiancé. I am engaged to be married to a wonderful man named Alec Rauland in Seattle.' She closes her eyes. She can't bear to look into the faces of this man and this boy.

But she can't escape the words. 'Why . . . why didn't you tell me? But you are planning to break off the engagement, na?' Ammar asks.

She stands there with her eyes closed. Kabir's voice arrives next. 'Mom! *Are* you? Breaking it off? But . . . why? Are you really planning to stay here? Marry Baba? I don't understand. Mom! I need to know what's going on!'

She cannot luxuriate in her despair any more. She must snap

out of it. Her son is suffering. 'No. I am not breaking it off. I am not staying. And neither are you. It's all a big mistake.'

'Last night was a mistake?' Ammar says in an instant. 'You . . . you were so sincere . . . that was a trick? A pre-planned seduction? *Why?*'

'Ammar! Show some discretion. Do you have no sense of how to speak around a child?'

'What are you guys talking about? What happened last night? Oh my God, I want to vomit. Mom, is this true? You *disgust* me!'

'I was trying to . . . I wanted to see if Ammar would show his true colours. I thought he would . . . throw us out.'

Their voices echo around the woods, oozing into the lac on the palas trees and stunning the spores on the gulmohur.

'You wanted Baba to throw us out? You wanted him to throw *me* out? Why would you do that to me? Your own child!'

Ammar speaks now, in a voice of sudden calm. 'You are engaged to another man. You did this to that man, to me, and to our son. Do you ever think of serving anyone but yourself, Katyayini? And you wanted me to bring you with me to serve other human beings? People like Bajirao, who, it turns out, sold his kidney a few days ago so he could pay for his daughter's wedding? You thought you could ever feel the pain of . . .?'

'Bajirao sold his kidney? Mom! Did you know this?'

'No! No, I didn't. I swear to God I didn't.'

'You told me you were sure it wouldn't happen. I showed you the clues and you said you were sure!'

'Kabir . . . I don't know these things. I am sorry. I am so sorry. I don't know these things any more.'

'Then why are you *here*? Why are you telling me *I* shouldn't know?'

'I . . . just want to . . .'

Ammar steps in. 'All right. Let's stop this before we say things

117

that we will regret later. Kabir, your mother and I need to talk about a few things. We'll walk a few steps ahead. You follow us and let us sort this out.'

Kabir looks like he will burst into a hundred more cries of outrage, but he nods. As the three of them walk back out of the wooded area now, in a triangle of pain, the beat of Kabir's footsteps behind her is the only thing that slows Katya's heartbeat down to where she can speak again.

She fights back her urge to ask Ammar to describe in detail the taste of his own medicine. Instead, she summons up the sincerest of voices and asks for his forgiveness. He asks for time to think. She asks for his understanding that Kabir must go home. He asks her why. She throws her angry voice into the thin wind. He asks her to quell her anger. She asks him how she could do that. They go on this way for a few hundred steps until all she can hear is words and no footsteps behind her.

In the instinct of mothers the world over, in the single second before she turns around, she already knows he is gone.

They run into the woods behind them, screaming out his name. She looks from the ground to the bark of trees, to the darkness beyond it all, looking for the flash of a neon-green backpack somewhere within it all. He couldn't have run too far, she keeps hearing in the voice of the man with her and yet, she knows that he could have. If that's what he wanted to do, her son could have run too far.

Twelve hours later, there is still no sign of him. Seven men and three women have hunted all corners of the woods and beyond, in the darkness.

In a smoke-filled dawn that sheds some light upon their hunt, these men and women have stumbled through the alleys of the village marketplace, questioned men at bus stops, and run in and out of homes of strangers in the village, just on a feeble hunch.

Then, they have informed the police. Katya has given them the photograph she carries in her wallet. She has described the circumstances of the minutes before the boy fell behind in the woods. She has spoken of every detail. She has bitten back her rage when the policeman asks her to examine why her boy keeps running away.

Another woman, too, has searched, but in a different way. Gayatribai has walked through the cotton fields in an aimless wander. She has stared at the yellow, blue and pink horns of cattle, and she has run her hand over the trunks of the trees that know her name in the woods. Soon, she has leaned into the thought that the boy has not just run away but has been taken.

9

Like Startled Crows

When the men of a village leave the arms of their women and stumble into the arms of death instead, the women look to each other to keep their secrets. The widows speak to the wedded. I should have seen the signs, they say. He spoke this way or that. He ate this, not that. He walked here, not there.

They speak also of other things, the things that happened on the road to their men's resolve. There are quotidian things—the visits from moneylenders, the long hours at Mr Sachin Patekar's office, the documents and letters that start arriving in the mail. There are the other things, spoken of only in riddles and suggestions—men who will help (and the husband never needs to find out), the best places to go and cry out loud, and the places not to let your children roam, especially your daughters.

Gayatribai knows she must now go to one of these places. She tells herself it is just to rule it out, this hunch she has. And she must go alone. The police would find nothing there. The men of the village would be loud in their approach; they know far less than women about stealth. The boy's mother should be the last to know.

She realizes she is on her way to this place already. Step upon barefoot step, she moves quicker with every passing moment until she is running—running harder than she has in years. She knows her slight frame makes almost no sound and her breath is only gasping in her head. The morning sun is already a demon that breathes without mercy upon her, as if she is the only human in the world left to cook. She turns that thought quickly on its head. Surya Devata. Don't insult the sun god, Gayatri. You need all the gods on your side.

Soon, she can see her destination and she is frightened by the desolation of the path on which she must now tread. She doesn't trust concrete. Places built with precision are the herald of men with a different bent of mind. Yet, a few years ago, she did not want to say this to anyone. This godown, now abandoned, was once bursting with activity and was fattened upon the early yields of Bt cotton. It was built to store the excess from the happy harvests many droughts ago. It was built as a temple of greed. Today, it is a tomb. It is a receptacle for the always whispered, forever unconfirmed stories of the widows.

Nothing moves around the concrete structure. She has no faith in what lies inside—or who. What would take her from here, hiding behind this tree, to there—standing before the door? She closes her eyes.

What she sees behind her eyelids is the boy's face, not from any gathered memory of the past few days, but a scattered one—the look on his face from two days ago when the man on the motorcycle had spit on the ground near his mother's feet. The boy looked shaken, like he had never witnessed such a thing before. What land did he come from, where his mother had not had her ground spat upon? Why did he have to see that scene, witness that worm? The boy's face had changed in an instant into that of a young man, soiled by the indignity of some of the men of his homeland. No. No part of him should come to harm at the hands of those men. If she waits here a minute longer, she could never live with herself.

She's at the door in all the brightness of the morning, in all the wide openness of this place. The door has no lock, just a bolt. This gives her pause. Has her hunch been wrong all along? Has she come to the wrong place? Why would those men put no lock on the door?

Faith. The men have faith that no one dares lift the bolt, shake it, and send secrets and shame flying like startled crows.

But they don't know that she has faith, too. Faith that comes from beyond her muscles and bones and joints. Faith that settles on her shoulders as she wraps the bolt in her fingers and lifts it. It squeaks. She drops it, along with her heart. All is silence around her. She does it again. This time, she moves the bolt slowly. It moves a fourth of an inch. Her sari blouse was damp with perspiration from running before, but it is now soaked with terror. She can't believe her hand is still moving, slowly, up and down, as she stands stark against the door, her haldi-yellow sari screaming its presence in the whiteness of this place.

With every half inch of loosening of the bolt, she can smell the recent presence of men. The stench of beedi upon paan upon sweat is clear and close, but she doesn't know how close. She doesn't know that barely sixteen feet on the other side of the godown, two men are walking around, trying to find a cell phone reception so they can get orders on what exactly is to be done with the captured boy. Their faith deafens their ears to the squeaking of the bolt. But all faith can be broken.

Gayatribai pries open the door and there, before her, lies the boy. He's on the floor, curled up in a heap. He looks asleep, or unconscious. On the walls all around him are beehives, and in the air just over his head, an army of bees hovers in waiting. She rushes to him soundlessly and puts a hand on his bruised chin, taking care not to fan the space claimed by the bees. The boy wakes up with a gasp. She clasps her hand down upon his mouth. He jumps to his feet with her, trying to take in the scene. The bees scatter and then spin around in rage.

Gayatribai rushes with the boy to the door. And then, it arrives, a cyclone in her chest. She coughs and then coughs again and again, until her body is racking and reeling, and she is immobilized, doubled over.

'Koan?' a shout comes out from behind the godown.

The boy says something, shaking in fear. He pulls at Gayatribai's coughing frame in panic.

She shakes her head and pushes him. 'Za!' she says through her coughing. 'Za!'

'Koan ahay?' The shout is closer now. They hear footsteps and then a scramble growing close.

'Za,' she says weakly. 'Ayi . . . Mom . . .' she waves her hand in the direction of the village.

She pushes the boy, hard, and then slaps him when he tries to grab her hand. She crumbles to the floor. The boy is stunned but he gets the message. He turns away in an instant. He runs. He flies out of the door and runs into the clarity of the day and she watches him go and go and go until the shouting silhouettes of two men appear at the door. One of them turns to look at how far the boy has run. The man screams in frustrated rage. The other one looks quietly, stoically at Gayatribai hacking through her breaths on the floor. The men enter, and, just as they shut the door behind them, she thinks she sees the slightest sliver of the boy twist around to look.

'Za,' she says into her sobs, and she falls into prayer for him. She prays also for Bajirao, for Meera, and for all those in the village who should find the boy but not hear his story of the men, the shutting door, and her.

☙❧

Katya has taken to gazing at the horizons. All night, she looked at shadows cast from light bulbs and lanterns swinging in frantic searches. She'd know his shadow anywhere. But now, in the morning hours, it's the horizons upon which she stares, with dry eyes, waiting for a clear shape to loom up and say, 'I'm sorry I frightened you, Mom. It was just me being stupid and running away. No harm, no foul.'

The barren horizons tell her there is harm and there is foul. There was something about those two lights in the wooded area yesterday. It was as if they were leading, luring Katya and Kabir deeper inside. The police made nothing of it, but she knows Kabir's disappearance has something to do with those lights. So she's standing now, somewhere at the edge of the wooded area and the village, looking on either side of the horizon while other searchers fan out further.

This land is growing frighteningly alien without the one human being that had tethered her to these shores for the past few days. Still, each boy in the village is beginning to look like Kabir. The goatherd who is approaching now, in a cloud of dust raised from the hooves of his goats, looks like Kabir did at the age of ten. The crooked teeth, the long stare, the clear skin of young boyhood, all make her want to hold the goatherd and hug his face into her belly, hide it there until it does indeed turn into Kabir's face and he struggles out of her grasp saying, 'That's way too inappropriate, Mom. That hug lasted five seconds too long for decency.' *Come back with all your irreverence, my son.*

But the goatherd keeps his distance. He doesn't stop staring;

he knows her story and the reason for her frantic sorrow. He's curious about how foreign people wear their misery. She doesn't know what to show him. She doesn't know what he can see. She shuts her eyes even though it's dangerous to do so. In the darkness within, there is a surge of hope that when her eyes are opened, the horizon will present that shape she longs for. *You were supposed to be here for ten days, Kabir. Not fair.*

As if to drown out the sounds of pleas to Kabir in her head, the goatherd's little sea of goats start to bleat around her. She keeps her eyes closed. She doesn't remember from all those years ago whether she is supposed to get out of their way or just stand there and let them create their own path around her, bump into her, step on her toes or steer clear.

If only Alec could see her now, lost, outlandish in her own land. What had she said to him? *If I need you, I will call. I promise.*

She feels one of the goats come up to stand snug against her right leg. She fights her instinct to shoo it away. She gives in to the comfort of the goat's heartbeat against her shin.

The goatherd shouts out. She turns to tell him it's all right, she doesn't mind the goat, but the child has turned away from her, pointing at the horizon, at a shape running towards them.

She had hoped for this but she hadn't really expected it. Kabir is running up to her in the clear day. He looks unbroken.

She stands there, unable to move away from the goat pressing against her now. Goats and goats and goats stand around her, trapping her in the ground, keeping her from running to her son.

As he draws close, she can see a bruise on his chin and more on his arms. Oh dear God. Someone had given him a beating. What else had . . .

'Mom! Come with me . . . it's Gayatribai! She's being . . . she's being assaulted. I . . . I have to go back. Come with me!'

'Kabir, wait! What? Who took you? Go back where? I don't know what . . .'

'Dammit, Mom. I shouldn't have left. She told me to run. She told me to run to you and I ran. But I should have fought. They're assaulting her right now, Mom. Please understand. Do you understand?'

'Who?' Katya fights for breath. Why can't he just run to her and stop here with her? Why can't they just stop all this?

The goatherd has leapt to action and is clearing the goats away from her. He senses the urgency, even though he doesn't understand a word Kabir has said. He opens a path, straight and narrow, between her and Kabir, but Kabir has turned around and is running away from her, back into the horizon he came from.

'Kabir! Stop! We can't go back into danger . . .'

His words are flying away from her but she strains to run after him and hear his shouts. 'We have to, Mom. I have my Swiss Army knife. I was afraid to use it when they had me. Now I'm not afraid. We must save her! They're cowards, Mom. We can take them. They didn't beat me much. They were waiting for orders or something. I'm fine. But I know something really bad is happening to Gayatribai. We have to go back!'

She has no idea what she is running towards. If she can just get her hands on her son, she will slap him to his senses. He knows this, so he's running, faster than ever, despite that backpack still on his back, across shrubs and thirsty ground, jumping over roots and rock and rubble, and all she can do is follow and keep herself from falling down.

Desperate thoughts crowd against her skull. Her eyes scour the landscape around them, looking for just one more human being to bring along with them. Words of warning from Alec, years of hearing him talk about police and criminals, fall by the wayside as she follows her son towards clear and present danger.

Suddenly, he has stopped running and she can't believe she has actually made it to him, panting, almost collapsing in exhaustion. Kabir grabs for her arm. He is shaking. She must be strong. Not just strong; she must be brave.

They stand there for a moment, mother and son, on a wide stretch of concrete, staring at a godown, so far, far away from any earth of their combined comprehension, hearing each other's heartbeats beating in unison to a fear so insanely foreign.

They hear a muffled cry, in no particular language.

'It's Gayatribai,' the boy says. His voice is lower than a whisper, but it still sounds like a shout. Her hand flies up to cover his mouth.

'You have to tell me what's going on,' she whispers, glad for the contact of his skin under her hand. 'Tell me what to expect. How many men? Are they armed?'

Kabir shakes his head. 'I don't think they are armed. They hit me with their fists. I . . . I fell behind when Baba and you were fighting in the woods. I just didn't want to hear your voices any more. These two guys grabbed me and stuffed a rag in my mouth. They dragged me to this place and kicked me around. Then they started making phone calls to someone. They left me locked up at night. I shouted and no one heard me.'

Every parent has nightmares of their child shouting for help and no one hearing them. Hers came true last night. It came true and it was over and done with. Now, she would make sure it never happened again.

Waves of darkness swim around her, threatening to claim her into the sleep she hasn't had for two nights. These waves and each word from her child's mouth are terrifying and she just wants to sink to the ground and wail.

'They came back in the morning and started making calls again. That's when Gayatribai came and found me. She just

walked in the door and shook me awake. She told me to run to
you and those men trapped her behind. It's been almost an hour.
Oh my God, Mom, do you think they killed her? No, wait. We
just heard her cry out. Are they beating her?'

Katya stands there, frozen. Inside the godown is a woman
who hadn't hesitated to save Kabir's life. Such was her insanity.
Now, was Katya to do the sane thing or the insane?

'Give me your knife,' Katya says.

Kabir reaches into his backpack without a moment's
hesitation. 'Not you, Mom. At least, not you alone. I will . . .'

And then, there's that coughing. It's unmistakable. Even
though it's mixed with cries like that of a dying beast, it's
inescapable. It's Gayatribai crying for help.

They start to run, both of them, without saying a word to
each other. They run towards the door of the godown. *No, no.
This isn't right. She can't let her child run into danger.*

She grabs his shoulder and yanks at it so he stops. She can
tell his eyes are turning crazy.

'You wait here,' she whispers to him through her panting.

'What? That's ridiculous. We need to run screaming towards
her so we frighten those men away.'

'No! Be quiet a moment. You will have to wait here. Both of
us will shout and scream so we can interrupt whatever is going
on. But you have to stay away. If I scream out your name, you
can come and help. Okay? We can't both run towards this at the
same time. You are my back-up. Be my rock. Be the one who
saves us. *Do you hear me?*'

He nods. But she doesn't trust he will obey.

'Please promise me you will do this,' she says.

'I *will*. Now, go!'

Kabir crouches behind a tree. And she runs. They scream
and shout and she rattles the bolt on the door.

'The police are coming!' she shouts in Marathi. 'The villagers are all coming here in a minute! Don't you dare run!'

She leaps and ducks right out of view to the side of the godown as the door flies open. She sees the back of the head of a man who runs, in a straight line, out and away. Behind him, trailing, seems to be a sheet of dusty yellow fabric. The man is clutching it and running. All she can think is: *At least he is running in the opposite direction from where my child stands.* In this moment, she slumps in gratitude for that single blessing.

She waits a moment, glancing at Kabir crouching behind the tree. All is silent but for the coughing. Where is the second man? Her knuckles are throbbing from their whiteness around Kabir's knife in her hands. Is she to experience plunging this blade into the back of a human today? Could she do this? Who would die if she didn't?

She feels her legs propel her from her hiding place and in through the door of the godown. She looks down to see Gayatribai lying naked on the floor. There's no one else around. The woman is clutching about her for her clothes but her hands are coming away empty. Katya stares at her, trying taking it all in. She can hear footsteps running towards them. *Is the man coming back?*

No, it's Kabir! She turns around and screams, 'Don't. Not yet. Stop, Kabir. Stop! There's no danger here, but stop!'

But the boy is upon them and his eyes are aghast at the sight before him. Katya sinks to the ground and tries to shield Gayatribai from view. Kabir turns away in the same instant.

'Oh my God! What happened? Mama, is she alive at least?'

Mama. He hasn't called her that in years. He is frightened.

'Yes, she's alive,' Katya says. Gayatribai is whimpering but is also trying to struggle to her feet. Katya can see in front of her the instinct of a mother—it kicks in before her mind has had a chance to react. For the boy's sake, the two women need to pull the world together.

The fabric the man was running away with was a sari. Gayatribai's yellow sari. *Why the fuck would that man take her sari?* To deepen her humiliation? Of course.

Katya finds Gayatribai's blouse and petticoat thrown in the corner of the room. It's only now that she notices a hundred bees, buzzing in the air, but none of them are attacking. Leave the violence to the humans, they seem to say.

Gayatribai is shaking and her fingernails are slick with blood, from clawing at the floor during her rape. Katya gets a firm grasp on Gayatribai's arms and holds them down to stop the woman's shaking. She puts Gayatribai's blouse and petticoat on for her. The loops in the back of the blouse are ripped off and the little hooks are broken. The men had obviously torn the blouse off her body.

'Don't turn around yet, Kabir. But tell me you still have the bag from the marketplace.'

'What? Yes. Yes. It's still in my backpack, I think.'

'Toss it to me. Gayatribai will not walk into her village naked. Those men will not have their way.'

Minutes later, the three of them are hobbling together on the same road upon which each of them had run today. A boy who can't stop shaking, a woman whose mind is racing and another woman dressed in a silken sari befitting a virgin bride.

Gayatribai tries to speak through her hacking cough, her bloodied hands joined in prayer and pleading.

Katya holds her close. She's incoherent. Let her cry. Let her get it all out before Katya throws questions at her. Was it one man or two? Did the men have a weapon? Did Gayatribai know who they were? Would she be able to identify them? Was she grievously hurt? How violent had they been? Should she take

Gayatribai straight to a hospital or should they go home and fetch the men first? Would the men have killed Kabir? Raped him? Or held him for ransom?

It's as if Gayatribai can hear all the questions in Katya's head, for she starts to give answers to those exactly.

'Sahukar,' she says through her coughing.

'Sahukar? Moneylender,' Katya says. The second term comes out of her instinctively. Why is she translating for Kabir? His knowledge of what happened to Gayatribai must stop right here, right now.

Gayatribai says something Katya cannot understand. But she is using a gesture that everyone all over the world understands. She rubs her thumb and forefinger together.

'Money? He wanted money?' Kabir says.

Gayatribai nods at the boy, probably in understanding of the English term that might have been used around her. Then, ignoring Katya altogether, she leans over and places her hands on Kabir's mouth, cupping it, just like Katya had done a few long moments ago, when they had been standing outside the godown.

Gayatribai jumps back when she realizes she has covered Kabir's face in her blood. She falls to the ground and starts to cry.

'It's okay, it's okay,' the boy is saying to her desperately, his eyes whiter than ever through the stains of blood, imploring Katya to translate.

They hold Gayatribai together, their arms around her and on each other's shoulders. They wait until her sobs and coughs ebb. They keep quiet and listen.

She tells them that the men had kidnapped Kabir to teach Ammar a lesson. They don't want the farmers' protest rally to go ahead. They work for the moneylender and were taking orders from him. But when Gayatribai rescued Kabir and he ran away, the men changed their plans. They argued. One man thought Gayatribai should just be beaten and sent back to walk through the village naked to serve as an example. Another man decided on . . . more. Bajirao owes the men money. That man who violated her . . . he often comes to their door, threatening all kinds of things. That is why Meera needs to be married off quickly and that is why Meera doesn't roam the village freely and that is why Meera is told to shrink into the kitchen when anyone arrives at their door.

Despite the horror of the present moment, Katya is startled that she hadn't noticed any of these things with Meera at all. How could she have been so oblivious to a young girl's captivity? She had just assumed that Meera was a homebody.

Katya feels a foreign shame wash over her. How far from the ground was her ear that she hadn't heard any of the whispers in the home of her hosts?

Gayatribai is still talking. The sahukar has been frustrated that he couldn't go to the house with his threats any more because the foreign guests were there, people with connections. His men had decided that humiliating Gayatribai would send a message to the village, to Bajirao, to the farmers planning to protest. One of the men left and the other man stayed behind to do the job. Gayatribai didn't struggle because she wanted to live. She didn't fight back because she didn't wants cuts and bruises on her body. He had punished her as a threat. He said that if the farmers' rally wasn't cancelled, the next time she would pay with her life instead of with her shame.

Bajirao must not know what happened.

Katya stiffens. 'What? That's insane. That's not possible. You can't ask for that.' Katya's words run into each other. Gayatribai looks frightened, even more frightened than she had while lying there naked on the ground.

'Gayatribai . . .' Katya says, struggling to find the kindest of words in all of Marathi.

'Gayatribai, you don't have to be frightened of that man any more. He will be brought to justice. The law will be on your side. The police will be on our side. They will not take this lightly. Kabir was kidnapped and beaten. And what happened to you today is the worst kind of injustice. Bajirao will want justice for you, for him. The whole village will back you. The whole world will back you. The press will make sure you . . .'

Her voice trails off. She sees it now. She sees these dark woods into which she is urging Gayatribai to go. The village. The law. The world. The press. Each of these words must seem to this woman like her sari was being wrenched from her over and over again.

What is one to do? What is the way here? What is the right thing? Katya pauses to think of things she has never had to think of before. She has only reported news in the aftermath. News is what happens after the event. She has never been on the other side of an event, the side on which something could easily never have happened at all.

Her mind returns to the present. Kabir is naked. Why is he naked? The sight of his skin, so soon after the sight of Gayatribai's skin, is a shock to her. She has to struggle to understand what's going on. He's not naked. Only his T-shirt is off. He is wiping the blood from his face and wiping Gayatribai's hands, soaking up all the blood from them and then giving her another corner with which to wipe the tears from her face. She accepts all this very quickly and then rakes her fingers through her hair and stands up. Apart from the wretched look on her face and her coughing, it's as if nothing ever happened. Except, she is dressed in a rich sari.

'We can't tell Bajirao,' Kabir says, folding his hands in a plea and imploring Katya to look at him.

How has he understood what Gayatribai was saying? This boy has his ear close to the ground.

'I . . . have to think. Those men could come back. They could harm you. They could harm Meera or Gayatribai. We might not be so lucky next time. I have to think.'

'No, you don't. You have to *listen*. You have to respect her wishes,' Kabir says.

'You don't know anything, Kabir. She doesn't know how dangerous this is. She could be attacked again. She can't let this go . . .'

'Is it possible that she *knows* what she's doing?'

Who *is* this child? How could he be saying what he is saying? How could he sound like he knows what's going on?

He continues, 'I understand what you are saying. I feel the same way you do. I also don't understand how anyone can want what Gayatribai wants. I come from a place where people would call the cops for much less than what happened tonight. Right, Mom? Isn't that right?'

He isn't trying to tell her anything. He is really just asking. He's asking her a question. *Listen, Katya.*

'Yes, right. Right.' This much she knows.

'But we can't mess up her life. That's all I am feeling right now. We have to listen to her. Right?'

She stays silent. She has to think. She has to.

But they are almost upon the village now. She has no more steps left in her journey towards thought.

'We won't tell Bajirao,' she hears herself whisper to Gayatribai. The woman looks almost normal now as relief washes over her. 'We won't tell anyone. But . . . you and I . . . we won't let Kabir out of our sight. We won't let *you* out of our sight. Is that understood?'

'No, we won't,' Gayatribai says. 'And we will each watch over the other. Ayi shapath.' I swear upon my mother's life.

Kabir falls in step with Katya as Gayatribai walks ahead on shaky legs into the village. Watching her, Katya pictures in her head what the men in the godown had intended for Gayatribai's return to look like. Even if Gayatribai had waited until dark, she would have been seen, crouching or running naked through the narrow streets, the raped mother of next week's bride.

But now, few people notice Gayatribai. On seeing Kabir, people begin to run around, shouting, giving each other the good news. Fetch the boy's father, someone shouts.

Katya feels an odd sense of . . . arrival. These people are rejoicing in the safe return of her boy. Someone else here also feels overwhelmed at the sight of Kabir. What their shouts are telling her is that there are now a few more people in the world to love her son. After all the hours of feeling alone in the world, in her waiting, she can find some joy in this strange reunion.

As the crowds gather to celebrate Kabir's return, Ammar arrives with a naked look of relief upon seeing the child he has only known for days. Gayatribai slips into her home, washes away the scent of a beast from her body and dissolves the caked blood on her fingers, letting it all flow into the soil beneath her home, knowing that the earth will receive her secrets and her skin the same way it had once received the truths and the flesh of the goddess Sita.

Outside, Katya listens with a falling face as Kabir lies like he has never had to lie before. He had run away, he tells his father and the villagers. He wanted to spite his parents and then he got lost and he stumbled and hurt himself in the dark, and in the morning, he found his way home and ran to his mother.

Nobody here knows how Kabir's voice rises a pitch when

he's nervous nor how he turns more and more eloquent with every frightening half-truth he speaks. Nobody suspects a thing. No harm, no foul.

☙

Late in the night, Katya hears Meera scramble out of bed to open the back door and let Bajirao in. The young woman tells her father that her mother is sick and wants to sleep by herself in the far corner of the hut. She has asked that Bajirao not worry. She will be better in the morning if she can just rest well for one night.

Three people in the hut lie awake almost all through the night. In the safety of Bajirao's slumber, announced by his light snoring, Gayatribai allows herself a few muffled sobs. She coughs blood into her pillow. Katya puts her hand on Kabir's head again this night as he lies shaking in his sleeping bag, startling himself awake every time sleep tries to claim him. Katya's mind roams from Gayatribai's nightmare to Kabir's. What will this event mean to his life from here on?

As her thoughts run into each other, she feels a flicker of heat on her face. She opens her heavy eyes but she sees nothing. She has imagined it. The heat seems to have sprung out of the beginnings of a dream in which she is standing before a blazing fire with other people huddled around her, crying.

She sits bolt upright. No. Bajirao should not find out what happened today. It would send him to his funeral.

10

The Waters of Drought

HOLDING A PILLOW soaked in the blood from your wife's chest
can send the scent of death into your lungs. But this was not
the time to dwell on that. This was the time to arrest her illness
and make her whole, healed, for she was and must always be
the hardier one.

Bajirao sat facing her, but he didn't want to look directly at
her. It would seem shameless, insolent, especially to the foreign
woman, who was sitting so close to Gayatri. So he kept his eyes
beyond them at a point in the distance, on the road stretching
away from them as the bus trundled along on its journey to town.

He understood why the foreign woman wanted to be on this
journey. She was the one who insisted that they take Gayatri
to the city hospital when they saw the bloodied pillow in the
morning. But he wasn't sure why the boy had come along. At his
age, shouldn't the boy want to spend his day playing in the village
or riding around in the jeep with his father? Instead, there he
was, sitting crushed between his mother and Gayatri, squirming
every time the two women grasped him in their anxiety that he
might fall off the bus.

Obviously, neither the boy nor his mother had ever made a journey seated on the roof of a bus. The four of them had arrived late at the bus stop and there were no seats available inside the bus. The driver pointed to the roof, where already, a crowd of people had perched themselves. The driver seemed to have taken pleasure in watching the foreign woman struggle at first with the suggestion and then with the climb to the top on a ladder. The boy, of course, would be delighted with the adventure. But it was hard to read this child's face. He looked, sometimes, like an old man. He looked like he had grown older since just yesterday. His ordeal of being lost and separated from the village had clearly taken a deep toll.

Bajirao could talk to the boy. Yes, he would. He spoke to the foreign woman over the noise of the bus. She spoke to her boy, who seemed to perk up just a little at the explanation of what was going on. Riding on the roof was common here, Bajirao told them. The transportation authorities made it safer by putting a rung around the four sides, for people to hold on to. Those who were in the middle were expected to be shepherded in by the people on the periphery. But it was harder here in the middle, because they had to squat and and did not have a firm perch.

The bus hit a bump and Bajirao jerked forward. He stopped himself just in time from falling upon his wife and their guests. Gayatri jumped like a startled animal. Why was she so uneasy? Would it be so shameful if a husband were to accidentally touch his wife?

Here it was again, her cough, which they all knew wouldn't stop for a good few minutes. It was also a reminder of why they were on this journey, carrying the blood on her pillow and the blood in her chest all the way to a doctor. Bajirao tried not to think of the money the doctor would ask for. The boy had asked the other day about what they meant in the village about 'one little thing'. Would today bring that one little thing? Bajirao reached into his bag and fingered the sachet of pesticide.

Ammar Chaudhry had seemed surprised at the foreign woman's desire to go with Gayatri to the hospital. He seemed perplexed, too, with the boy's demand to accompany them. Naturally, he wanted to spend more time with his son in the days before the boy left with his mother—especially after the boy had gone missing.

Out of nowhere, the boy's mother had suddenly started to plead that the protest rally be cancelled. Ammar Chaudhry was shocked at her suggestion. The woman looked like she wanted to say more but she had stayed quiet for a while and then she went back to worrying about Gayatri's coughing. She talked about some research about women's health in rural India. She said she had barely slept all night from Gayatri's coughing and would be uneasy until she learned what the doctor had to say.

Ammar Chaudhry also seemed reluctant to give up Bajirao's work for the day, in the field and in the organization of the rally, but he relented. He seemed, for a moment, to want to drive everyone to the hospital in his jeep. But then he had suddenly seemed to change his mind. Everyone was left with a feeling of things being odd, askew, like a plough on an ailing bull.

The bus was picking up speed now. And in this land of stillness, there was suddenly a breeze. A ripple of sighs went through the crowd on the top of the bus, but Bajirao's heart skipped a beat. The wind lifted the flowing end of Gayatri's sari and raised it into the air behind her, as if mistaking it for the flag of a strong country. It stayed flying there now, rising and falling gently to the swaying of the bus. And Gayatri, sitting before him, watching him through her sleepy eyes, turned into a fairy from a verdant land, her green wings soaring behind her, lush against the sky that led them out of Dhanpur.

Bajirao couldn't take his eyes off her, no matter how rude it looked. These glimpses were the waters in his drought. They washed away the remnants of the images that otherwise played before his eyes all day—his fingers digging, digging, digging into the cracks in the earth of his field, coming up with nothing but weeds.

Two hours later, the verdant fairy was trapped and pinned down into a box. The doctor said that the machine into which Gayatri was being rolled as she lay on its bed would make a loud noise, which was necessary, to take a deep picture of her insides. The X-rays he took were not enough, he said. The doctor swore that this machine, which looked like nothing Bajirao had ever seen before, would be harmless.

Bajirao watched as his wife was swallowed almost whole by what looked like a shallow well lying on its side. He wondered what she could hear and if she could bear the noise the machine was making. Would he need to shout into her ears from this day on? He hid a smile at that thought.

While they waited for the results to arrive, the boy's mother took them to the canteen and bought lunch for all four of them. Bajirao wondered whether to tell her that his stomach would always get upset the day after he ate food cooked by anyone other than Gayatri or Meera, or their older daughters before they married and left for their husbands' homes. He would feel sick, especially if the food was cooked in a hotel. And this was a hospital.

He looked at Gayatri, hoping she would tell him what to do, with a twist of her nose ring. But she kept her face lowered. Bajirao noticed the skin around her nose ring was a little red. Had it caught in her long hair again? He hid away the image that leapt into his mind, of their lovemaking, of Gayatri with her long hair shaken out and flowing around her bare body. When her hair caught on her nose ring, his fingers would gently pry them away. He blinked. This was a hospital. It was a place for disinfected thoughts.

The boy and his mother talked a little, smiled every now and then, but always seemed to sober up quickly. The foreign woman looked pensive. She appeared to have grown tired in her days here, and she seemed to be lost in her thoughts. Her voice had grown quieter since the first day she had arrived in Dhanpur. But then, in recent years, these villages did such things to their inhabitants.

Another thought came to him, as it had for a few days now: did Gayatri know just how deep they were in debt? Did she know about the dowry he had to pay for their daughter? Did she know about the kidney that had bought their daughter's groom? Dear God, she must not know. Did she know about the men who worked for the moneylender? Did she know that those men were threatening to take away the family's last acres of land? Did she know about the terrible threats the men made to Bajirao on his way home from the fields? Bajirao could never let those men get to Meera or Gayatri. Meera would be gone to live with her new husband in a few days, but how would Bajirao keep his Gayatri safe?

He had little time to dwell on these thoughts. The doctor had sent an attendant to fetch them from the canteen. The boy's mother frowned at this and possibly sensing his eyes on her, she changed her expression to a shaky smile. She asked the boy to stay in the waiting area outside the doctor's room. The boy protested. Gayatri insisted she would stay with the boy. She said she was in no hurry to find out what was happening to her insides. She would wait to learn of it from Bajirao.

And so it was that Bajirao saw what lay in his wife's lungs even though her body was not next to him. The doctor spoke to the boy's mother in English and only nodded at Bajirao every now and then. He jabbed at the smudge on the shadowy images of his Gayatri's inner being.

Bajirao knew the word 'cancer' but he could understand little else. The foreign woman said something to the doctor, who then turned and spoke to Bajirao in Marathi.

The cancer was new, the doctor said. They had done well to bring Gayatribai in so quickly after the coughing started. Most people wait until the patient is not just coughing up blood but having seizures, and by then it is too late to stop the cancer from spreading to the bones, the brain, and the liver. The doctors could remove Gayatribai's tumour with a surgery. It would be no problem. And the cancer was not spreading too quickly. So they had at least a month to raise the money for the operation.

The doctor kept talking but Bajirao could not hear him any more. His mind was nowhere, but it wasn't here either. He had to struggle to keep it from leaving him entirely.

A woman's hand held a glass of water before him. It was the boy's mother. Bajirao looked at her face, hoping she was crying so *he* didn't have to. But her face looked pinched and she kept her eyes on him in a fixed stare.

She said something. At first, Bajirao thought he hadn't heard it because his mind wasn't with him yet. But then she repeated what she said. 'How can so many terrible things happen to just one woman? Do you know why this has happened?' she said. She didn't wait for an answer. 'It's because of *you*. It's because you have been irresponsible. You are not fighting back. You . . . you smoke beedis. Your wife inhales what you exhale. The smoke of your beedi is more dangerous to her than it is to you. Surely, someone must have told you at some time to stop?'

The doctor translated numbers, lists of research that the foreign woman was discussing with him, of women across the country whose health and safety comes last on the list of priorities for their men. Bajirao heard each word, sharp and clear. His mind was here. And now it refused to run away.

The foreign woman turned back to him and spoke, '. . . and the fires she burns all day. In the kitchen, in and around the household . . . all from wood. She never stood a chance.'

Then, the foreign woman's voice rose to a higher pitch. Even the doctor looked startled. '*Why couldn't you keep her close? Why couldn't you keep her close? Why couldn't you keep her close?*'

The boy came darting through the door. He ran to his crying mother and put his arms around her, begging her to stop.

                                              ◦≈◦

They didn't have to ride on the roof of the bus on the way back. They found seats easily in the thinning crowd of mid-afternoon, though the seats were paired for two and set apart from each other. Gayatri asked the boy to sit with her. She hadn't asked any questions about her own test results. The boy's mother, her eyes red from the events of the afternoon, sat by Bajirao. She now joined her hands and asked for his forgiveness for her outburst.

He joined his hands and shook his head, begging her not to consider him worthy of an apology. He spoke to her slowly so she would fully understand: Gayatri should not know of her condition until after their daughter's wedding the following week. Soon after that, he would have the money ready, and they would take her in for the surgery.

The foreign woman sighed and shook her head. She said she was tired of the secrets in this village. Bajirao had to tell Gayatribai, or she would do it instead. The foreign woman asked to be allowed to pay for the operation. She said something about owing Gayatribai a debt.

The woman didn't wait for him to answer. She didn't wait to hear him tell her that he would not accept a single rupee of charity and that he had no idea what she meant by owing Gayatri a debt. She simply rose and walked to her son on the bus. She smiled at Gayatri and nudged her to go and sit by her husband.

Bajirao saw Gayatri glancing around to look at him at the back of the bus. He caught his breath. She looked more alive than he had ever seen her look.

She came to sit by him. She listened as he told her, word for word, what the doctor had said. As he talked, she put her head on his shoulder and fell asleep. Bajirao could still smell the scents of the hospital in her hair—plastic, medicine, disinfectant—he inhaled it all. On the exhale, he tried to hold all the air back in his lungs. But he couldn't hold his thoughts back: he had slowly murdered his Gayatri with the fire of their hearth. He was killing her with his own breath.

When they arrived at the village, the boy's mother asked for them to stop off at Ammar Chaudhry's home-office for a few minutes. When they got there, there was a lock on the door. The boy who sometimes ran errands for Ammar Chaudhry was outside, sipping tea. He told them that Ammar had left in his jeep mid-morning and had said to tell them that something had come up in the city and he wasn't sure when he would be back.

Even through his own state of dull shock from the news about Gayatri's lungs, Bajirao couldn't help but notice the boy's face—for a moment, the child's lips quivered and his eyes carried the threat of tears; in the next instant, he pulled on a mask of nonchalance. And although he pulled his shoulders back and up, his mother's arm found its quiet way there. The woman looked like she was about to say something, words of anger or of comfort, but she seemed to change her mind.

The four of them walked in silence to their home. As they

approached in the falling light, Bajirao saw the shadow of a man seated on the porch of the hut. His heart started to beat painfully in his chest. Gayatri gasped and sprang towards their home, shrieking Meera's name.

The man leapt to his feet, startled. He joined his hands in greeting and Meera came hurrying out of the house. It was just a messenger from the home of the sarpanch. They had been invited to dinner in the home of the sarpanch. The sarpanch's wife wanted to welcome the visitors to the village, and the sarpanch wanted to discuss plans for the protest with some of the village men.

Bajirao knew better than to refuse an invitation from the sarpanch. He hoped the boy's mother wouldn't make a fuss. She didn't. Bajirao told the others to go on ahead without him. Yes, even Meera. He would follow after he had rested for a little.

Gayatri held his gaze for a moment. He did not deny her the look. Something in his face seemed to reassure her. Yet, she said to him that he should think of Meera and her wedding day. She nodded at him and led everyone away, even the boy, who said he was tired and didn't want to go. You will go wherever we go, both his mother and Gayatri said to the boy.

He waited for their voices to slowly fade away. He waited until the louder voices sank into the distance. Then he heard Gayatri's voice—almost a whisper at this point, but unmistakable in the way it suddenly rose and fell. It was only when everything was silent that he knew why he was here and what he wanted from this room.

He walked over to where Gayatri kept the family's few clothes, in neat piles of the washed and the unwashed. He hadn't noticed it before but there was a new pile now, clothes for Meera's wedding—two silk saris, and another one in polyester, whose bright floral pattern made up for the cheapness of the fabric.

There was the red sari that Meera borrowed from her mother the other day. The yellow sari wasn't here. Did it get torn or become too worn? Was Gayatri now using it as rags in the kitchen? It always hurt him when this happened.

But tonight, he was looking for something else. He plunged his hands into the small pile of clothes that Gayatri was to wash tomorrow. Within that pile was Gayatri's pink sari, the one that always carried best the scent of her perspiration. He teased it out gently from amidst the other clothes. He pulled it to himself and didn't inhale until his face was buried well into the fabric. How long would this sari last? It wasn't right that it should survive for so long, that it should plan to outlive its wearer.

He ripped the sari with his hands, surprised at how little effort it took.

The pieces were beautiful. Each one fluttered to the ground as if there were a wind in this room, in this village. The pieces fell upon those places in the hut that were all too familiar. Each piece of this sari must have touched those parts of the room before. The garment had lived that long and the woman who wore it had moved and sat and prayed and slept and made love and cooked and cleaned and been sick and had nursed and kneeled and swept the floor. And now, in these strewn pieces, it was as if she was everywhere, doing all these things at once.

Bajirao let the pieces sit for a while. He heard a noise outside. In a panic at the thought of someone coming in and discovering what he would never be able to explain, he scrambled and picked up each piece. He had nowhere to hide the pieces so he hid them in his bag. He rushed out of the hut. No one seemed to be around. It must have been a passerby he heard.

On the way to the home of the sarpanch, Bajirao took a detour and walked down to the river. Here he tossed the pieces of the sari into the water, not waiting to watch them float or drown.

This is all you will have of my wife, he told the river. You can have her clothes, not her ashes. Take this and no more. She will live and speak of sweet things. Her man will send her daughter off as a bride and then he will put the life back in her breath. He will put their land beneath her feet. She will live and breathe and walk on her own land, with or without him.

He didn't once turn around. He didn't see the way the gold threads from the borders of the sari caught the light of the moon as they rose up in the water like hands trying to strain against the undertow.

11

'Can You Really Help Me?'

IF THE THINNEST cloud had indeed floated by the skies of this village, it would see a hundred storms below. It would see men and women moving their feet over fields that looked like the grey, cracked shells of hard-boiled eggs held together by their deeper membrane. It would follow them down the skinny gullies of their homes to the wider, crooked lanes with their bullocks and their carts and their ploughs and their baskets, all in motions practised and familiar for generations.

It would see one farmer first ring a prayer bell, sprinkle holy water upon his sacred beast of burden and then push it past the point of cruelty in the field. It would see women bent over with baskets on their brittle backs. And yet it would seem to the cloud that all was well. All these rituals of the day kept the myth going that very little was out of place; that no terrifying news and resolutions need be revealed between husbands and wives and children and unwed mothers from long ago or dejected men who sired sons they could not hold, or brides-to-be who longed to burst out of the threshold of their homes and into the arms of grooms who had been purchased for them.

If this cloud could see the knots of old and new pain each one of these people carried in their chests and the million misgivings in their heads, the cloud would surely gather up all its strength and rain down upon them, if only to say *shhhhhhhh* all over the land. Dear God, would it rain?

But because it didn't, the other rituals of water are set into motion on this, the sixth day of Katya's lodging in the village of Dhanpur. Gayatribai gathers her two urns in the early morning and quietly slips out from the back of the hut to fetch water from the village pump. An aberration to the rituals, Katya leaps up from her perch by the window and asks the woman to wait a moment. She hustles Kabir into wakeful briskness and the two of them join Gayatribai in the long walk to water. Katya tries, over and over again, to open a conversation but no words come.

Kabir is too sleepy to say anything. He has been promised a morning with Ammar, roaming the village in the jeep. Could Katya trust Ammar to keep a hawk's eye on the boy, or should she hint at her anxiety over the boy's safety? How would she do this without arousing suspicion and keeping Gayatribai's secret? She had the feeling that Ammar and she needed a long talk and that they would have it soon, but with the beehive of all the untruths and half-truths hanging over their heads, a single sharp word could leave one of them stung beyond any hope of healing.

She quickens her step, seeing that she has fallen behind. Gayatribai is weary in her own step, yet her weariest is quicker than Katya's. And Kabir has sprinted ahead. Katya is about to call out to him when she notices something. Gayatribai's step is actually brisker than usual because her eyes are riveted on the boy and she is hurrying down the path after him. She could call out too and ask him to slow down, but she doesn't, not once.

From what Katya can see of Gayatribai's torso, jaw and brow, they are alert but carry no sense of urgency. The three of them are the first ones to arrive at the water pump. Kabir bounds up over to Ammar's home-office. Katya can see that the door is unlocked and Kabir walks in with a happy step. Ammar must have returned late at night. 'Ask him to give you some breakfast,' Katya calls out to her boy.

Katya turns around and hurries towards Gayatribai, who is bent over at the pump, positioning the first urn under the tap. Katya stands, shuffling her feet for a few minutes, her hands on her waist, still ploughing through her mind for words with which to begin speaking to Gayatribai. The woman is bent before her, facing her, and the vermilion kunku in her hair is zigzagging before Katya's eyes as Gayatribai throws her frail frame into pumping water. No water comes out of the mouth of the tap. It could take a while, Katya remembers. She looks closely and sees Gayatribai's arms quiver and slip from their grip on the pump. Her fingers look sore from the bleeding of two days ago. Her face is taut, frowning with the effort, and for a fleeting moment, she seems to roll her eyes from weakness.

Katya jumps towards her and gently takes the pump from her hands. Gayatribai protests, but Katya firmly pushes her arm into Gayatribai's shoulder, urging her to sit down. Gayatribai gives in, wipes her face with the corner of her sari, and squats a few feet away from Katya's vigorous pumping.

In a few long minutes, water spurts out of the pump. The two women chuckle quietly. And then the water comes out in a healthy trickle. As she pumps, Katya's body falls into a rhythm, and the sound of the pump's rise and fall begins to seem to her like a concert between a drum and a violin.

'Gayatribai?' Katya says.

It seems to take Gayatribai some effort to pull herself away from her thoughts and respond. 'Bola,' she says tiredly. Tell me.

'No, *you* tell *me*,' Katya says. 'Did you know where to go looking for Kabir that day?'

Gayatribai nods.

'Then why didn't you take anyone along?'

'Because I didn't have the time. Every minute mattered. And because a million storms would fall upon my village and my sisters and daughters if too many people rushed into that hell.'

Katya stops the pumping. Then, afraid that the trickle would dry up, she starts again. 'Gayatribai . . . I owe you more than you can imagine,' Katya says. 'You knew you could be in danger and yet you went to rescue my son. I owe you the debt of a lifetime. Please let me give you . . . some money . . . so you can have that surgery. And so Bajirao and you can build a better life.'

Gayatribai sighs deeply. A film of water comes over her eyes as she looks past Katya and shakes her head. The straight, thick line of red kunku in her hair now seems to wag itself like a finger in Katya's face. 'Can you really help me?' she says.

'Yes! Yes, I can.'

'Then help me save my husband's life.'

Katya catches her breath. 'I don't understand. Is he in danger? Do you think those men will . . .'

'My husband is in danger of himself. Our devastation is bigger than the greed of two or four or twenty men. Those men have their own reasons for what they do. They have their own desperations, their own lot in which they suffer. We are all living in a time of very little moisture. Drought can send some men to their death and it can send others to seize what isn't theirs. My husband has his own desperations. If you want to help me, please help me keep him alive. Please make sure he doesn't kill himself.'

Katya feels her chest tighten. Straining against this feeling, she says, 'And how will I do that?'

Gayatribai lowers her face now. 'I don't know.' She stands up and changes the urn at Katya's feet. Katya hadn't noticed that the first urn was now overflowing. Gayatribai gently takes the pump from Katya's hands and gestures to Katya to sit down.

Gayatribai speaks again. 'I don't know. But I wish for your help in finding out. I think I am asking for too much from you. Please forgive me and think no more about it.'

Katya knows, then, that Kabir and she will not be on that flight to Seattle. If she has to find out how to keep Bajirao alive, they will have to stay a while.

When Gayatribai is done filling water and is preparing to head home, Katya walks with a hesitant step over to Ammar's home-office. It's dark inside and there is no one in the front room where the office space is. Are they in the kitchen? Katya quickens her step when she notices that she doesn't hear any voices in the home. In the kitchen, a maid is sweeping the floor. She looks up at Katya and then goes back to her work.

Katya scrambles into the bedroom, breathless with panic. No one.

But wait. There on the bed, curled up, is Kabir. Fast asleep. Katya steps up to him quietly. He is lying on his side and his leg is dangling off the bed. She picks it up gently and straightens it onto the bed. The boy takes a deeper breath, but doesn't otherwise move in his slumber.

Looking closely at his face, Katya notices a tiny pool of tears in the dip between the inner corner of his eye and the bridge of his nose. On his pillow is a damp spot, a map of tears the boy has carried in two countries.

Where is that man? How could he disappoint her son over and over again like this? Could he ever make a promise he would keep? Did he think Katya was just going to stay here and watch her child be pulled in and then tossed aside at whim? She wants to stand up and storm out of this place and demand that people go fetch Ammar Chaudhry from whatever hole he has disappeared into. But, instead, she sits there, watching her child's puffy-eyed face in its slumber, loving him more and more with every passing moment, feeling stronger on his inhale and weaker on his exhale.

What do you want, Kabir? Mommy will get it for you.

She curls up then, feet to head on the bed with Kabir, and allows sleep to claim her. 'Sleep when your baby sleeps,' a voice in her head says, a voice from long ago, when she was alone with her newborn and the hospital nurses were teaching her to be a healthy mother.

When she awakes, nothing has changed but the light in the room. Katya sits up in alarm. It's late in the afternoon. Kabir is still asleep, but someone has shut the door to the room they are in. Katya rushes to it, almost expecting it to be locked on the outside. But it isn't. The maid must have shut it so they could sleep.

Katya walks outside and all is still quiet. But there, at his desk, is Ammar. His back is turned to her, but she can tell he knows she is there. His neck is straight as a rod and his hands are gripping the edges of the desk.

'Where were you?' she says, stopping a few feet from him.

Ammar turns his chair around slowly. He looks unkempt. His clothes look rumpled. She recognizes them as the same clothes he had on yesterday morning, when he saw them off at the bus stop. His hair looks like he hasn't washed it in days and his face has a stubble. But worst of all are his eyes—bloodshot, shifty.

'Nowhere,' he says. 'I mean, nowhere important. I had to pick a few things up from Nagpur.'

'Like what? And why didn't you tell us? Why didn't you tell anyone? Jesus, Ammar! Kabir and I don't know anyone here. And there's enough going on in Gayatribai and Bajirao's life that

. . . well, I, we all needed . . . what if we needed something?' She has no idea why she can't launch a coherent attack.

'It's really none of your business where I was,' Ammar says, quickly, but without passion.

'Oh?' Katya says. She frowns. 'Okay. It isn't my business. But back in that room is a boy who came here from America, looking for his father. All I need to know is—shall I take him back, or should he hang on here for a while longer while you totally stomp on his heart by showing him how he can't trust you to ever be around?'

'No!' Ammar says. He turns his bloodshot eyes right on her. His hands start to shake. 'No. There's no need to overreact. I was just gone for a little over a day. I needed to go. I came back sooner, sooner than I'd thought. I'm here now. Please don't ask me where I was.'

'It's okay, Baba,' Kabir's sleepy voice catches them both off guard. 'It's okay.'

Ammar jumps to his feet and runs his hands through his hair, trying to rearrange the curls into respectability. Katya tries to shield his body from Kabir's view, but Kabir helps out anyway by looking away.

'Baba was just heading into the shower,' Katya says. She can't believe she has just referred to Ammar by that term and turned this into some sort of quotidian family scene. But it seems to get a hearty nod out of Kabir.

Let him have a few nods. Better than sobs. 'Shall I make us all some breakfast?' she continues.

When Ammar has shaved and showered, and they have eaten in silence, Katya says, 'I need to use your phone. I need to call . . . I need to make an international call.'

'Your fiancé?' Ammar asks.

She feels lighter all of a sudden. She could choose the truth now, this time and each time to come. 'Yes,' she says. 'My fiancé, Alec.'

Kabir is looking from her to Ammar. Maybe because of this, or maybe because the truth telling is also some sort of relief to him, Ammar nods, and, walking to his desk, writes down the codes that Katya should use to make her call.

'Take your time,' he says to her. 'We're heading out.'

'What?' she says. 'I don't think so.'

'I promised Kabir we would go canvassing for the protest. We should go,' he says.

She thinks for a minute. She looks at Kabir's face. Then, taking Ammar aside, she whispers, 'Please tell me you did not do anything yesterday, did not go anywhere, that would present some sort of danger to my child.'

'I did not. I promise,' Ammar says.

Katya nods. 'I'll pay for the phone call, of course,' she says. 'And ... don't let him out of your sight, okay?' she adds, running her hand through Kabir's hair until he ducks out of her reach. But, he's caught her eye, and his look says, 'Yes, I'll stick close to my father. You don't have to worry.'

The call to Alec's mobile phone goes through instantly. Alec's voice, so loud and clear in her ear, catches Katya by surprise before she has had a chance to assemble the words she wants to say to him.

'Hello?' Alec says. 'Katya?'

'Yes,' she says. 'It's me. Hey Alec.'

'Hi, beautiful! Jeez, where have you *been*? I have been so worried. What's going on, honey? Are you guys on your way home?'

'Oh God, Alec ... I don't know where to begin.' She just wants him to go on talking for a while. His voice—deep, American, declarative—seems strange amidst the tentative voices of her past few days. Yet, she feels like she wants to sink into it.

'Is everything okay? Is Kabir okay? What's going on? Go on. Tell me.'

'I . . . there's so much . . . these people here . . . Alec, none of this is going to make sense, but . . . wait, yes, we're okay. We're fine.' She wonders whether to tell him about Kabir's kidnapping. How could she not? And about Gayatribai's rape?

She can't believe she isn't going to tell him about these things. Him, a policeman. She can picture him getting on the next plane, lumbering into Dhanpur and trying to figure out the criminal activity here. That's all Dhanpur needs—an American cop chasing Indian rapists.

'We really are fine. But we . . . I didn't realize how things might turn out.'

'With Ammar?' he says.

She can't believe she isn't going to tell him about her tryst with Ammar. Just a few moments ago, she had chosen the truth. But the truth is something you say to someone's face, not on a long-distance telephone call. No matter how clear the telephone line is, these truths would not be clear.

'No, not with Ammar. That's the least of our troubles right now. It's this family we're staying with. Well, there's a farmer and his wife and daughter. They need our help.'

'Okay,' Alec says. Tell me more. What sort of help?'

'I don't know yet. All I know is . . . well . . . Kabir was lost for a whole night and Gayatribai . . . this farmer's wife . . .'

'Kabir was lost? What do you mean? For a whole night? Did he run away again?' Alec's voice seems closer than ever before now, as if he's right here, in Ammar's office, looking at her and also looking around this office for clues.

'This is a new place. It's a confusing terrain. Kabir got lost, Okay? He didn't run away. Anyway, Gayatribai is the one who took a lot of risks to find him. She sort of risked her life, actually. I'll explain later how. And so . . . anyway, now she has been diagnosed with lung cancer and I asked if I could help and I wanted to give her money and she said she didn't want the money but she wanted my help to keep her husband alive. I don't know, Alec. I should probably find a way to do something.'

'Keep her husband alive? Is he sick, too?'

'No, no. He's not sick. He's . . . he's a high risk for suicide.'

She listens to Alec's silence, wondering how he is piecing her confusing bits of information together. 'Suicide?' he says.

'Yes. Hundreds of thousands of farmers in the country have committed suicide recently, especially in regions like this one. I think I'll send you a few links to articles you could read that will explain the conditions here a bit better. Actually, Kabir's started to write about all this in a blog. I'll send you the link.' She knows she sounds like she's having just any conversation, about plans for a date night or something. She may as well have been saying, 'I'll send you the link to this great new Italian restaurant.'

But Alec seems to have heard more in it. 'Holy crap. I'm surprised we haven't heard of these suicides here,' he says. 'Yes, send me the links, especially to Kabir's stuff.'

'So, anyway, because Gayatribai helped save Kabir's . . . I mean, she helped find him and because she's asked me to help keep her husband alive, I feel like I need to stay a few more days and do something, help out in some way.'

'But your tickets are . . . well, I guess the tickets can be changed. But I don't understand. What can you do to help?'

'I don't have a clue. But . . . I can't walk away either. If anything, I must stay and be absolutely certain that I can't do anything. I don't know. What do you think?'

'I want you home,' Alec says.

Her heart sinks. But this could be for the best, she tells

herself. She could just hand this decision over to him. After all, he has waited two years for her to pick a date for their wedding. And he has strong instincts about danger, about physical harm. He would not have let Kabir fall behind in the wooded area. She could just tell Kabir that Alec had given her an ultimatum and they . . .

Alec's voice comes back. 'I want you home, but I can tell you have work to do there. You have things to figure out. And it looks like some people are asking for your help for some reason. They must have a sense that you are able to help in some way, beyond money. Hey, that's what brought me into my profession, you know. And I suspect that's what brought you into yours, as a journalist. We wouldn't be so wrong to follow that instinct, right?'

'Right,' Katya says. She is surprised at the smile in her voice.

'Just promise me one thing, will ya?' Alec says.

'Oh, no. Are you going to ask me to help save your life?' she says.

His laughter is like an embrace in which he has picked her up, spun her around, and set her back gently on the floor. 'Just promise me that you will stay safe. And also . . . promise me you will . . . stay faithful to me. So, I guess that's two things, not one. Promise me those two things.'

'I will,' she says in a heartbeat. She knows she can tell him right now that she's already crossed that line, but no, he isn't asking if she had been unfaithful. He is asking for her to stay faithful from here onwards. That, she will promise.

'I promise. And I know we'll be home soon,' she says.

'At least you're still calling this "home",' Alec says. 'I love that.'

'And I . . . I love you,' Katya says.

When she puts the phone down and turns away from it, her

next few physical steps seem like the hardest and heaviest she has taken in a long time, even though just about forty-eight hours ago, she was running beyond her breath, holding a knife in her hands. These steps are of the deepest uncertainty. *What is she to do?* This notion that she could help Gayatribai in some way, to keep her husband alive, is it just a delusion of grandeur?

That map catches her eye again, with its bright red drawing pins. She steps closer to it, moving deeper into the faded print and watery colours. She recognizes this village name or that, squinting at the Marathi script. The district of Yavatmal is laid out within the span of her arms. Katya puts her finger on a village she had travelled to years ago—Ralegaon. From here, her finger winds its way to Rajurwadi, then dashes to Sakur and then trails over to Pandharkawada. The loops of her finger grow smaller as it knocks up against drawing pins and either circles them or rides over them until she finds Dhanpur and its cluster of red pins. She places one finger and then another on each pin, frowning, until all ten fingers of her hands are sitting atop red drawing pins and she's still frowning, trying to put together some kind of pattern.

She jumps back when it hits her. Her fingertips turn numb and then start to tingle. The pins represent the suicides. Each one in the wall counts for a man or woman who has turned to ashes. Katya stumbles backward and steps hastily away from the map. But she can't take her eyes off it. Her head starts to swim and then all she can see is a wave of red before her. She clasps her hands together to stop them from shaking. When her eyes are able to focus again, she steps back closer to the map.

Once more, a shaky finger finds itself on the ageing paper. She runs it over Dhanpur, imagining its lanes and gullies, her finger following her thoughts until there it sits, right upon where Gayatribai's home should be. There's no drawing pin here, no red. Her finger comes away with a slim layer of dust on it. Bajirao is alive. This space must stay covered in dust, not in a tack, not in ashes. She puts her finger back on that spot, standing there for several minutes, letting her fingertip pulse against the paper.

12

'There is No Crisis-vrisis Here'

THE CREMATION GROUNDS are the best place to find farmers to draw into a protest rally. That is where Katya finds Bajirao, handing out flyers to farmers and families whose eyes are rimmed with red. The flyers are orange, with bold black writing on them that says:

'Come to the protest rally tomorrow. Make sure the chief minister of Maharashtra hears your cry. Don't let your loved one's death be in vain.'

Katya ignores the looks she gets from the men at the funeral and walks over to Bajirao, startling him with her approach. She reaches out her hand for a flyer. He gives her one quickly, with a hesitant half-smile on his face. Katya studies the wrinkles on his forehead.

'Bajirao,' she says. 'If it is all right with Gayatribai and you, I would like to stay here a little longer.'

The lines on his forehead deepen into a frown. He clears it away quickly as he realizes she is watching. He bobs his head from side to side in assent.

She wants to make him a little more comfortable. 'I want to

stay for Meera's wedding. I am like a young maushi to her, no? As her aunt, mustn't I stay?'

Again, the bobbing of his head, from side to side.

'But, if you are not letting me pay for my son and me to live in your home, I have the right to help pay for my niece's wedding, no?'

Bajirao looks away. He takes a few steps away and hands a flyer to a young boy, not much older than Kabir. The boy's face is swollen from crying, his lips are tight from holding back his sobs. Who was this boy to the man being cremated before them? Katya waits until the boy has returned to his duties at the cremation before she steps closer to Bajirao to pose her question.

But Bajirao speaks instead. 'Son,' Bajirao says. 'He is her son.'

'*Her*?' Katya says in a hoarse whisper, glancing over at the burning pyre, as if the flowers and flames on it would give some clue to the gender of the corpse. 'How . . . how did his mother die?'

'Atmahatya,' Bajirao says. Suicide.

Yes, she knew women killed themselves here too. How many? How often? Were their reasons the same, born from the same despair? Katya once again felt frozen by how little she knew. But, then, what was it that she told her students in Seattle? Ah, yes: don't be overwhelmed by how little you know; be empowered to find out more.

'Bajirao . . . 'she says. 'Let me stay and let me pay. Please.'

Bajirao walks a few more steps away from her. Then, as if realizing that his silence and his physical distance could be taken as rudeness, Bajirao turns towards her and says, 'You don't have to ask me if you can stay. Our home is your home. But about payment—that is up to Gayatri. Please discuss that with her.'

'But I want to know what *you* think. I want to know what *you* want from *your* life. I want to find out . . .'

Katya is about to protest some more, but her words catch in her throat. In turning around, Bajirao is standing stark against the fire of the cremation. Watching the flames jump and snake around behind him like that makes Katya feel a little unsteady on her legs.

Taking her silence for assent, Bajirao breaks away from their conversation and hurries over to a group of other farmers who are stooped over a map, tracing the exact route the chief minister's motorcade would take tomorrow. Katya's eyes sweep over the grounds. Where do these grounds begin and where do they end? No one can tell. There are no walls or boundaries, as if just about anyone could stumble in and out of death.

The grounds are close to the river so the ashes can be taken quickly and scattered into the water. The river also flows as a witness and receptacle of the hair that is shaved clean from the heads of the men whose relative has died. The boy she saw just now will soon be taken to the river to have his head shaved. Where would that boy be in a few years? Here, close to these grounds, this river, these dying fields? What would he say of his mother when he grew up? 'She killed herself because she didn't believe I was going to make life better?'

As she watches Bajirao sitting with the other farmers, nodding quietly, his eyes distant but his body hunched into itself, Katya wonders what would make this man want to live. Meera? Gayatribai?

And what would make him want to die? The belief that they could not make life better, or the certainty that he could not make life better for them?

The roar of an engine punctures her thoughts. The men she is watching spring to their feet and look at the source of the sound—the Chief Agricultural Officer on his motorcycle. His name leaps to Katya's head—Mr Sachin Patekar. No one had heard him approach, but now, as his motorcycle coughs and sputters in precision, idling for a few moments as its owner glares at the people he has been watching, even the priest at the funeral stops chanting. The dead can stay suspended for a few moments. The Accountant of Suicides was here to have a word.

The man shouts over the noise of his motorcycle, 'Again, I am warning you. Beware. No foolishness tomorrow. Tumhi Maharashtra cha ani Marathi lokan cha apmaan karat aahat. You are insulting Maharashtra and the people of Maharashtra. But never you mind. If you are not taking this warning seriously, then the police will know how to tackle you. And I will personally teach you a lesson.'

It takes all her strength not to walk towards Mr Sachin Patekar and ask him a question or two. Katya can hardly bear to look at him, with his pock-marked face, his thick nose, his neatly slicked hair, his perfectly trimmed moustache. He doesn't even seem to have noticed her here.

She turns her gaze back to Bajirao. In the few seconds that she had looked away, Bajirao's face, his body, his posture have all changed. His hands are on his hips, his chin is higher than she has ever seen it, his eyebrows are knit together in a determined rage and from his mouth is rising something . . . a guttural sound and a thick glut of saliva. Bajirao spits this out now, loudly and sharply, on the ground at his own feet.

The men around him look to Mr Sachin Patekar and then back at Bajirao. On Patekar's face is disbelief, for a moment, and then, outrage. He turns his machine off with a flick of the key in its ignition. Silence spins itself tighter and tighter around this whole landscape of humans.

The man swings his right leg off the motorcycle and then takes a few slow strides towards Bajirao. He is neither very tall nor intimidating in his girth, yet all the men he faces start to take tiny steps back, receding with as much dignity and as little drama as they can muster. When it is clear that Bajirao intends to stand his ground, one of the men clutches Bajirao's forearm and tugs on it. Bajirao shakes the man's arm off and looks right into the eyes of the government official standing less than a foot away from him.

'You bloody bastard,' the man says, in English. Then, in Marathi, he utters a few more profanities. The men recede a little further. Bajirao seems to noticeably, decisively, widen his chest. Katya watches, listens, her body tense, holding back her head and heart, both of which want to run into this scene before her, screaming, threatening, maybe even slapping. But something tells her that her intervention may do more harm than good. Besides, Bajirao seems to be doing fine on his own.

'Let your policemen come,' Bajirao says. 'Let them come.'

'What?' Sachin Patekar says. 'Do you know what you are saying, you fool?'

'Yes. I know what I am saying. If I do anything wrong tomorrow, let your policemen try to arrest me. Let them try.'

A shocked murmur goes up in the group of farmers. What is he doing? It is one thing to stand up to this small man from the government. It is quite another to throw him an open challenge. *Does Bajirao know what he is doing?*

Mr Sachin Patekar laughs. He shakes his head. He kicks a stone out of his path. He turns around and starts to walk to his motorcycle. That's when he spots Katya. The laughter vanishes from his face. He looks about, all around her and behind him, over his shoulder. She can tell he is wondering if Ammar or anyone else is around her. He seems puzzled by her presence. Puzzled and repulsed.

On an impulse, Katya joins her hands before him in a namaste. He ignores her greeting. Katya hurries over towards him but he mounts his motorcycle, spurts dirt in her direction and rides away.

Katya, Bajirao and the whole assembly of people at the funeral listen to the sound of the motorcycle driving away. The other farmers start to chide and question Bajirao, who stays silent. The priest resumes his chanting. Only Katya hears the sputtering of the motorcycle suddenly halt not too far away. Her instincts from her years as a journalist were correct—despite his swagger and his display of contempt towards her before these men, Mr Sachin Patekar is curious and is willing to talk to her. He is waiting, out of view.

Katya leaves the cremation grounds without much ado. She hurries towards Patekar's motorcycle, parked under a gulmohar tree, faced away from her, yet somehow attentive to her approach. The canopy of bright orange over him from the bursts of gulmohur flowers in full bloom gives him the look of a cruel king revelling in a moment of ill-earned opulence before heading into battle on his trusty steed of steel.

She is unsure of what exactly she will say to him, but she thinks of Gayatribai and the horrors Bajirao may have invited upon his family this afternoon. Somehow, she must endure this man Patekar and undo some of the damage Bajirao has done. Maybe she should just give him a chance.

'Kasa kai, Mr Patekar,' she says to the back of the man's head.

He turns his head with studied nonchalance, then cranes his neck with deliberation to watch as she walks past his motorcycle and stands facing him, her hands again in a namaste. Katya is aware of his eyes on her clothes. He doesn't lift his gaze from her hips. She can tell he wants her to watch him leer at her pants.

'How do you do?' he says.

All right then. He'd rather speak in English. 'I am fine, sir. How are you?'

He finally looks up at her face. 'I am not having time to talk nice-nice things with you, madam. What do you want? Hanh? Why have you come here?'

Katya takes a deep breath. 'I came here to take my son home, sir. We are leaving soon. But I know you are working hard here with the farmers' crisis and I . . .'

'This is a time-waste, madam. There is no crisis-vrisis here.'

'Sir, are you saying there are no suicides?'

Mr Sachin Patekar smiles widely. 'The one or two people who attempted to do suicide here in our peaceful village are nincompoops. They are being instigated by that fellow . . . what is his name . . . your lover . . . Ammar.'

She was expecting a rude remark or two, but this man's hostility now seems to her to be clearly a defence mechanism. He wants to be so obnoxious that they never get around to talking facts. He puts his hand on the ignition of his bike as if to signal to her that their dialogue is over. Katya steps right in front of his bike. She smiles at him.

'What is this, madam? You are being American? This is the American way, no? They just go wheresoever they want. They put themselves in the way of anyone as if they own the whole world. Why do you want to be American so badly? Not happy with your motherland?'

'Sir, there are more than one or two people who have committed suicide. They must have some reason and I believe that a man with as much power as you can help,' Katya keeps a blank look on her face. He must not think she is mocking him.

Mr Sachin Patekar doesn't fall for it. He laughs a sharp, quick laugh. 'These small farmers are wily people, believe me. Killing themselves off to get the government compensation only. Not to mention all the drama of your Muslim lover. The government is investigating this whole foolishness. We have a saying here in

Marathi—kunachi mhais kunala uth bais. Sometimes we have to get stuck in cleaning up other people's work. But you will not understand this. You are from neither here nor from there.'

'I am from here,' Katya says. She feels stupid the second she has said it.

He leaps on it. 'Oh yes, madam? Then you should know that interfering in other people's private lives is not something we do here. These men are dying because they have ghosts in their heads. They have started drinking and they want the government to give them money now for their alcohol. What will they do next? Ask to be paid to go to rundis, to prostitutes? Shayh! You visit for two days and you think you understand everything? What do you know, madam visiting professor?'

'All right, sir. I don't know anything. Can you please help me understand? Can I make an appointment with you and . . .'

Mr Sachin Patekar draws up his shoulders and in the most official tone of voice he can summon, a voice that Katya can imagine never fails to silence many of his subordinates in the taluka office, he says, 'You should know one thing—we have a list of at least forty criteria that a farmer's suicide must meet in order to qualify the farmer's family for the government compensation. Do you think most of these so-called suicides meet these criterias?'

'I suppose not, sir. But I am requesting that you . . .'

'And you should know one more thing. We believe here—before a man takes his own life, he also throws it away in some way. I am the officer in charge and I will get to the bottom of it for every case. I will find out how and why each and every farmer throws his life away. No pity for your stupid farmer. No compensation for the chootiya who doesn't know how to make a living. No need whatsoever.'

'My stupid farmer? Who are you talking about?' Katya tries

to keep the alarm out of her voice.

'That swine, Bajirao. You don't think I can see it in his eyes? You don't think I know why he stood up like a bloody crazy donkey before me today? Madam, take my advice. Take your son and go back to your country. Go and drink a cup of coffee there. Go home. Out of my way!'

He revs up his engine. Katya steps out of his way. She shuts her eyes against the spatter of dry dirt that flies into her face from the deliberate skid of Mr Sachin Patekar's tyres.

If what this man said was true, Bajirao was closer to death than she'd imagined. How close? When would he do it? Where? Who would find his body? Gayatribai? Meera? Kabir? What would keep him from doing it?

Standing there, on a spot of land she had so badly wanted to leave just a few days ago, Katya racks her brain for all its learning, through all the books it has read, through all the news and lectures it has stored. She finds no answers. And her heart? All it can do is beat against her chest in its dull way, like a clock with no hands for hours, no indicator for when an alarm was set to ring. Just ticking away . . .

⌖

In the hours that she waits on the steps of Ammar's office for Kabir and Ammar to return, Katya is gripped by a feeling long unfamiliar. When did she last feel this way? A memory comes to her of herself sitting among boxes. It was the day she had arrived in Seattle for her new job, holding a doctoral degree and a seven-year-old boy in her hands. The movers had set all her boxes down in the tiny second-storey apartment in the Wallingford neighbourhood of the city. The property manager arrived to note down some details. Among the things he wanted was the name and number of an emergency contact person. He wouldn't take the name of old friends in India and he wouldn't take the name of her advisor or other graduate student friends from Austin. 'You don't know anyone in this city?' the man had asked, trying not to look her in the eye, trying to save her the embarrassment.

'No,' she had said, struggling to hook the cable to her television so Kabir would have something to do when she began to unpack.

'Well, what about your employers? Maybe we can put their name down?' the man had asked.

So, she had given him the name and office number of the chair of her department, whom she had met only once, at her job interview. After he left, she opened her calendar, and under a messy to-do list of supplies to buy for her new home and school admission applications to fill out for Kabir and grocery stores to scout for in the neighbourhood, she wrote 'Make friends. Fast.'

Looking out of the window that day, she had seen a lot of rain and very few humans. When she took a break from emptying box after box, filled mostly with her books and Kabir's toys, she put a box down by the window, put her elbows on the sill and gazed outside at the new street Kabir and she were now to live on. She saw people driving up in cars to pick their kids up from a school down the block. The school seemed to have a carpool system, and Katya watched as children ran from the playground and piled into the backs of SUVs and their parents waved at other parents and the sounds of their white laughter carried over to Katya through the rain. She noticed that Kabir had left the television and come outside to stand by her. 'Are those children going to be my new friends, Mama?' he had asked. 'Can I go play with them?'

'Not yet,' she had said. 'But soon.'

She had then turned up the volume on the TV, given Kabir a peanut- butter-and-jelly sandwich, shut herself in the bathroom, and cried. An hour later, she was still trying to blot out the sound of laughing strangers and splash out the swelling of her teary eyelids.

Buy hand towels, she wrote on her list when she came out and joined Kabir in singing, 'Who lives in a pineapple under the sea? SpongeBob SquarePants!' along with a very loud television.

She had sworn then to never feel lonely again. Once it was on her list, she did it in two ways—one, she made friends, for her and for Kabir, and two, if loneliness ever threatened to creep up on her, she just fucking snapped out of it.

Sitting here now, picking Patekar's dirt out of her hair, avoiding the long stares of passersby, even if they might offer up conversation, and unwilling to go inside the office for fear of looking at that map again, Katya encounters loneliness. She has no emergency contact and has little claim of participation in all the emergencies storming around her. There is no laughter of strangers, but their cries are cause enough for her rising sense of desolation.

Most of all, Kabir is not hers alone. He has grown up, found worlds beyond her and also found that no one lives in a pineapple under the sea.

Katya wonders now if Kabir has written anything new on his blog. Going inside Ammar's office, Katya avoids looking at the map and drawing pins on the way to the computer. She finds one new blog post from Kabir. No pictures.

This is the part I don't understand—these folks here, they don't for a second expect a man or woman in any part of the world to widen their eyes and say, 'Wait a minute . . . what's going on here? What? Men and women just go and tie a rope from a tree and break their necks by hanging from it? They do this even though they have seen the hideous dead faces of other men and women hanging from a rope? A woman throws herself into her village well even though she has seen the broken skulls of other women lifted out from it? A father drowns himself in a river even though he has heard the wailing of a child whose father's bloated body has just been fished out of the river?'

These folks here don't expect any of us to talk like that. Zero sense of entitlement here. I just don't get it. It's like they're beginning to think that this is the circle of life or something. This is how they live and this is how they're meant to die. It's like you and I say, 'Oh, yeah. Your grandma was ninety and she died?' Or, 'Crap. The school principal's physician didn't catch his prostate cancer until it was in its third stage?' These folks just say, 'Oh, Kalnitkar's crop failed and he couldn't pay back that loan for his kid's appendicitis operation? He died by hanging? Ah. When is his funeral?'

They pick up the local newspaper every day and read about elections and movie stars and—I kid you not—what Lady Gaga wore at the Grammy Awards. They don't shuffle through the pages looking for news about their crops or the government's plans for irrigation projects, or what the guys at Monsanto are saying about their crappy seeds. They don't expect to get any news of themselves.

WTF.

She isn't sure how long she waits there, sitting, letting her mind wander as she stares at the computer that she has switched off. When she hears Ammar's jeep approach, she finds it hard to get to her feet. Outside, she looks into the faces in the vehicle as they grow closer, watching closely to see if any of them will widen into a smile. One of them does. It's Ammar. Her eyes search the other shapes in the shadows of the jeep but she doesn't see Kabir. Her breathing quickens and she runs up to the jeep as it halts.

'Don't worry. I left him with Gayatribai,' Ammar says, grinning at her. 'He said they had plans.'

'What kind of plans?' she says, although she exhales and feels the tightness lift.

'He wouldn't say,' Ammar says, gathering up papers from the driver's seat. 'But Gayatribai and Meera seemed thrilled to see him and they were all chuckling.'

Katya stands there, frowning. Ammar stops what he is doing and puts his hand on her head. 'Don't think so much. You've got to let him have some secrets, you know. He's growing into a man.'

Katya shakes her head. 'Why doesn't that sound comforting?' she says.

Ammar's laugh catches her unawares. Before she knows it, she has joined in. He seems different now, far better than he had this morning. He still won't look at her for more than a second, but that was something she would inquire into later. They look over at the men picking their things up from the jeep. They smile at Katya and Ammar. Katya is surprised to see Bajirao among them and his brother Kisna-kaka. Bajirao is not smiling. He doesn't even seem to have noticed the laughter or the smiles around him, or that there are people around or that the jeep has come to a halt, for that matter.

Katya touches Ammar's arm and juts her chin in the direction of Bajirao. Ammar looks over at him and then back at Katya. 'Why does that bother you? He's pensive. He has worries. He has a daughter to marry off in a few days and a wife with cancer, not to mention a million other . . .'

'I am aware of that,' Katya says, annoyed that Ammar

assumes she is still clueless. 'But doesn't he seem . . . more . . . a little more faraway than others?'

Ammar doesn't look back at Bajirao. His eyes are now, finally, steady on Katya, studying her face. Then, he says, 'Do you think we should talk to him about something?'

Katya nods. 'I'd like to do that. In fact . . .'

'In fact, what?'

'In fact,' Katya says, putting her hands on her waist and her feet firmly on the ground so they won't move in any direction other than where her words are going. 'I want you to know this—I am here, Ammar. I am staying for a bit longer. I am cancelling our departure. I will stay for the protest rally. We will stay for the wedding. I want to . . . help. I want to do whatever I can. I'm in. I'm all in.'

Her voice seems to falter and get firmer with the changing expressions on Ammar's face. He looks bewildered at first and then he widens his eyes. His face breaks into a smile so full of pleasure, it stuns her. Does she need to clarify? Does she need to tell him that this has nothing to do with . . .?

'Brothers,' Ammar is saying to the farmers, 'We have some good news. This wonderful, learned, strong, influential lady will join our cause. She is pledging to put her might behind our march.'

The men join their hands together and exclaim one thing or the other not very loudly, but with a sincerity that makes Katya lower her eyes, it seems so intense. This isn't quite the applause from that auditorium in Seattle, but the butterflies raging in her stomach tell her that the stakes here are higher. This one won't be about the right turn of phrase or sparkling wit. This one will be about keeping to her word and plumbing the depths of her grit.

'What needs to be done? What remains to be done?' she asks Ammar as they settle maps and pamphlets and flyers down on his desk. Bajirao is with them, looking a little more attentive now that he has been specifically asked to stay behind to talk.

'Attention,' Ammar says. 'We have to make sure that we attract the chief minister's attention. The plan is to create a human wall on the road at the very hour during which the honourable chief minister travels by in his motorcade to a meeting on farming policies. This is a meeting to which none of us is invited. Can you believe that? So, we have to make sure we catch the eye of the press that will be travelling with his motorcade. I am told there will also be foreign press. They have been far more receptive to the stories of our farmers than our own national press has.'

'That's odd,' Katya says. 'What happened to all those rural affairs correspondents here?'

Ammar chuckles. Without hesitating, he puts his hand out and ruffles the hair on Katya's head. 'My Katyayini is frozen in the early 1990s. Everything's changed. It's all about free trade. Liberalization. It's celebrities all the time in the papers now. Any chance you could invite Angelina Jolie or George Clooney?'

'No, but I do know some really good journalists here who couldn't have changed that much. I will make some phone calls,' Katya says. She turns to Bajirao and is surprised to see how closely he is listening to what Ammar and she are saying. She feels guilty for keeping the conversation going exclusively in English. She quickly translates the gist of what they've said.

'The journalists will come?' Bajirao says. 'They will come and write about our demands?'

'Well . . .' Katya hesitates. 'I hope so. If they come, they will write at least something. Unfortunately, they like drama, not numbers. If the chief minister stops to listen, they will write about it and then they will have to write about what the farmers are asking for. Sadly, they want a dhamaka, a stunning event of some kind. Hundreds of thousands of their countrymen dying quietly probably doesn't make . . . but, Bajirao, we can't be so negative. I will make some phone calls. I am sure something will happen.'

Katya wonders if Bajirao realizes what he is doing: he is frowning, listening with rapt attention to her, and he's running his fingers over the area on his torso where his scar must be, from the operation for the kidney. Does it still hurt?

She knows she cannot ask him about it. But, maybe some journalists could. Katya excuses herself from the two men and gets busy on the phone. Call upon call leads her to a few good people from the past. She allows them only five minutes of catching up on fourteen years of lives lived. And then she tells them why they must come to Dhanpur. Behind her, Ammar and Bajirao listen. Only when she has exhausted every possible contact, been turned away by many and piqued the curiosity of a few, does Katya finally eat the meal of chicken curry and rice that Ammar has brought for them from the truck-stop dhaba nearby. Bajirao declines, as always. He eats the thick roti that Gayatribai has packed for him, with a large piece of lemon pickle.

Katya hasn't realized how hungry she is. She licks her fingers clean but for the deep stains of turmeric and red chilli that stain her nails and flavour her skin.

Ammar has been writing down points for his speech at the rally. He looks pensive. 'If something is to get into the papers,' he says, 'we will need to be sure that people come out in large numbers. And we need to be sure that Sachin Patekar doesn't find a way to shut us all down. He has the police in his pocket. One wrong move on our part and he could send the policemen charging at . . .'

'I met him today,' Katya says.

Ammar puts his papers down on his desk and turns to look at her. Bajirao, too, pulls his shoulders up from their slump, as if assuming the same posture he had presented to Patekar not a few hours ago.

'Yes. He threatened the farmers again. Bajirao was there . . . do you want to tell Ammar about that, Bajirao?'

Bajirao shakes his head and looks away.

Katya isn't sure whether she should continue to tell Ammar about that event. 'I . . . well, he made some threats to the farmers about consequences if they marched in the rally. So, I followed him and he stopped and agreed to talk a little. He was rude and aggressive. Really insulting. But he said something that was intriguing. He said his office had forty criteria by which they determined and decided whether a farmer's suicide is officially deemed a "suicide" or not. Only if a death meets these forty criteria, will the family be paid the government compensation for the loss of the earning family member. Do we know anything about these forty criteria?'

'Chalees?' Bajirao says. Forty? His eyes are wide, even panicked, Katya thinks.

'Yes, why?' she says. Now, it's she who is watching closely. Why should this interest him so much?

Bajirao catches the intensity of her glare and he softens his face, clumsily. 'Nothing,' he says. 'Nobody . . . none of the farmers knows of these things. Their families don't know. So many families have not got their compensation money. This list of Mr Sachin Patekar must be the reason for that, no?'

They both jump. Ammar has slammed his fist on the table. 'Shit!' he says. 'I knew they had criteria, but I didn't know they had as many as forty!' he says, shaking his head, looking suddenly tired. 'Our work just grows and grows every day.'

Katya looks from Ammar to Bajirao and back. Both men look like someone has slapped them and walked away comfortable in the thought that they will not reach out and slap back.

'Please . . .' Katya says. 'Please . . . let's not lose heart. You have worked too hard and come too far for that. Maybe . . . maybe we will find a way to get journalists to investigate the forty criteria.'

'What? Are you daydreaming?' Ammar says.

He sounds more bitter than Katya has heard him sound in all the days she has been here.

'I'm sorry,' he says with a sigh, realizing his tone could have hurt her. 'But you said yourself that journalists don't like numbers. Forty criteria? They won't even investigate four.' He shakes his head.

Bajirao takes his topi off and uses it to wipe the sweat from his face. He sighs deeply and then he looks at Katya and says, 'You please try to bring those journalists. We will be . . . we are worthy of their writing. They will write about us.' With that, Bajirao puts his hands together in a namaste, bobs his head at Katya and then at Ammar, and leaves.

'I don't like the sound of that,' Katya says after the few minutes of silence following Bajirao's departure. 'I worry about Gayatribai.'

Ammar is quiet. He watches her, waiting for her to say more.

She speaks into this quiet. 'I know you and I both see Bajirao and Gayatribai and think of . . . what a love they have. It's as if they are two people living a . . . a single life. They have a commonality of purpose. They have one language. They come from the same earth.' She stops. She has no idea why she has taken the conversation here.

'Is that important for love?' Ammar asks.

'What?'

'Isn't it important that you come from the same earth, Katyayini?'

She turns to look towards the window. It is shut. She can't keep looking at it if it is shut and there is nothing to look at beyond it.

'Sometimes, the same earth does not give you enough ground to stand upon,' she says.

'Not if you keep leaving it,' Ammar says. Katya can feel him walking up to her.

She turns around quickly and says, 'Do you think he will do something foolish?'

Ammar stops a few feet from her. 'Who?' he says.

'Bajirao. Do you think he will do something foolish?'

Ammar doesn't look at her. He crosses his arms over his chest and walks back to his desk. He starts to shuffle through some papers there.

Katya clears her throat and says, in a low voice, 'They do kill themselves for the compensation money sometimes, don't they?'

Ammar grunts, in disgust. It doesn't startle her as much this time, but she steps away from Ammar nonetheless.

'You too, Katyayini? '

'But . . .' Katya says.

'No "buts" Katyayini. Don't speak such nonsense again. Dangerous nonsense.'

Katya blinks at him. 'I . . . I wasn't implying that the farmers are *greedy* or anything. I do understand . . .'

'Please. Stop. I have little patience for this,'Ammar says, covering his face with his hands and shaking his head more vigorously.

Katya wants to let it go, but instead, she hears herself say, 'I understand how hard this work is. Every suicide must be heartbreaking. You might be showing signs of PTSD, Ammar. You must . . .'

'PT-what?' Ammar says. His expression seems to be almost a sneer.

Katya takes a deep breath. 'Post-traumatic stress disorder. It's not uncommon for . . .'

'Tell me, Dr Katyayini Misra, is this disorder treatable?'

Katya stays quiet and looks to the floor. Her feet are caked with dirt. Her sandals are frayed. Her toes curl in and draw lines of sweat into the sandals' footbed.

'I am sorry,' she says, not raising her eyes. 'I wasn't trying to . . .'

'I wonder how much it costs to treat this disorder,' Ammar says.

Katya cannot bear to look at his face to see if the sneer has turned any deeper. She assumes it has.

'I wonder if it costs less than Gayatribai's surgery,' he says.

'All right, enough,' Katya says, putting her hand up and turning away from Ammar. 'I care about . . . I am concerned about Gayatribai and Bajirao. I can't help it if I have views and experiences from another country. Please forgive me,' she says.

'If you are here to dip only your toe in, Katyayini, please just stay on the shores. Don't try to get in deeper than that. This place is only for those who are ready to plunge in and are willing to be swept away. Not for people who are afraid of syndromes and disorders.'

Plunge in. Be willing to be swept away. Katya feels her face burning and the water welling up in her eyes. She blinks hard and walks out of the office. She is startled to see that it is now twilight outside. She wonders if she can find her way back to Gayatribai's home on her own.

It doesn't take more than a minute for Ammar to come up behind her. He places his arms on her shoulders and draws up close. She stiffens but she doesn't want to push him away, for fear of inviting more vitriol. She will be more patient.

'Katyayini . . .' he says. 'I don't know what got into me . . .'

Katya puts her hands on his forearms and tugs them away

from her body, gently turning towards Ammar with a sliver of a smile. 'Never mind,' she says. 'Let's go find Kabir.'

'Oh, Kabir!' he says. His arms soften under her hands and his face loses the tautness of deep thought. 'Yes, Kabir—we have to let him know that you both are staying.'

13

The Young Dhanpurean Theatre Company

A CLOTH TENT is set up on the grounds near the peepal tree. In the growing darkness, it stands out like a bright jewel with red and green and purple glints. Had there been a breeze, the scalloped skirt of gold that circled the top of the tent would have flapped around, waving people inwards. But there is no wind, so the skirt sits, curled up and stuck in the precision of its own pattern. All is still and picturesque in this centre of the village, but for the scurrying of humans, excited, ready to create shifts in seasons through stories, where their weather gods will not do so with water.

Men, women and children are seated on blankets and sheets laid out inside the tent. Lanterns dot the inside and run in a straight line down the middle, creating a glittering aisle. It takes so little to make a place of death come to life.

'Are they screening a film? Is that the surprise?' Katya says to Ammar as they are ushered to the front and seated on a mat. Ammar looks at her and smiles.

'Where's Kabir?' Katya asks.

A hush falls over the tent. A row of people walks past them, in a manner that seems slow, ceremonial. Katya spots Gayatribai and Meera and a group of other young village women. And, in the middle of them all, is Kabir.

She leaps to her feet. Is *this* Kabir? Here is the smile and shell of Kabir, but the rest of him doesn't make any sense. His chest is bare, and from his waist down, he is dressed in a blue silk dhoti. Tied tightly around his waist is a brocade sash of blue and red, embroidered in beads and gold. From this sash dangles a sword, its gold-coloured handle gleaming against his naked belly. Around his neck is a large gold necklace and a garland made of fresh flowers—jasmine and marigold. He is barefoot, but on his head is a turban, as opulent as the sash. It isn't until Katya notices the peacock feather rising erect out of the turban that she realizes that Kabir is in costume. He is Krishna.

Her first instinct is to rush up to Kabir and take all these ornaments off, apologize for the spectacle he has somehow been enrolled into. But Kabir is grinning. How nice it is to see his grin after these days of misery. She hasn't been able to look at her child's face with any measure of peace ever since she saw it covered in the blood from Gayatribai's fingers.

But he looks so clean now as he swishes his sword around. This isn't quite the Young Shakespearean Theater Company he loves in Seattle. There's no lighting manager making last-minute displays of his prowess under the ruse of rehearsal. There's no drama critic or talent scout being ushered in with an urgent flourish. No one has brought bouquets of tulips and lilies to hand to their young protégés in the green room. But Kabir isn't letting these details cramp his style. Not in the least.

Ammar leans over to explain to Katya what is going on. Gayatribai had smuggled Kabir away for the day to prepare an impromptu theatrical performance. An artists' group had once donated to Dhanpur an arsenal of costumes and props and from time to time, the village brings these out and gathers around to enjoy a good story. 'Tonight,' Ammar says, 'it's as if they're all celebrating our new resolve.' Ammar's eyes linger on Katya's for just a moment. He has looked away by the time Katya's eyes widen in shock as she realizes how Ammar might indeed have misconstrued her intentions for staying behind.

But there is no time now to explain anything to him. He steps up to the front of the gathering and welcomes everyone. Tonight, he says, Gayatribai wants to tell her guests the legend of Lord Krishna and Rukmini, the princess of Vidarbha.

Meera is dressed as the princess, in a gauzy lilac fabric sequined with gold. The fabric is draped as a sari, but the pallu cascades down her shoulder and trails dramatically on the floor behind her. A group of other girls and boys is also standing around, shy but beaming, in cheap satins, silks and brocades. Voices and laughter break out around the tent, all the more shrill for the silence that hung there just moments ago.

Katya tears her thoughts away from the possibility that Ammar has misunderstood her reasons for staying. No. No, she can't have him thinking that she wanted to stay and create a family with him. She will have to speak with him and clarify things after tonight's programme. She allows herself to be entranced now by the sight of Gayatribai readying herself shyly and solemnly for some storytelling.

So this is how Gayatribai reclaims her spirit. This is how she drives the demons of the godown away. This is how she beats her cancer. This is how she turns from victim to woman.

Katya looks around the tent for Bajirao. Her glances grow more searching as she looks from the face of one man and another and another and can't find Bajirao among them.

Suddenly, as if sensing her searching, Bajirao takes a step forward from a corner of the tent, reveals himself, and then steps back into the shadow he seems to have claimed as his chosen point for viewing tonight's performance. He seems to have no intention of sitting down. Katya wants to believe she is imagining it, this force around him, this readiness to recede, this preparation to bolt.

The talking in the tent dies down when Meera and Smruti, the other bride-to-be from Dhanpur village, walk to the front of the crowd. Giggling, they pass around a straw basket filled with slim wristbands made from jasmine flowers. Meera has also brought with her a bag filled with groundnuts roasted in their shells.

Katya watches Gayatribai give last-minute instructions to Kabir, with Meera's help. She feels something catch in her throat. Is Kabir playing along with all this because he believes Gayatribai is going to die?

The crackle of groundnut shells, the flicker of lanterns and the anticipation of a tale told in a raspy but merry voice is a strange salve at the end of this strange day. Katya stretches her legs out in front of her, letting them sink into the cooling earth beneath. Her lavender linen pants are unrecognizable. All her clothes have taken on deeper and deeper hues of the earth; there is never any telling when or where she might have to sit down in the dirt and dust.

Ammar announces that the storytelling will move in two steps—Gayatribai's voice, followed by a quick, silent enactment by the amateur theatre troupe. Ammar returns to sit with Katya. Gayatribai settles down in her comfortable squat not very far from Ammar and Katya.

The story is about what happened to Vidarbha's Princess Rukmini on the day of her wedding. This village knows the story well, Gayatribai says. It springs up here and there, from the soil in this region, in references and artefacts.

In keeping with the tradition of storytelling in her land, Gayatribai first declares the underlying motif: a universal truth is that a woman will love but once, and when she sets her heart on the man she is meant to claim, no wind, no waters, no rules, no rituals may hold her back.

Katya bites her lip. She can see from the corner of her eye that Ammar is smiling, trying not to look at her. Again, Katya distracts herself with Gayatribai's voice as it unfurls itself into the night, clearly audible in the centre and the periphery of the crowd, no matter how much it falls or rises. Katya can't bear to think of how the woman might start coughing any minute now.

'A long, long time ago, the mighty King Bhishmak of Vidarbha was blessed, after many years of longing for a child, with a lovely baby girl, Rukmini.'

Meera steps up to the space in front of the crowd and bows. She looks radiant. A fan placed a few feet across from her goes on, noisily, and her pallu catches the breeze. It rises and blows perfectly in the air behind her. The crowd applauds. Meera keeps her eyes demurely on her feet.

'The fair Rukmini blossomed into a startling beauty, unparalleled in her gracefulness. Her skin was flawless, her bosom ample and her waist slender. Revered and adored by her father's subjects, Rukmini always had in her companionship a hundred female slaves and a hundred virgin handmaids.'

Meera covers her face in her hands and shakes with mortified laughter. The young women in the audience laugh louder.

Gayatribai goes on, her voice gravelly in the smooth, warm night. 'Every day, Rukmini was bathed in floral waters, her hair was braided with jewels and flowers, and her body bedecked in gold ornaments. Stories of her beauty reached lands far and wide and also rose up into the heavens, where the souls of the gods were stirred.'

The titters are a little subdued this time. Katya watches the faces of the younger women in the crowd. They look expectant, as if this emerging story will somehow give them dreams to store away somewhere in the folds of their fading sarees, out of harm's way.

'In those days, the maidens of India married the men they truly loved,' Gayatribai says. 'So Rukmini was aghast when she was betrothed to Prince Sishupal, the son of another powerful king. For singing in Rukmini's ears since she had been but a girl were the glories of the man she had determined she would marry: Krishna, the Prince of Dwarka.'

At this point, Kabir strides to the front, holding a flute up to his lips. Katya is startled as a lilting tune rises up from the flute. She realizes in the next instant that a flautist is hiding on the outside of the tent. Children rise from the audience and scamper around Kabir, trying to upset the synch.

Kabir laughs aloud in a voice as deep as he can manage, startling the children and sending them running back to their mothers. He holds up the palm of his hand, on which is tied a chakra, made from cardboard and gold paper. Katya tries to catch his eye, but Kabir is in character now. He looks with a benevolent smirk over and above the heads in the crowd, holding his back straight and his head proud. He starts to pace up and down the length of the space in front of the crowd. This is a cue to Meera to strike a pose of yearning and despair.

'Rukmini had heard of many a gallant deed by Krishna, through the words of those who visited her father's court. An unspoken passion was nurtured in the young royal maiden's heart. He was the only prince in the land worthy of her love.

'Now, Rukmini had five brothers . . .' Five teenage boys from the village walk to the front of the crowd, each one with a swagger all his own. 'Rukmini confided in her brothers about her love for Krishna and her will to marry no other than him. Her oldest brother, Rukmi, the crown prince of Vidarbha, was livid. He did not favour her alliance with Krishna, and he convinced his four brothers and his father, the king, that Rukmini should be married immediately to Prince Sishupal, her betrothed.'

On stage, the actors are following the cues from the spoken story. Very little has moved among the people sitting in the audience as the story and enactment slowly spread themselves out like the weave of a cool, white cotton sheet over them all.

'Rukmini broke down and begged her brothers. 'No, valiant brothers,' cried she. 'I have given my love, my heart to Lord Krishna of Dwarka. No other man may plunder my will.' But Rukmi was arrogant and adamant. He stood by his decree like a rock. 'No suitor is better for you than Prince Sishupal,' he declared to his sobbing sister.

'Princess Rukmini was forlorn. She sought solitude from her handmaidens, lost the colour in her cheeks and plunged into a deep melancholy. But then, the memory of a kind and elderly sage, a Brahmin, came to her mind. The princess sent for the Brahmin, a member of her father's court. The Brahmin arrived swiftly and sat by the dainty feet of Rukmini whose virgin handmaidens were brushing her shiny hair. Rukmini sent her attendants away and bowed before the learned Brahmin. "O kind and knowledgeable sir, please heed my tale and advise me," Rukmini said.

'Upon seeing the beautiful princess's heartbroken yet courageous state, the Brahmin said, "O loveliest of princesses, Krishna is unparalleled in his valour and you in your loveliness. It is a match made in the heavens, one such as the world of mortals has never seen nor will ever see. Generations of humans and gods will speak of the legend of Krishna and Rukmini."

'Please praise me in this very manner to . . . to the prince of Dwarka,' Rukmini said shyly to the Brahmin, for she could not say her man's name directly. Promising to relay tales of her beauty and devotion to Krishna, the Brahmin rode as fast as he could, through treacherous terrain and dangerous foes. Upon his arrival in Dwarka, he sought an audience with Lord Krishna, who lavished his hospitality and courtesy on the wise Brahmin.

'Then, Krishna enquired with reverence, "Dear sir, may I enquire about the mission of your visit?" The Brahmin dug into the deepest folds of his shawl and produced the parchment upon which Rukmini's letter lay written. He told Krishna of the virtues of Vidarbha's princess.

'Krishna was soon lost in the words of the princess, laid out in luxurious ink in her meticulous hand, "My lord, my ears are ringing with the stories of your splendour and justice. You may perceive my conduct to be unmaidenly in approaching you in a matter so tender but I am driven by my will and my belief that you are, indeed, my true love. I am sure you will be honoured to accept a woman who lays her heart out for you—for it is every young woman's right to choose her husband as much as it is a young man's to choose his bride."'

Katya is startled out of her trance. In the shadows and in the secrecy lent by the audience's attention to the enactment, Ammar has reached out and touched Katya's face. He rubs his thumb on her temple, his brows furrowed. Katya realizes she must still have faint stains of mud from the spray from Patekar's motorcycle earlier today. Ammar wipes these away and tucks a lock of Katya's hair behind her ear. Just as she is about to pull away, Ammar turns his attention back to the enactment.

She turns, too, to the sight of Kabir standing in a pose of valour, moving his lips silently as if reading the prop that serves as Rukmini's parchment. All of this is beginning to feel like she had never left India, like Katya's exile of fourteen years had never happened.

She watches her son. How could Kabir suddenly move his body in ways to which he was so unaccustomed? She watches as he folds his hands in a namaste, bows his head and broadens his chest in a manner so intrinsic to this earth. He isn't shrugging his shoulders—that was a Western mannerism. He is raising his arms and shaking them at the heavens. In the role he is playing, Kabir has steeped himself in some good old Indian melodrama.

Gayatribai's voice draws Katya back into the story. 'Krishna read Rukmini's letter. "Pray, my lord, do not deny my love for fear of offending the royalty of this land. What king, what father, what brothers can stand before the heart that loves as fearlessly as mine? Do not seek to ask my father for my hand. Come to my kingdom one day before my appointed wedding day. As tradition demands, I shall be in worship at the temple of Goddess Ambika. Find me there and claim me, seize me and take me away. If not, I shall certainly die of a broken heart."

'Krishna said to the Brahmin, "I shall leave right away with you for Vidarbha and carry this brave and beautiful princess away with the dignity and passion that she deserves."'

A cheer goes up in the audience. Some of the young men whistle. Katya turns to look at Ammar, relieved that he is looking away and into the crowd, laughing with the others. She wonders if he had ever felt these stories the way she had. These lyrical legends . . . had he realized that they carried the truths of human love and longing? Or had they always been just stories to him? How could he just laugh, when she was condemned to a lifetime of either being deeply moved by stories of love or to beating back all depths that threatened to pull her under? She fights the urge to say something to him about dignity, passion, and deserving. She wins the fight. If he hadn't thought of it in all those years of abandoning Kabir and her, what good would it serve to bring it up now? Maybe she could finally learn what people meant by 'letting it go'.

'Krishna ordered his charioteers to command the strongest steeds. Along with him came an army of Yadava soldiers, and they all rode swiftly through the land to the kingdom of Vidarbha. At the same time, Prince Sishupal arrived in Vidarbha in a blaze of opulence, a fine wedding-procession indeed. King Bhishmak laid out the grandest of regal ceremonies to welcome the prince who would be his son-in-law. Noble kings and stately princes thundered into the kingdom of Vidarbha on elephants and horses, bringing with them their armies. The men sat on thrones and were handed garlands of fresh flowers and emeralds and rubies to wear. Servants brought them bowls of rich kheer, sumptuously garnished with almonds, pistachios, cashews, kewra and saffron.'

The audience is at its most silent now. These descriptions of excess, of food, are riveting.

'In her chambers, Princess Rukmini sat adorned with jewels and fine brocades but her eyes were filled with tears. It was the eve of her wedding and there was no sign of the Brahmin nor of her lord. If she had been given her true right to a swayamvara, she would surely have placed her garland around the dark-skinned Krishna's neck.'

Katya is mesmerized by the sight of Meera wearing a forlorn, distant look on her face, holding a paper garland in her hands. For a moment, it seems to Katya that Meera has left this place in which she is standing and is in the realm of that time and space where she will be a few days from now, on the threshold of a new life, ripped out of this landscape that seems to be drying and crumbling into itself.

'At that moment, Princess Rukmini's left eyelid began to

flutter. This was a good omen, heralding a meeting with her one true love. Rukmini rushed to the doors of her chambers and welcomed the Brahmin inside. "O kind one, please tell me you delivered the letter." The princess was unable to ask the Brahmin any more, lest she appear rude. The Brahmin told her everything.

'Outside, Krishna made a grand arrival into the kingdom, and was given as royal a reception by King Bhishmak as had been accorded Prince Sishupal. As they rode through the festive streets of the village, Krishna once again spoke to his companions about the right of a woman to marry the man of her choice. Together, they were determined to make this true for Rukmini.

'The princess arrived at sundown at the temple of Goddess Ambika. She thanked the goddess for bringing her this far and prayed with all intensity that Krishna may be her husband. As she left the temple, the princess took but one look down the steps outside and she saw a grand golden chariot below, bedecked with a flag that had an eagle embossed on it. It was he!

'Krishna's eyes fell upon the milky white hands bedecked with bangles, the limbs supple as young saplings. Princess Rukmini's body was adorned in an entrancing river of mauve silk and chiffon. Her face was as radiant as the moon. Her hypnotic gaze, that now met his, danced with shyness and playful abandon at once. Krishna felt like his heart would burst, it swelled with so much love.'

Kabir falls to his knees. He keeps his gaze on Meera and throws his arms up towards her in a dramatic gesture of enchantment. Meera starts to giggle. The audience bursts into laughter and Meera is forced to collect herself.

'After the shrieks and sighs of the handmaidens, a hush fell around the temple as Princess Rukmini's heart went out to the one she so loved. She addressed Krishna and said, "I will be with no man or god other than you. No matter that they set death upon me, by fire, by water or by the noose." Krishna's chariot galloped up the steps of the temple and he carried Princess Rukmini into his arms and rode away with her in the chariot.'

Cheers break out in the audience as Kabir puts his arm around the much-taller Meera's waist and leads her to the chariot, a human pyramid created by the teenage boys. None of the actors giggles.

Ammar continues, 'As they rode the chariot, Krishna said to Rukmini, "Do you know how much I love you, O Rukmini, my partner of seven lifetimes?"'

'And then, Krishna begged the princess's pardon and explained to her why she may not want to marry him. She was a princess and he was a pauper. He could never give her the comforts she would receive from marrying a true prince who would take her to a rich land. But Rukmini explained to Krishna the real measure of her love. Princess Rukmini had defied her father, her brothers, her kingdom, and now she knew more than ever that it was the right thing to do. She had been true to what her land had truly willed for its daughters. She now said to Krishna, "We are not strangers nor have we ever been. Perhaps we have known each other before; perhaps we have met in a place I no longer remember, in a different birth, a separate lifetime."

'Krishna was moved beyond measure. He said to the princess, "O fair Rukmini, from this day forward, I shall be thy faithful consort. I shall delight in your words, and stay forever yours."'

Katya's thoughts grow so large in her head, she wants to cover her face and hide so Kabir wouldn't somehow read them. She longs for reason to arrive before her on a chariot. She longs to find a telephone and call Alec.

And then, there it is—the coughing. Gayatribai muffles it into her sari, as usual, but it seems to grow a life of its own in this tent, where ears are tuned in especially to her voice.

Katya's eyes search the shadows in the corner of the tent for Bajirao. She spots him, still standing, looking right at her. Again, she thinks she sees him shrink away a little, as if from guilt. Ammar speaks over the coughing. He urges Gayatribai to call it a night and narrate the rest of the story some other time. Gayatribai shakes her head and fights back the storm rising from her lungs. She speaks again, a little softer this time, and the audience draws closer.

'When Prince Sishupal and Prince Rukmi learned of Princess Rukmini's abduction, they flew into a rage. Prince Rukmi gave chase to Krishna's procession and Krishna challenged Rukmi to a duel. Without a thought, Rukmi agreed and leapt upon Krishna with his sword. Metal clashed against dazzling metal as the swords glinted in the sun, the sharp edges striking terror in Rukmini's heart.'

Katya tears her eyes away from Bajirao to watch Kabir fencing with the teenage boy playing Prince Rukmi. Both boys throw themselves into this act, and the audience cheers. She smiles as Kabir leaps about. *He's having the time of his life.*

Kabir looks up at her from the fencing, as if he has stumbled upon his mother's thoughts. No, that look is more deliberate. Katya squints at him in the dark. He faces her as he fences, and he seems to be urging her to recall something . . . *someone?*

Alec. Kabir and Alec took fencing lessons together.

'Krishna soon defeated Rukmi in the duel. As his sword stood poised over Rukmi's head, the kind-hearted Princess Rukmini begged Krishna to let her brother go. Of course, Krishna let the prince go, and then he carried Princess Rukmini into his small, poor, but happy kingdom. It is said that no fairy has ever glided with more grace, nor has any bride looked more dazzling than did Princess Rukmini at her spectacular wedding with Krishna, her true love.'

As the story draws to its close, Katya makes use of the darkness to peer into the faces around her. This moment, the climax, has brought them from its tender beginning, through its twists, all the way to this uplifting end. In the few seconds after the legend releases them from its hold, these captive creatures of timeless stories struggle for air and slowly emerge from their private throes of love and longing.

The moment is over as quickly as it had crept upon her. Cheers and applause have broken out. The village girls are shouting out to Meera and Smruti:

'We hope your story ends with the same kind of happy wedding, Meera.'

'I hope your husbands don't have to duel with your brothers.'

'Oh, and are you pining yet? Are you yearning, Smruti?'

'Are you marrying the men of your choosing?'

Katya looks for Kabir as people start to rise to their feet. She wants to walk with him quickly. She must get to him before Ammar says anything to him about his notions of why Kabir and Katya are staying back.

But Kabir is walking up to Gayatribai. Katya is about to shout to him to ask him to remove his hands from his waist before speaking to the lady, but then she sees him mouth the words, 'Thank you, Gayatribai.'

Katya stands watching from this distance as Gayatribai pulls Kabir into a fierce embrace. Kabir doesn't struggle. Bajirao and Meera walk up to them. Even from where she stands, Katya can see the creases on Bajirao's face ease a little as he sees his wife's eyes shut in deep affection, her bony arms around Kabir's head. Bajirao gently touches them both on the shoulder and bobs his head at Kabir. The boy looks both relieved and relaxed.

Their hosts turn around and start to walk away together. Kabir's eyes stay on Gayatribai. Katya notices a watchfulness there—she can't be sure in the dark, but she thinks she sees a soft smile playing on the boy's lips, almost as if he were comforted by watching Gayatribai's gaze turn upwards to meet her husband's and her arm link with her daughter's.

Someone is tugging at Katya's elbow. She turns around and draws in her breath. It's Ammar. He is standing close.

'I need to talk to you, Katyayini,' he says.

'Now?' Katya says. She knows this is probably the best time to tell him about their miscommunication, but she feels exhaustion wash over her. She hasn't thought her words through. She will need the night. She says, 'I want to talk to Kabir, and it looks like our hosts are heading home. Maybe Kabir and I should follow them? I'm still not sure of my way . . .'

'Yes, yes, you're right. I will need more than a few minutes to talk anyway.' Ammar cocks his head to indicate to Katya that Kabir is walking towards them. 'If you'd rather talk to the boy alone . . .' he whispers.

Katya is surprised and grateful at his offer. 'Yes,' she says. 'I think that's best.' Then, she adds in an urgent whisper, 'Ammar, please understand this. We will leave in a few days. We are not staying for good. I . . . I know who I belong with. He is waiting for me at home.'

She can't see Ammar's expression in the dark, but she is surprised, again, when all he does is nod. 'I'll try and catch you tomorrow, before the protest. By the way, it's best not to bring Kabir to the rally. Let him go with the village women to the prayer procession they have planned tomorrow.'

Katya nods. 'Why aren't the village women going to the protest?' she asks, but Ammar has already started to walk away. She watches his back, and then he turns around, looks at her, and says in a voice so low that she can barely hear him, 'Goodnight, Katyayini. I . . . I feel so happy now that you are here.'

Katya feels a pair of arms wind themselves loosely around her waist from behind. She turns around and draws Kabir tightly into an embrace. The boy puts up a feeble struggle, unlike a few moments ago. So he's had too many hugs for the night? Katya overpowers his protests with kisses all over his head. His hair smells different. His shoulders feel bony and his face is turning angular. She wants to crush him a little; would it all then spring back into the childish roundedness she aches for?

Kabir struggles out of her grasp and begins to skip down the path to their hosts' home. 'You coming, Ayi?' he says.

Katya laughs. 'Yes, I'm coming, you silver-tongued Indian boy. What did you think of tonight's story? Complicated, huh?'

She sees Kabir shake his head vigorously in the shadows ahead of him. 'Not at all. It was simple. One of the simplest stories I have ever heard.'

Katya quickens her steps behind him. 'But the contexts and the subtexts of Rukmini's so-called *rescue*...'

'To sit with elders of the gentle race, this world has seldom seen...' Kabir's voice sings into the night. Katya slows her steps, watching her boy—in his silks and brocades and peacock feather headgear—skip barefooted over pebbles and stones, singing Led Zeppelin.

They talk of days for which they sit and wait and all will
   be revealed
Talk and song from tongues of lilting grace, whose sounds
   caress my ear
But not a word I heard could I relate, the story was quite clear
Oh, oh . . .

He stops then, and waits for her to catch up. 'Ayi?' he says. Katya grins at him.

'I have the money for Gayatribai's surgery.'

'*What*?'

'I got someone in Seattle to put all my electronic stuff on sale. The Xbox, Wii, Nintendo DS . . . it's unbelievable the stuff you can sell on Craigslist these . . .'

'Wait. Stop.' Katya grips Kabir's arm.

'Please don't be mad at me. I *had* to. And it's all done now anyway. The money's being wired to your bank account as we speak. Please tell Bajirao tomorrow. Tell him it comes from your university or something, okay?'

'*Why*?' Katya tries to keep the quivering out of her voice. 'Why did you do it?'

They stand for a moment in the silence and then, Kabir says, 'What kind of question is that? Because she must live, that's why. Because she's the only one that makes any sense to me here. Not to mention the fact that she rescued me.' Then, he shrugs. He's back to his American mannerisms.

'Besides, there are all the new versions of those game systems coming out, and I'll just hound you to buy me those,' he says, slipping out of Katya's grasp and breaking into a run.

'You got it, my son,' she says. 'And, guess what?'

'What?' he says, turning around to look at her, walking backwards.

'We're staying for a few days. Until after the wedding. Until Gayatribai and Bajirao . . . until things settle down a bit for them.'

'Holy crap!' Kabir says, pulling his peacock feather crown off, tossing it into the air and catching it again. 'Dr Misra will get four hugs from her son . . . tomorrow!'

'One more thing . . .' Katya calls after him. 'Who helped you sell your stuff?'

'Some of my friends who are really beginning to follow my

blog. I think some good stuff is going to come out of it,' Kabir's voice rings out into the night even though she can't see him any more in the darkness into which he runs, singing. Kabir, the sure-footed sufi.

14

Protest

IF THERE WAS a seed of doubt that the men of Vidarbha would answer the call to action, it turns into thin air on the morning of the protest rally. Six decades isn't long enough to diminish the fervour of protest that still carries itself thick in the winds of India. This is the land where a man of slight build rose from the porch of his ashram on the banks of the Sabarmati on the twelfth day of March in 1930 and set out on foot, gathering people along the way. At first seventy-eight men followed, then 3,000 men and women and then 50,000 or more, walking, walking with him until he arrived at a seashore 240 miles from where he had started.

Twenty-six days after setting out, the man stood before a tide of humanity, picked a lump of salty mud from the seashore, boiled it in seawater, made illegal salt—and defied an empire. Mahatma Gandhi's call for satyagraha and ahimsa turned men and women across the nation into non-violent warriors.

And now, watching farmers stride out of their homes, walk down the paths of their hamlets, leaving their useless fields behind them, to surge like a rising crowd, like countless fingers turning into a fist, Katya recalls a speech she memorized as a girl in a history class at school. Mahatma Gandhi and Jawaharlal Nehru, after that historic Salt March to Dandi, had together penned India's Declaration of Independence:

> We believe that it is the inalienable right of the Indian people, as any other people, to have freedom and to enjoy the fruits of their toil and have the necessities of life, so that they may have full opportunities of growth. . . .

Katya follows Ammar, Bajirao, Kisna-kaka and other farmers into the growing, unstoppable tide of men shouting a Hindustani slogan that has stayed fertile over the decades since its originator, Bhagat Singh, a strapping young revolutionary from Punjab, was hanged by the British at the age of twenty-four. '*Inquilab Zindabad*,' they shout. Long live the revolution.

Ammar slows down and waits for Katya to catch up. He smiles as she strides towards him. They fall in step, treading their common ground, faster and faster now, but still marching together. The crowds turn from hundreds into thousands, gushing like blood pumping into a furious heart. Each village sends its men—and a few women—with placards carrying protest slogans in Marathi. Ammar and Katya receive these people together, their faces turned towards each other, smile folding into smile. Slogans go up into the skies, and the two of them chant these to the rhythms of their hearts beating each to each.

'Karz mukti!'

Ammar shouts out translations for the foreign press.

'Freedom from debt.'

'Asaa kasaa hote naahin?'

'Why won't it happen?'

'Jhaali paije!'

'It must happen.'

These were the cries, this was the land and these were the men she had left behind. And this is why she is here now, this day— for Kabir, for Bajirao and Gayatribai, and for her countrymen. Ammar has to break away and lead the crowd now, so Katya links her arms with two women by her side, and falls in step with the restless army of Marathi men and women going into peaceful battle.

She can see that Bajirao, too, looks stunned at the response that has come forth in the few days he has spent relaying the call. Word has spread during the night, as he had lain sleepless, no doubt, thinking of Gayatribai's cancer. Men, and some women, are still arriving from distant villages, in trucks and buses and on bullock carts.

The heat of the day is nothing in the face of the fire of protest. The foreign reporters stare, open-mouthed, breathing in the clouds of dust that rise up around this spectacle of heads—bare and black-haired, or clad in topis and turbans—all walking, marching in step towards the highway on which the chief minister's motorcade is to pass.

Katya hurries in her step, trying to catch up with Bajirao to tell him it would all be fine, they have the money for Gayatribai, that he simply cannot, must not refuse it. But she loses him in the crowd, and then they are all converging before a stage set up by the side of the highway. The slogans grow louder and the crowds seem to grow into a tighter weave, and it's all she can do to not let go of the hands she is holding. She is almost relieved to see men in khaki uniform—local police—standing in a silent circle around the crowds. Along with them are a couple of men who look like classic lowly bureaucrats. One of them is sitting slouched yet alert on his motorcycle. This is a peaceful protest,

Katya wants to tell the police and the bureaucrats. Keep the peace.

The slogans rise up in the air once more, louder, and the din of drums rends the air, until the chanting, too, seems like a drumbeat—loud, resonant, vibrating against the hearts of all those who stand here. Ammar climbs onto the stage with some of the farmers, and the crowds eventually fall silent.

Katya cranes her neck from the crowds and she sees the faces she is looking for—two old friends, journalists from Mumbai, sitting near the stage. They look a little sceptical. She will have to talk to them later and tell them all they need to know.

Ammar makes a few announcements and a brief speech. He then invites the two brothers—Bajirao and Kisna-kaka—to talk about their farms, about their debts, about the impotence of the government relief packages, about the need for farming subsidies, and about the need to reclaim their freedom from the companies selling genetically modified seeds.

Kisna-kaka breaks down and speaks in sobs at the microphone. He grows slowly incoherent through his tears and his brother leads him away to be seated among other sombre farmers.

Ammar is talking again. The farmers' crisis must inspire the whole world, Ammar says. 'Farmers like Bajirao must stay alive. What does he have to do to be on the front page of tomorrow's papers?'

A commotion breaks out. The peripheries of the crowd begins a murmur and it rides quickly through the sea of people— the chief minister's motorcade is approaching.

Ammar's voice takes command of the microphone. 'Brothers . . . how are we going to make the chief minister hear our cries? How shall we get him to look at us and listen to us? How do we tell those journalists with him that *we* are a story the world must heed?'

Katya begins to feel uneasy. The two journalists behind

Ammar rise to standing, also sensing something. The commotion in the crowds seems to swell.

'How do we get the chief minister to get out of his air-conditioned car and come here on stage?' Ammar shouts into the microphone, his fist clenched, his arm raised in the air.

Stop, Katya wants to cry out. *What are you doing?*

But it's happening now, all around her, exactly what she had feared without thinking it. People break away from the crowds and run towards the highway, forming a human blockade designed to stop the motorcade in its tracks.

Katya can think of only one place that anyone should run to. She hurtles towards the police, shouting, 'Don't do anything, please! This is all peaceful! It will all be nonvio . . .'

But the policemen are now running too. Their sticks are raised up in the air, poised for a lathi charge. The chief minister's car comes to a halt. His bodyguards jump out of it and surround the vehicle. Katya cannot see anything any more. She is carried along by the flood of people around her, stumbling, pushed and dragged in the direction of the cars. She must not fall. She must keep the ground beneath her feet.

The rising dust is mingling with the water streaking from her eyes, turning to mud on her lashes. And through this, she sees something and freezes.

Bajirao has broken away from the crowd and is running, straight and fast, towards the chief minister's car. The trajectory he is on, the speed and tilt of his frame, turn him into a precise human missile headed right for the crack between two bodyguards, right towards the window of the passenger seat where the chief minister is seated.

Within seconds, two police constables, their faces contorted in rage, are pounding their thick sticks down on this missile's very human neck.

Katya screams, louder than she ever has in her life, but no one hears it over the din around them. She scrambles through the crowd that is still swaying around her. Her head darts about to keep Bajirao in view through the jungle of bodies in which she is trapped. She fights against fainting, keeping her eyes on him, as his own face seems to twist into soundless screams of pain, dodging, shielding his head from the men's sticks, taking the blows on his arms and his back.

Stop, stop, stop, she thinks she is shouting, but the noise comes out like those voiceless shrieks of one's worst nightmares. She looks around her, snatching, grasping at people's arms and shoulders, but all around her are strangers. She has lost the people she came with, and the faces around her all look back at her as if they hear her shouts as slogans of protest, not cries for help.

When she turns back to look, she can't see Bajirao any more. Oh God, has he fallen to the ground? Please don't let him be trampled in a stampede. Katya screams again, and stops. But she is pushed in the next instant by the crowds behind her. She scrambles to stay on her toes and tries to spot the space where Bajirao may have fallen. And then, she can see him once more, standing. She screams again, until her throat seems to rip away and fall into her stomach.

Bajirao hadn't fallen. He had turned around to face the policemen, and from what she could see, he was holding . . . no . . . *grappling* with the stick in one of the men's hands. As she watches, Bajirao gives a final heave and breaks the instrument of his torture free from the man's grasp. The other policeman aims a blow at Bajirao's head. Bajirao springs aside to catch its momentum on his arms.

Katya sees it coming, the instant in which Bajirao realizes . . . she sees it on his face—that briefest moment in which it occurs to him that the stick in his hands could be more than just a shield. And then, there it is, the blow from Bajirao, down on the . . . Katya shuts her eyes.

A shot rings out, clear as the cracking of a dead man's skull. Katya's eyes spring open again, but they don't want to see. Her brain fights against making sense of anything, but it does. She sees no blood, she sees no fallen man or woman, just a police constable with his hand holding a gun to the sky. He has fired into the air.

Bajirao is right there, standing. Oh thank God, he is standing. But his arm is still raised, with the stick in his hand. *Lower it, Bajirao, lower it before they . . .*

'*Hit back, Bajirao! Strike him. Fight for your life!*' a voice shouts out. Katya staggers in her step as the familiar ring of the voice catches up with the foreign whip of the words. It's Ammar, standing no more than a few feet from the spectacle.

'*No!* No, Bajirao, no! Think of Gayatribai! Think of Meera!' Katya shouts in the next instant. Bajirao's head turns to see her in the crowds. He looks dazed, but he has heard her! Over the tumult of people running for cover on hearing the gunshot, Bajirao has heard her, or sensed her, or sought to hear some voice of reason, and maybe he has imagined it, but it has carried to him somehow. There he is now, lowering his stick, casting it with contempt on the ground at the feet of the man from whom he had wrestled it.

15

Prayer

A FEW MILES away, across seven fields and six dirt roads, Gayatribai misses a step in the gentle dance she is swaying to with the other women of the village. The women around her laugh as she shuffles her feet to catch up—two little steps to the left, and then a large diagonal one to the right, two little steps to the right, and then a large diagonal one to the left. There, she has it again, and her waist still has the sway of her younger days. 'Lead with the foot, let your hip curve forward in a coy tilt, then sweep the upper half of your body into the move,' her mother's voice says to her from years ago, playing in her ears with the sound of the silver anklets on the women's feet. *No filthy animal can take this away from me.*

Now, she is teaching Meera the dance, adding another coil to the long rope of dancing women that makes its way down to the temple. Loosen those wrists, let them dance with their own grace. Let them know that they should ready themselves for those green glass bangles that will trap you into wedded bliss tomorrow, sing the teasing sisters, the cousins, the sisters-in-law, the aunts and the grandmothers of Dhanpur, as their children skip alongside. Flowers will settle into your palms and stars will embed themselves into your sari, Gayatribai sings through the discomfort growing in her lungs. She keeps her eye on her smiling daughter and another eye on a sulking Kabir.

She hadn't liked it either, the decision to leave him behind. It told her of other things—the possible dangers of the protest rally, the plans and secrets that were being kept from her. Yes, it was for his good that the boy wasn't allowed to go, and yes, it was for her good that she wasn't allowed to know, but, for once, she wants to know more, she wants to do more than . . . go to prayer.

Gayatribai looks into the skies and notices an almost transparent mist so subtle, she is afraid to talk about it. Yet, today, she feels a yearning for words, for a language in which to tell her sisters and daughters and her guests that she feels well. Her daughter will be married, the village would have its story told to the world, and Bajirao and she will soon take back the land. It makes her blush, this thought of growing old with Bajirao, together on their land.

But then she remembers what lives in her chest. Bajirao hasn't really looked closely at her since that day at the hospital, except from the dark shadows in the tent during the theatre performance. Maybe the doctor thinks Gayatribai isn't meant to grow old. Whatever happens, Bajirao will talk to her soon after their daughter's wedding, and they will together find a way. She will spit it out, whatever it is that is sitting in her chest. But no, she won't leave Bajirao to grow old alone.

Some of the younger girls of the village are now teasing Meera and Smruti, the two brides-to-be from Dhanpur, who will soon join almost 300 others from the region for their shared wedding day. Giggles and good-natured taunts add a deeper twang to the singing. How many times has she shared in this joy for the sake of others' daughters? And, now, it is her turn.

Gayatribai sings louder, giving vent through song to her new need for words. She watches as the boy looks up at her and smiles again, in the same ready way. It seems to her that if this child were to open his mouth and laugh some time, she might see the sun upon his tongue and the whole universe swirling in his mouth.

This thought prompts her to lead the song they are singing into another one, a bhajan singing the glories of Krishna as a child. Gayatribai once again hovers around Kabir, dancing in his periphery, but distant enough so that he can keep kicking the stones in his path, skip or stretch his arms in the adolescent abandon that is so becoming on him.

'He's Indian, but he's a foreigner!' says a teenage Dhanpur girl, making the other women laugh.

'And *you* will never get to be one!' hisses Gayatribai, smothering the girl's teasing into a shame it doesn't really deserve.

The singing dies down as the sun rises higher in the sky. She knows the shimmer of light on the curves of the aluminium pots can be seen from miles away, like flashes of lightning that have lost their way and stumbled into another season. Gayatribai keeps a keen eye out for signs of sunstroke. She sees Meera grow weary and Kabir more silent, if such a thing were possible. Gayatribai begins to realize that the path she trod so often is longer than ever.

Cows with their horns coloured kunku red and popat green pass by, moving almost as slowly as the dancing troupe. A jeep comes hurtling down the road behind them, forcing the women off the path. The vehicle, its canvas roof flapping wildly as if in warning of the clouds of dust that would follow, is crammed full of men, at least fifteen of them contorted into a single membrane of humanity that has heaved itself gratefully onto a set of wheels. As the jeep passes, the women hear hearty slogans of protest over a loudspeaker on the jeep's roof, and they know that these men are headed to join their own men at the protest rally. Gayatribai whispers a prayer so it could be carried along in the winds stirred up by the jeep.

Suddenly, there it is. The temple that Gayatribai had promised was all the more spectacular for the journey.

But even more suddenly, Gayatribai wants to turn back. It isn't *here* that she needs to be, at least not for very long. It isn't *here* that she would fight for her village. It isn't *here* that her battle would be put into words—words as clear and as sharp as prayer.

And yet, she holds these thoughts inside her, even though they rise like a tide over which she has no control. She is poised now at the top row of the temple steps they have climbed. Before her is the cool, dark, stone interior of the temple, with its orange-and-red adorned deity, its familiar rituals of blessed waters and incense and lamps. Behind her are girls and women growing listless, loveless in the sun.

Why is she thinking these thoughts? Why does she want to disappoint both the deities and the women?

It's because of that child, the boy, and what she had heard him say! Gayatribai hadn't paid it heed when she had first heard the words in the activity of this morning. It was what he had said as he watched the men leave for the protest rally and the women get ready for prayer. Meera had translated for Gayatribai the boy's words of disappointment, and a single other sentence: *I think this is so twisted—shouldn't it be the other way around? The men should go and pray and the women should . . .*

She can't take a young boy's words seriously. This event, this day of prayer, is for her daughter. Today, she is just a mother.

Her eye catches a glimpse of something familiar, something that she knows well but something that shouldn't be here. She senses this fact before she comprehends what she is looking at—a woman in the line of devotees at the temple. A stranger. What is so familiar about her? The sari she is wearing . . . it belongs to Gayatribai. It's *her* yellow sari, the one the beast had dragged away from the godown that morning.

She stares at the woman, who is going about her prayers, smiling, laughing, chanting with her own group of women. Could Gayatribai be mistaken? After all, it is possible that there are two identical saris in the vicinity of . . . . no, there it is—there's the blue fall that Gayatribai herself had stitched on, mismatched with the yellow, but the only one that had been available at a cheap price.

The beast had given the sari to . . . his wife? *What kind of man does that sort of thing?* Gives the sari of the woman he raped to his own wife? Why would the wife take it? Why would she wear another woman's old sari?

Before she knows it, Gayatribai has walked up to the woman and asked her where she got the sari from. The woman is puzzled but she replies, with a faint smile playing around her mouth, 'My husband said he found it among the sacred offerings made at his ancestral temple. He said the priest told him that any woman who wears it will soon bear a son.'

Another woman standing beside this woman giggles, 'Her husband makes her wear this sari every night when they . . .'

Gayatribai recoils from their laughter and stumbles backwards to where her own women are standing. She wants to throw up her lungs for the wife of her rapist to take back with her and feed to her sick husband.

She spins around at the top of the steps, where the Dhanpur women are still queued up. She looks for her daughter's face in the crowds. No, it's not *prayer* that she must pass on to Meera. It's *protest.* Meera calls out to her, and Gayatribai sees her daughter looking anxious. The boy, too, is staring at her in panic. She says, with all the calm she can pull into her voice: 'We will go inside and pray, but it will be short. Then, we will ask the temple priest to arrange for transport for us all to go to the protest. It is *there* that we will put to right use these offerings of beautiful things we are carrying with us: bangles and garlands and turmeric paste.'

⌒≋⌒

And so it is that just when Bajirao throws down a policeman's stick that has beaten welts on his back, a row of women comes marching down the road. The women are singing, no, *declaring* songs, swaying in step, clanging pots and pans together, all of them led by a woman in a green sari. Skipping along, by her side, is a long-haired, large-eyed Indian boy.

The reporters that are part of the motorcade turn away from the occasional picture of the police showdown. They turn their cameras, flashing like lightning that indeed strikes in the same place twice. The policemen and bodyguards watch, slack-jawed and squinting, their hands limp on their sticks—this procession looks neither dangerous nor unruly. The bureaucrats shuffle on the outside of the crowd, unsure of what orders to shout to the policemen.

The women break up into groups as if on cue, accost each one of the bureaucrats and policemen, and singing wedding songs, throw garlands around their necks. They make offerings to them of green glass bangles, and smear their faces with a turmeric paste meant for blushing brides. An occasional lathi rises and then grows limp again. The cameras are watching. This can never be explained as violence . . . this is . . . a *carnival*.

It goes just as Gayatribai has planned. The policemen are too startled to do a thing. They shrink back, but they can't run or put up a fight, for that will set them up for ridicule forever. After all, what man would run away or turn violent at *this* pageant of protest? The garlands are meant to mockingly pronounce them as husbands, protectors. The bangles and turmeric paste are symbols meant to emasculate them into the state of passive femininity that these women themselves have abandoned on this auspicious day.

The police cordon recedes. The men in uniform scatter. Behind this line of force, Gayatribai sees her man. He is squatting on the ground, a policeman's knee is digging into his back, putting his hands into steel cuffs. Red welts are growing angry on his neck and arms. She searches the familiar contours of his head and is relieved to see no blood or swelling there. Bajirao meets her eye for a brief second and then looks away. Meera screams.

The only thought that comes to Gayatribai's mind is: the dying should fear nothing. If the doctor believes I am to wither into my lungs, let these lungs have one more shout.

〜

'If you want to throw my man in jail, do it.' Gayatribai's voice rings out over the microphone. She has somehow found her way to the top of the stage. She has never heard her own voice this loud before, but here she is now, hearing it echo back to her as deep as she had intended all day.

Ammar Chaudhry springs up from the crowd onto the stage to stand behind her, as if to hold her if she falls. Gayatribai turns around and nods at him, urging him to trust her, to go and sit down.

'I don't know what my husband did, but I know him to be the gentlest human being for miles and miles. If he was driven to do something for which he deserves the cuffs on his hand, at least find out what drove him. Don't have pity for him. Have questions for him. Ask him why there are more women in this village than men.

'I can say this now—my Meera shall be a sorry bride if she should leave behind a village of women in mourning! Of what use would be our prayers today, if tomorrow we should be widows? Of what use are our voices, if they are raised only after we turn into those widows? Listen to us *now*, hear us *now*, as *farmers* who till the land as much as our men do. Don't talk to us and take our pictures only when we are in tears. Ask us *now* what we have to say about subsidies, about irrigation, about loan waivers. Ask us how . . . how the sahukar gnaws and chews on us . . . and, yes, we will welcome you to our bare kitchens as much as we will lead you to our dying lands. We will still feed you until your bellies are full, but we will not let you go until you have fed our soil!'

Not for a moment does she feel lost as she stands before a thousand and more people and hears her voice booming over them. For among those thousand are three faces that look up at her as if her words have come for them after a long and thirsty wait. Her daughter, her man, and the strange young boy who has come here from America who, with little knowledge of where to place her in a world that is foreign to him, has placed her right here, on top of a stage, with a loud voice. Gayatribai's eyes now catch a movement at the back of the crowds.

The crowds are parting to let the policemen and bodyguards through. Behind them walks a portly, bald man in a white kurta and pants, a khadi waistcoat, and the cleanest leather shoes Gayatribai has ever seen. She doesn't know who this man is, walking up to the stage now as the crowds cheer.

The man joins his hands in a namaste to Gayatribai. She

on the man. His head bobs up and catches a shaft of moonlight. The woman sees him and throws herself in without a thought.

As the woman's body and her thoughts hit the waters, the river gasps in shock. This woman is unafraid. She is here with all her heart. She is here with all her will. She is here for the man and she will not be frightened away. She will get in deep. She isn't just willing to plunge in. She is willing to be swept away. The river whips around in a trance. She grows a hundred little hands to hold the man down and a hundred feet with which to push at the woman. From her belly, the river raises an undertow.

But the woman has strong limbs. She kicks deep into the water and her breath holds out for minutes on end as she gropes into the river's belly, writhes against the undertow, and stretching one arm as low as she can, grabs hold of the man's forearm. The river rushes a strong ripple at the woman and takes the silver and emerald jewels from her neck. The woman is undistracted. Her legs turn into the forked tails of the strongest fish and she starts to haul the man away. As the man's lungs begin to give way, his body loses its reflexive resistance and turns more and more limp, making it easy for the woman to tug out and away from the hungry waves.

Suddenly, the man's insides turn to fire. The substance he has swallowed on shore churns its own tornado within him, and his body starts to twitch and squirm. A scar in his body opens. The red river that humans carry within them gushes out to meet the waters.

Even in the darkness of the struggle under water, the woman sees the rush of red from the man's body. For the briefest moment, she shudders in shock. That's all the man seems to need. His legs throw a powerful blow on the woman's chest. Her hands lose their grip.

The river seizes her moment. She swiftly gathers up the man, an ever willing accomplice. She pulls him into her deepest folds. He rests.

The river gets no moment to relish this. On her shores, that boy of the strange twang of voice has arrived. He is crying out for his mother. He throws himself in. Within seconds, another man follows him in. The river shudders at the madness of these people.

She pauses to sense their movements. The boy can swim like his mother. The man cannot swim at all.

Their time has not come yet. The river grows tired with these humans who have so little sense of the tides of their humanity. When will they learn?

The river carries the broken woman to her son. The woman lays a strong arm on him. Their heads bob to the surface. The boy gasps and shouts something to his mother. The woman's body gathers itself up again. She gives the boy a mighty push, propelling him to the shore. The boy swims as he is told. The woman, who still has the feeblest of struggles left in her, dives around looking for the living man. With the frenzy of a woman who *will not* lose two men to the river in one night, she homes in on the man, her lover from that night of listlessness. She puts her arm around his shoulder and, with one final push of will, drags him to shore.

The woman, the man, and the child lie there for a while, on the river's shore. Their gasps and coughs slowly fall quiet. Their sobs fall helplessly upon each other. The rain seems unwilling to notice. It keeps up its plunder of the river that quivers and clutches at her own heart to calm the storm growing there.

20

'Has He Done it Yet?'

SHE WOULD NEVER forget the second in which a man's life slipped through her fingers. In the minutes after Bajirao's drowning, Katya's hands twitch and clutch involuntarily at the air. Her lungs ache from being denied air and her chest hurts from the blow from Bajirao's legs, yes, but the most pain she feels is at the tips of her fingers. Only days ago, her fingertips had been stained with the dust from a map of the land where Bajirao once lived. Now, these fingertips have come away with nothing.

In the darkness and gales of this night, crowds of people are beginning to arrive, running to the river's shores. Katya lays one hand on Kabir and the other on the man who had sired him and had, just minutes ago, thrown himself into the river to save the boy's life. Had he forgotten he couldn't swim? Or had his only thought been to save his son? Katya flattens her palm against the breathing chest of this man, Kabir's father.

People's voices rise as they realize that Bajirao is indeed gone. They had seen him bolt from his daughter's wedding. Most of them saw Katya break away from the wedding party and quicken her steps behind him. People outside saw him break into a wild run. They saw Katya's steps grow frantic and then they saw her give chase.

They saw her trip over the borders of her sari and fall to the ground. They ran to help, but they had seen her rise and run again. It was clear she was fighting against the pain of her skin breaking at the knee. As they watched her go, some people say they saw her tear the sari from her body and leave it on the ground so she could run unconstrained and follow the speed of her panic.

They saw the boy come running after her. They saw his father follow. They looked to the tent to see who else would come. Gayatribai didn't. Those inside the tent heard her ask the priest to complete the wedding rituals. They saw Meera's eyes widen in shock and then, steadied by her mother's unflinching stare, Meera did as she was told.

When no one saw any of the running people find their way back, people from the wedding party and from here and there gathered into a crowd and followed the path on which Bajirao had seemed to be headed. They arrived at the river.

So, Bajirao was gone. How could he have stood a chance against the rush of a recently rainfed river, especially if he hadn't wanted that chance anyway.

Katya listens to all these shouts around her. She keeps her eyes closed and her cheek resting in the mud, one ear to the ground on which the rain is trying to help her drown out all sound, but failing. She feels Kabir's body shake with childlike cries at all that he is hearing. She feels Ammar pull slowly away from beneath her hand to answer questions in a flailing voice.

'Who will tell Gayatribai?' someone asks.

They wait an hour by the river to see if the waters would offer up Bajirao's body to take home to his wife. People who have known this river and its ways with the rain say that Bajirao would not surface for a day or two. Still, they wait another hour, staring at the glittering silver sari in which the moon covers the river. The rain starts to abate and now they can see gentler drops fall, puncturing the sari like sequins. These two hours of waiting are also to allow the rituals of the mass wedding to come to a close, for Meera to be fully wedded before her mother is to be widowed, for Gayatribai to be home, a place where she may grieve in the quiet company of her gods.

Katya pushes through the growing pain in her knee as she walks closer to Gayatribai's home. Someone has brought her the sari she had ripped from her body when she ran. It is soaked and muddy, but needed for some semblance of decency. Katya has now wrapped this carelessly about herself.

In the last stretch of the bylane that leads to Gayatribai's home, Katya tells the group that this terrible job is hers to do. She is relieved that no one puts up a protest. Even Ammar acquiesces. His arm is wound tightly around Kabir's shoulders. The boy looks ready to fall from the insanity of this day that began with a dance in the rain and ended with a death in a river. In this, the fourteenth year of his life and his first Indian monsoon, her boy has seen enough. Ammar offers to take Kabir to his own home. Katya accepts. She plants a stream of kisses on her child's face. He begs her to go to Gayatribai.

Gayatribai's home is dark when Katya arrives. The blue door is ajar, the porch looks steady and the toran of flowers that Gayatribai had hung on the door for blessings before heading to the wedding still looks fresh. For a moment, Katya is assailed by the thrill of the vision she had walked in upon on one of her first evenings in this home—Bajirao and Gayatribai were locked in a moment of intimacy. Gayatribai's mangalsutra beads were entangled in Bajirao's kurta as he was trying to undress her in a frenzy. The man and woman were woven together in a way that Katya couldn't unscramble in her brain even after she quickly, quietly had stepped away. In her memory of that vision now, she still can't pull them apart. She does not know where Bajirao began and where Gayatribai ended.

She longs for this to be just another night that would lead to just another morning when Bajirao would rise to the sound of Gayatribai's dented aluminium kettle readying his chai, so he could stretch, untether his bullocks and leave for his fields.

Katya puts her foot on the porch and pain shoots through her leg like a warning. She crumples onto the floor, inhaling the dung that is caked here in layers, over years of keeping this hut going. Holding onto the threshold of this home, catching her breath, she suddenly feels lost. Is she at the wrong hut?

She stands up to turn around, to run back. From the corner of her eye, she catches the shape of Gayatribai, sitting with her back to the outside world, facing her assembly of gods.

It seems like a silent eternity before Katya can steady herself on her feet. She can't take her eyes off Gayatribai's head, and yet, she doesn't want it to move, doesn't want her to turn around. But, in the next instant, Gayatribai does turn around to look right at her.

Katya wishes she was sitting down. Not because she is in pain, not even because she is tired from running, but because she doesn't know any more where she is standing. And she can't bring herself to take the single short step between the threshold and the interior of Gayatribai's home.

What does Gayatribai know? Why didn't she follow the people who ran after Bajirao? Was she confident that Bajirao wouldn't kill himself? Or was she sure that his time had come? Katya pushes the door open with the same arm with which she had let Bajirao go. She struggles to read Gayatribai's face. The woman looks older than ever before. The evening's mother-of-the-bride is midnight's ghost.

'Gayatri . . .' Katya says. She feels more foreign with every passing moment.

Gayatribai speaks, in the single language she knows. 'Tyaa ni kaylat kai?' Has he done it already?

It is now that Katya notices Gayatribai holding in her hand her little box of kunku, poised mid-air, mid-question. Her hair is freshly washed, and it hangs damp around her shoulders and down her back. She hasn't applied her brilliant red streak of matrimonial certainty yet, in the sliver of scalp that separates her hair into two halves.

Near her feet, Gayatribai has placed dinner utensils for two. Two copper plates and two copper tumblers filled with water. In the centre is a brown-paper wrapper flattened out, on which she has placed two pooris and a clay pot of shrikhand. Katya looks at this strange assembly of food, this odd ritual of dining that seems incongruous to everything else going on. She recognizes in the next instant that this ritual holds some meaning for Gayatribai tonight, some significance that will making the coming pain all the harder to bear.

Katya is overwhelmed again by a desire to run. But she knows that she will only run around in circles, run on beyond, farther and farther out, past the cattle and the temples and the river, over the dips and rises in the landscape, right through, into the fields, where, for years, Gayatribai and Bajirao have wordlessly worked the cotton from seed to bud to bale. And all the circles will bring her back here, to the biggest failure of her life, the hardest moment of Gayatribai's life.

She starts to shake. She nods at Gayatribai. 'He is deep in the river,' she says.

Gayatribai nods and slumps to the floor.

21

'I Grinned at Her'

WITHIN THE HOUR, Gayatribai's hut is claimed by mourning relatives and by the rituals of grief. Drained of all struggle and aching to surrender to solitude, Katya recedes. This home is no place for her now. She will only bring to it questions from the lonely people of another land, trying to make sense of all that has happened. What has happened is a death. Sense can wait.

She walks for an hour into the night. The rain has abated. A fuller moon has emerged and it shines down now on all that lies on a beaten, slippery earth—leaves and branches, bits of roofs from homes, footprints and hoofprints. Even through her unseeing exhaustion, Katya is aware of how familiar she has become with the bylanes of this village. She wonders if she can stretch out under a gulmohur tree, close her eyes and fall asleep.

Instead, she walks on, limping, to Ammar's office. Katya wants to claim a corner of Ammar's inner room, where there is a bed, a lamp and a hundred books. When she arrives here in the dark hours, she finds Kabir asleep on the bed, still dressed in his kurta. Ammar awakens as she enters and he quietly lays out a spare mattress on the floor. He leaves the room without a word, a touch or a single look at Katya. Yet, she senses no hostility between them—only the solidarity of a man and a woman whose child is alive and asleep before their eyes.

She awakens with a start at midday, lost in an unknown room but caught firmly in the grip of the knowledge that few things are well with the world today. She sits up to look for Kabir, but he's gone. So is Ammar. She can hear their voices in the office outside. She gives herself a few minutes of thought. The first one that strikes her—she doesn't know where to be today. The second—she doesn't know how long to be here now. The third thought arrives as an answer—be where you are asked to be; leave when you are irrelevant.

She steps into the office, where a letter is being read out to a small group of people:

To my daughters—

When you have children of your own, you will learn how difficult it is to leave them alone for even a minute. When they grow up, they will leave on their own and this will make you happy. But you will spend the rest of your life waiting for those days on which you can see them again, with children of their own and with love and struggles of their own. That is the third part of a parent's life.

What, then, makes a father give up the joys of the third part of his life and choose to walk into death instead? I don't know. I cannot think any more. I feel weak when I think of how I will not see your faces again. I feel paralysed when I think of how I will not see your mother's face. But more than anything, I feel dead already when I think of you and her without me in this world. It makes me angry to think of the grief you will feel upon hearing of my passing. It makes me feel like setting the world on fire to think of the days and months you will spend feeling lost, wondering if you could have done anything to change what happened, holding each other and crying and then getting to all the work that must be done once I am gone.

I feel like protecting you from my own decision. But I can't. This has to happen. I have lost everything. You must understand this—the pain of me living is worse than the pain of my death. A man is only alive if he has land to stand upon. And I am losing more and more with each passing year. This has to stop. Your mother must have a home to grow old in. She must have land that yields cotton and feeds her. She must have money from the government as compensation for the death of the head of her household.

Your mother is sick. She needs an operation for cancer. I am letting our guests pay for some of this but no more. The compensation money will pay for other things, especially for getting our land back.

And, when your mother is well, she will know what to do. I know she will fight. I know she will earn back our land and earn back our dignity. She will also fight for the village. She will fight for the rights of each farmer of Vidarbha. I saw her do that a few days ago. The only person who is standing in the way of all this is me.

It is difficult to explain. Your mother looks at me and thinks she sees the complete world. But this world I made for her has failed her. It is incomplete. She must make one for herself. It will be better than mine, you know. She must not be crippled by memories of me. She must not think of me as a strong man. She must find her own strength. She must be more than just my wife and your mother. She must be a true daughter of Vidarbha.

I hope you will bring your children to see this woman that

I will not live to see. And I hope you and your mother will forgive me.

    With all my blessings,
    Your father

Ammar wants to publish Bajirao's letter in the papers. Meera Deshmukh, who should have left for her new husband's home but has instead, changed her clothes from bridal finery to the rags of mourning, refuses to let the letter go. Her husband Dinesh Deshmukh, who is by her side, nods his head at her decision. Her sisters and their husbands all agree.

'I don't think this letter was meant for the world to see,' Meera says. 'I don't think it was meant for my mother to see.'

Watching Kabir's face now, Katya realizes that the letter wasn't quite meant for him to see either. Here he is, her boy, caught in a frighteningly foreign world. His face is distorted from his effort at holding back his sobs.

Katya moves quietly through the seated people to the edge of the room, and tugs on Kabir's arm, nudging him to follow her outside. This is his first encounter with death; it's the first time that someone he has smiled at, touched, or talked to, has stopped doing all those things.

The skies have opened up again and sheets of rain are pouring down outside. Katya and Kabir walk in silence under Ammar's umbrella until they arrive at the grand peepal tree in the village. They sit down on the concrete, circular platform—Kabir's place of architectural genius from their first day together here. This time, no one is around. Those people in this village who are not in mourning are either celebrating or preparing for the rites of rain.

His words come out in a tumble. 'I went to meet Gayatribai. A couple of hours ago, when you were asleep. I went on my own.'

'What? Why? How did Amm . . . how did Baba let you?'

'He didn't know. He was out. They found Bajirao . . . I mean . . . his body.'

'*What?*'

'Yeah. It floated up to the shore early this morning. Baba went when he heard about it. He said not to wake you. But I wanted . . . I really needed to be there to . . . I felt stupid sitting here. I thought we should all be with Gayatribai.'

His face is soaked with tears now. His breath is rancid and his clothes and skin still smell of the river.

'You did the right thing,' Katya hears herself tell her son. 'It's okay.'

'I wish I hadn't gone. It was horrible. Mom, it was horrible.'

He puts his face in his hands and lets his sobs tear themselves away from his head. Katya watches him. Had he seen Bajirao's body? Was it grotesque, bloated, bitten? Would he ever be able to erase those images?

He fights against his sobs, fights for breath. 'I go there, right? And I hear this god-awful howl. I want to turn back, but I go in. I see Gayatribai inside her home and it's dark. And she's standing by this . . . this body lying in the middle of the hut. It's covered in a white sheet. She's shaking and weeping and I realize it was her that was howling. Then it gets worse. She sounds like a dog coughing. And she's doing this thing.' He shuts his eyes.

So he hadn't seen the body. Thank goodness. She feels a sensation rise in her. Again, on her fingertips, a tingling, a feeble current, of being connected and then being prised loose from a body. That body that she had let go of had resurfaced, in a form that couldn't be held on to.

She yanks her thoughts away from their new drift and returns them to Kabir's voice. 'She's doing this thing. She's ripping locks of her hair out of her head. I don't know what the hell that is. Why was she ripping out locks of her hair from her head?'

259

'Grief,' Katya says, weakly.

'And then she turns her head for a moment, as if she senses me standing there. Her face is tilted really awkwardly. She seems to stop, like, for a breath. And I think it's all done, it's all over and that she'll stop crying. And I couldn't help it, I couldn't stop myself, and I . . . I grinned at her. Just like that. I *grinned* at her. Can you believe it? As if nothing had happened. As if she's a teacher at my school or something and I am saying, "Hey, Mrs Andhale! How're you doin'?"*Aaaaargh*. I am *so mad* at myself. Why did I have to do that?' He hides his face in his hands again and shakes his head vigorously.

He doesn't need her to say what happened was okay. He doesn't need her to comfort him for this.

'What happened then?' Katya asks.

'She . . . she looked away. She looked away. As if I wasn't even there. Like she didn't know me.'

'She probably didn't realize . . . '

But he interrupts her. 'And then this government official arrives, like, thundering on his motorcycle. We've seen this guy before. He's that Patekar guy. Now he's squeezing his shiny bike through that narrow path leading up to Gayatribai's home. And all these kids and chickens and stuff are squawking and flying out of his path. He says to us all that when there is some doubt about the cause of death, it is government procedure to load the body of a farmer into a government truck and take it to the Poison Ward at the nearest hospital. An examination is to be conducted, he says.'

Kabir gulps for air between his words and sobs. 'He doesn't ask to talk to Gayatribai. He just declares his statement to the crowds outside. He makes an official pronouncement that a death has taken place—of Bajirao Andhale, head of household, Hut Number 62, Dhanpur Village. Then, he pushes the ground with one foot to turn his motorcycle around, and he leaves all this muck spraying behind him. And just like that, they've taken Bajirao away again from Gayatribai and loaded him ... his body ... into a truck. And she's standing there now wailing over an empty space and filling it up with strands of hair she is ripping off her head.'

He stops speaking. The rain grows louder around them. It's the same rain that fell outside Gayatribai's home yesterday. It's all part of the same rain.

'And then I do another stupid thing. *Do you know what I do?*'
Katya shakes her head.

'I do something stupid. I know I shouldn't look, I know I should let her be alone, but I turn around to look at Gayatribai again. And she's lying down in the same spot where Bajirao's body was lying. And she's looking up at that little skylight in their hut and tugging at her nose ring, and nodding her head. She's nodding and nodding and nodding as if she understands everything.'

There's nothing to do but sit here, in the heart of the village, and slowly turn from sitting to lying down. The umbrella flies away and the rain beats upon them until their skin is numb. The sound of the water crashing upon earth makes all speech impossible, which is a good thing.

Gayatribai stands by the river at dusk, letting the shadows hold her and hide her. The river always lives, with at least a sliver of a stream, even in the worst drought. But now, she is fat like a raakshasi, a demoness.

Not a stone seems to have shifted since the first day Gayatribai came here as a little girl, visiting this village for an older cousin's wedding. She didn't know then that this would become the river of her adult years. She didn't know that the rim of the river, the spot that was neither water nor earth, would be the space where she would come every time she sought to touch that which was a constant. This river, that rim, have carried her through the sometimes turgid, sometimes still waters of her womanhood and they have also kept her on solid ground.

She sinks into a squat by the river. This is where he had drawn figures in the earth, even though he knew she barely comprehended numbers. Now, bits of familiar soap scum float around the pebbles, carrying with them pieces of the recent life of this village—a clump of broken earthen pottery, scraps of paper with a child's handwriting still clinging to it, a plastic bottle of hair oil, a broken sandal so perfect and fashionable that it seems to have arrived from another world, a half-globe of a child's broken rubber cricket ball, a glass bottle of Coca-Cola, a smashed piece of green jewel, a scrap of pink fabric, its golden threading soiled to rust by the river bed.

This would do. This is enough. This piece of time in this place where her husband had chosen his last breath, these few inches of space that separate unchanging water from the always changing pieces of humans' discards . . . this is all she would allow herself. There is work to be done.

She knows now what it had meant, that blank look he gave her when she stood up on the stage at the rally, searching his face for a sense of direction. He was preparing her for being alone. He was readying her for a lifetime of making her own decisions.

The first one of these was the one she had made today. No, she had said to her cousin who arrived from the city. No, Gayatribai wouldn't accompany her cousin to Mumbai to work as a maidservant in someone's lovely home. She would stay here, to carry on the fight that had begun at the farmers' protest. She would reclaim her land. She would use the money from the compensation for Bajirao's corpse to exhale the tumours in her lungs. She would reclaim the life that Bajirao had wanted for them. She would live it without him, but she would live it the way he had dreamed.

Putting her hands upon the earth near her feet, she pushes herself to standing. She starts to step away and pauses. She turns back and looks at the river. She spits into it and changes it.

⊙≋⊙

When Katya and Kabir return to Ammar's office, an army of press cameras has arrived. Word has spread that the man beaten by the police has drowned himself. The farmer's funeral against the backdrop of the monsoon would be a poignant image. The widow with the rousing speech would make a great interview.

Katya grips Kabir's hand and pushes through the camera crews. Among the group are both her old friends who had come to cover the protest the other day. Katya smiles and nods, but dodges and ducks past them. Kabir walks separately and passes right along without attracting attention. Someone takes Katya's photograph. Yes, of course, she must look terribly fascinating— this woman with wild, highlighted hair and a limp, soaked silk sari. What was her story? What did she have to do with this business of the suicides?

Ammar has asked the press to wait a few minutes as he readies an official statement. He looks relieved to see Katya.

'Gosh, I need your help. They're here, Katyayini. They're finally actually looking deep for answers.'

'What are their questions?' Kabir asks.

Ammar gestures at Kabir to sit next to him at the computer. Katya heads into Ammar's kitchen and brings back two slices of bread with jam on them. She sets the plate down before Kabir and is pleased to see him start to nibble.

Katya starts to read the file that is open on Ammar's computer. Kabir speaks again. 'What are their questions?'

'Well,' Ammar says, 'They want to know more about Bajirao's life. They want some photographs of Meera's wedding. And they want to talk to Gayatribai.'

Kabir falls silent. Katya keeps her eye on him for a moment. Just a hungry boy eating his sandwich.

'The press speaking to Gayatribai is a bad idea,' Ammar says.

Katya nods. 'She is in mourning. Maybe we can ask her for a written statement, sort of reiterating her points from her speech?'

'No,' Ammar says quickly. 'It's a bad idea, now, tomorrow, or any other time. We'll need to talk to her and tell her to step back.'

Katya looks up from the screen at Ammar. 'I'm not sure what you mean.'

'She got a little carried away, na? It will take a lot of work to undo what happened at the protest rally the other day.'

Katya tries to focus on what he is saying. What is Ammar talking about? What had she missed about Gayatribai's role in that day's events?

'I don't see what you mean. Aren't we happy that Gayatribai has emerged as a . . . ?'

'Are you joking? She can't emerge as anything. Haven't you been reading the papers? People are talking about how the farmers' movement is doomed if a woman has to take charge. It's a travesty!'

Katya turns to look at Ammar, her mouth gaping. Ammar pauses and sighs. 'I mean, I am really grateful and touched by her support in these past weeks, but . . .'

'But she should *support* and not *lead*?' Katya knows her tone is openly incredulous now. She is searching every pore on

Ammar's face. Where is the man who, like Mirza Ghalib, saw thousands of dreams, each one worth dying for?

'Katya, why won't you listen?' Ammar has raised his voice.

She remembers this voice, this tenor, from a telephone call from long ago. She tries to fight back her impulse to walk out of this door right here, right now.

'Katya . . . my Katya . . . you are more American than the Americans themselves. You think the sky is the limit for women. Please understand the local context here. She can't go to the chief minister's meeting. She won't know what to say.'

So, he calls her Katya now. All right. Katya it is. 'She seemed to do just fine the other day,' she says.

'Yes, she did a good job listing the issues. But don't you see, the villagers, the sarpanch, the agriculture office, all these people here . . . they won't be able to tolerate a woman as their leader. This is not the city. This is not America.'

Katya takes a deep breath. 'Actually, you're right, it isn't America. That country cannot tolerate the thought of a woman leader. But I know *this* one can.'

Ammar's face darkens. He rises from his chair and walks to the window and stares outside at the waiting news reporters. 'Those people there are waiting for me to say something,' he says.

'Let them wait,' Katya says. 'Better still, let them find the people who can really tell their own story. You and I, Ammar, we could try and be quiet. When one has a voice in the world, one feels like one can say anything, that one *must* always say something. We might forget when to be quiet and listen.'

Kabir's voice speaks into the silence. 'Baba, my mom is right. This isn't America. It's Dhanpur. And whatever is happening here is fine. It's fine for Dhanpur. Because it's happening here and now, whether you like it or not.'

Outside, the camera crews start a fresh clamour, their sounds urgent, unmuffled by the deluge of rain. Ammar presses his fingertips to his eyelids. 'Kabir, my boy, you don't understand. She will be misled. She will be manipulated and she will be silenced. She thinks they want her to speak, but what they really want is to keep her quiet.'

'Who is *they*?' Kabir says. 'Isn't that what *you're* doing, Baba?'

Katya and Kabir sit there, watching Ammar's back. He turns, slowly, and looks at Kabir with the most naked look Katya has ever seen on his face.

'But . . . the press is here. They're ready. They want to write about this. They need direction from someone who understands . . .'

'Sure,' Kabir says. 'And then?'

Ammar pauses for a moment. 'And then? Oh, I see what you mean. And then . . . they . . . well, I suppose they will . . . they can be led to writing about deeper realities.'

'Will they?' Kabir's look is direct, open.

'Kabir . . .' Katya says. She really isn't sure what to say next. Kabir doesn't turn to look at her. He is searching his father's face.

'Why didn't they come to Kisna-kaka's funeral?' Kabir says.

Ammar steps closer to the boy. 'Because . . . they didn't know he had died. Kabir, my boy, I understand what you're . . .'

'Do you, Baba? Because I'm not sure if even I do. I don't really understand. But I think . . . I think Bajirao kinda knew. I think he threw himself at the chief minister's car because he suspected that the press would write about that whole drama there. He was right. They did. I think these guys will keep coming back every time there's something more dramatic like this. And then it'll be like . . . old news . . . and the whole village will have to set itself on fire to get into the news. Right? Don't you think?'

Ammar stares at Kabir. Deep frowns are growing on the

man's forehead as he tries to comprehend what his child is saying.

'Baba, I don't know as much as you about this whole farmers' crisis thingy. I don't know about the cotton market and subsidies and price adjustments and loan waivers or whatever. But I know that people don't have the time to pay attention to this and read about it or watch documentaries on it unless someone's finding newer ways to kill himself. I think Gayatribai can do some work quietly. She can keep the cameras away and get some real work done and have some people who really care to write about it. I think we can get her some support to do that.'

'Kabir, my child, what makes you think she can do it?' Ammar asks.

'Because she's actually quite boring,' Kabir says. 'And brave.'

Ammar sits down. He laughs. He shakes his head and his laughter grows uncontrollable. Katya and Kabir look at each other and back at him as he clutches the corner of his desk so he doesn't fall to the floor laughing.

Katya wants to say something about PTSD but thinks the better of it. She sits there, her clothes still damp, raising the scent of sweat and the river into her nostrils. She is beyond caring about this now. It's as if she needs to keep these clothes on, stay right like this, until three days of rain have beaten enough branches off the trees.

Ammar re-emerges from his laughter and puts words together. 'Kabir,' he says, 'You might be right. In fact, I'm quite sure you are. Gayatribai is boring and brave. And . . . she has nothing to lose,' he says. 'She's readier for this than any of us.'

Katya watches as Ammar's smile stretches all the way into Kabir's. The boy jumps up and throws his arms around his father. 'I love you, Baba,' he says.

'I love you, too, my son,' Ammar says. 'Now, go find

Gayatribai. Ask her if she has something boring she wants to say to those people outside.'

Kabir can barely get his slippers on before he rushes to the door. For just a moment, he pauses and turns to look at Katya. She nods, just once. Yes, you may go on your own. Yes, she will be in a better state to receive you. She will know who you are.

Katya lingers for a few moments at Ammar's desk. She knows she must say now what she may not have the nerve to say ever again.

'You jumped into the river to save Kabir's life, didn't you? You didn't know if he could swim. So, you forgot that *you* were the one who couldn't.'

Ammar rubs his eyes. 'I . . . I was terrified of losing him in the river. I have seen children swept away in the . . .' His voice trails off. Katya sees his face darken with visions and memories of terror. Droughts and floods find the poorest of the poor. And among them lives Ammar.

'You've loved having him here, haven't you?' Katya says.

Ammar sighs. 'Oh, Katyayini, I cannot begin to tell you . . . you and I both know that I do not know how to be around a child, least of all my own. But . . . around Kabir . . . I feel like I want to learn. I want to learn so badly, you know?'

Katya nods. 'Yes, I know. But I also know this—you know enough. If you throw yourself into raging waters to save your son's life, you are a father. That's all you need to know. And that's all I need to know.' She takes a deep gulp of air into her lungs. 'Kabir came here and found his father.'

༄

Katya knows where Kabir would have thought to look for Gayatribai—the cotton fields. They have been in Dhanpur

268

long enough to know that the living would still be working in the fields.

She arrives at the fields and walks deep into them, through the rows of furrowed soil until she reaches a higher stretch of land that allows her a viewing perch. Katya looks at the sweep of landscape before them and her eyes meet with the sight she had anticipated, the scene she sought out. Farmers are bent over their land, plucking at it, prodding it, their feet at times treading the mud and at times planting themselves into it, mud and skin blending into one colour. It is as if these humans had themselves sprung like crops from this land, like an ailing yield.

Among these humans are the two people she is looking for—Gayatribai and Kabir. She is in no hurry to walk up to them. Katya stretches herself out on the stretch of land, on her stomach. She crosses her hands under her chin and lets the irrigated earth seep in and soak her clothes as if to slowly absorb its secret intent for abundance in this land.

Lying this way, she watches Gayatribai lead Kabir into doing with diligence what they are supposed to do this day—not mourn, not take charge, not talk or tell, but sow the seeds after the first day of rain in the kharif season. Katya thinks back to that day Kabir and she had walked around the villages with Bajirao. He had told them about the crop cycles, 'There are three harrowings—two after ploughing and one after the first monsoon rain before the seeds are sown.'

Katya wonders what Kabir is seeing on this land now. Bajirao's two-day-old widow faces him, bent over her small piece of land, her own eyes as dry as the dirt is wet, doing in solitude what she has done with her husband for years.

Into these quiet motions arrives a motorcycle. As the vehicle pumps wet soil from beneath it, forming a track that shows that the man on the motorcycle means business, one by one the farmers in their separate spots on the fields straighten up from their working positions.

Katya's instinct is to run to her boy, grab his hand and Gayatribai's, and run out of here. She fights it. Patekar can do no direct harm. Katya flattens herself deeper into the earth and strains her ears to listen. It's only now that she notices that for quite some distance in the horizon, just like always, the farmers are women. She recalls something now about women doing most of the sowing and the harvesting while men did the ploughing . . .

First come the mumbled greetings aimed at the figure of authority. Then come the questions from Patekar. He notices Kabir but ignores him. He is addressing Gayatribai. Katya can hear his voice now, but she cannot pick up what he is saying. Like the government official, she waits for Gayatribai to speak. But the woman slowly looks away and, turning her head back to her work, sinks down and lets her hands move back into their rhythm.

Katya can see Kabir's shoulders stiffen as Patekar steps closer to Gayatribai, towering almost right above where she is crouched. He asks another question, now speaking louder. Katya can decipher two words: Bajirao Andhale. And she can decipher what happens next.

The women around Gayatribai, their bags of seeds tied in pouches around their waist, step up and form a circle around her, placing themselves between the government man and the working woman.

From her perch Katya is witness to the clear geometry and physics of dissent—the chief agriculture officer has to stumble and take a few steps back as the humans before him rearrange themselves in silence.

Within this . . . crop circle . . . Gayatribai sits sowing her seeds as if nothing is happening around her. A chanting rises up in the field. Katya recognizes the words. They are from the speech Gayatribai made at the protest rally. The women have found a new slogan: '*Ti ek shetkari ahe; keval ek vidhwa naahi.*' She is a farmer . . . she's not just a widow.

Patekar recedes. He leaves. The farmers allow themselves a few smiles. They return to their sowing. When the sound of the motorcycle has been swallowed up by the horizon, Gayatribai pulls Kabir to her and gently smothers his head into her neck, her bony arms clasped around his shoulders, rocking him from side to side. It is a whole minute before Gayatribai lets him go, but the boy looks like he could have stayed there a while longer.

Katya can tell, even from here, that Gayatribai looks ashen with fear, but the woman is smiling now as she reaches out awkwardly and tucks some locks of Kabir's hair behind his ears.

'What do you want?' Katya hears her son say to Gayatribai. His voice is clear, loud.

The woman is trying to understand what he has said. She shakes her head but moves her ear closer to Kabir.

'What do you want?' he asks again.

With no one to translate for them, the woman and the boy strain against language and search each other's faces.

'Tu-ma-la kai pai-jay?' Kabir says.

He has found the words. Of course. That's what Gayatribai asked him every day at breakfast.

Gayatribai is chuckling. She touches the ground, laying the palms of both hands flat on the clean, wet mud before her feet. Digging her fingers into the mud and feeling out the earth like clay, she brings her fingers up, holding between her right thumb and forefinger a single seed. Katya knows Kabir can't tell what seed it is, but she knows he can tell what Gayatribai means. *Land. Seed. Water.*

Gayatribai places her hands, with clumps of mud running

down them, onto her chest. Her green sari and blouse quickly soak up the colour of earth. She takes a deep breath and exhales. *Breath.* Kabir is nodding. Gayatribai's next move catches him unawares. She cups his face in her hands, holds his cheeks in a gentle grip, and pulls them apart into a smile. Kabir laughs. She has wiped her hands clean on her clothes before touching him.

'Oh, I'll be fine, Gayatribai. I'll be happy, I promise.' Kabir says and stands up.

She tugs on his hand and pulls him down to the ground again. She reaches into the folds around the waist of her sari, from where she fishes out a clear plastic bag that contains what looks like a letter. She unfolds the plastic, keeping the letter shielded from the drizzle. Kabir looks at it. Even from this distance, Katya can tell he is looking at an official government document. Kabir is blinking. It is probably in Marathi. Why, then, does Gayatribai want him to read it?

Just before Katya can pull herself to standing and reveal herself to the farmer and the boy, Gayatribai flips the letter over.

'Ah, English,' Katya hears Kabir laugh.

Kabir reads the letter aloud with rising excitement in his voice. The letter is from the chief minister. He is formally inviting Gayatribai Andhale of Dhanpur village to join the taskforce working on farm subsidies for Vidarbha. The date of the meeting is a month away.

'Enough time for you to recover from your cancer surgery,' Kabir says.

Gayatribai nods, bursts into a low laugh again, followed by a cough. She bobs her head from side to side and pats her hands on her body, in the region of her lungs. She makes the gesture of scissors, cutting at her lungs. She keeps smiling.

And Kabir? He sits there, his joints hinged into a comfortable squat, his body and face looking more present than Katya had ever seen, right there in the mud and seed and manure of a field so far from the playgrounds of his known home, but so much less foreign to him, somehow, than a brick that had cost $35 to bear his name on it.

◦≈◦

When Bajirao's skull cracks, Katya knows it punctuates her purpose here. A full stop. In the United States, it's known as a period. The end of a sentence. The opportunity to start a new paragraph.

It's a picture-perfect moment for the cameras. They couldn't have ordered better lighting. The rain has abated a little, and the sun is peeping out from between the unending, grey clouds. The fire from the funeral pyre lingers over the burning body, thick and heavy in the muggy air. With the thundershowers now quiet, the sounds of wailing carry well to the recording machines. The lenses move briskly, trying to capture it all. The news reporters relish the excellent copy that a raw cremation serves up.

Kabir is standing beside Katya as Ammar moves among a clutch of men in the funeral.

'I am sorry we couldn't save Bajirao's life, Mom,' he says. 'How will we ever get over that?'

We! The word breaks her heart. At what point had he assumed this was his work to do, along with her? This young hand in hers, turning hot from the proximity to the fire, was her child. Her work wasn't his to do.

'But we should make sure Bajirao's last wish is fulfilled,' he says, wiping away tears from his cheeks. His voice, though, is steady.

'Yes.'

'We have to make sure Gayatribai has the best surgery ever.'

'Yes,' Katya laughs weakly. 'The best surgery ever. I have

scheduled it at the fancy hospital in the town.'

'Her surgery should be done from the compensation money for Bajirao's death. We must get it quickly,' Kabir says.

Katya sighs. 'It's not that easy, my son. The government bureaucracy will fight to make sure they don't have to pay the compensation. I wouldn't be surprised if Bajirao paid Patekar a bribe. I also wouldn't be surprised if Patekar pretends he was never paid. There are so many criteria Bajirao's death must meet. They may find out about his alcohol habit. That's the end of that. And . . . there are so many other things that an investigation may reveal. If there's some miracle and the case slips through all of those, there's also the issue of time. Paper pushing here takes . . .'

'Do you think that some things here don't happen because people don't believe they will?' Kabir says.

'Not sure what you mean.'

'It's . . . well, kinda like when I'm snowboarding, you know? Sometimes I'm really nervous . . . terrified even . . . that I won't make it over a rock in the snow. Then, in a moment, I just feel like it will be fine. And it is! It works each time. Each and every effing time.'

He's smiling a tentative smile. He's wondering if his mother is going to object to his use of the 'f' word.

She smiles back. 'Okay. So I should believe that the compensation money will come through. And it will?'

'Yeah.'

◦═◦

Right outside the cremation grounds, the cameras are now trained on Mr Sachin Patekar on his motorcycle. Katya can't help noticing how he seems to look so unaffected by the rain—his grey slacks, white shirt and his leather sandals are spotless, dry, unsoiled. In his hand, he holds a waterproof folder that looks thick with papers and documents. Clipped to the pocket of his shirt are a fountain pen and a ballpoint pen. He is guarding all these things under his big, black umbrella.

The man is talking loudly into the camera. He frowns and points his forefinger at the camera and into the face of a female reporter interviewing him.

'No compensation for the dead farmer. No need whatsoever. It is all a big, fat fraud.'

The steel in the man's eye turns Katya's heart cold. Not only will he crush Gayatribai, this man is going to break her boy's heart. He will break his will and optimism. She feels an urge to walk up to him and spit in his face, right here, for the television cameras and the whole world to see. Instead, she follows the point at which the man has focused his eye, unmoving, unflinching.

He is looking at Gayatribai. This man, this bastard, is looking at a widow who stands with her daughter and other female relatives outside the cremation grounds, and, although he is speaking in English for the rest of the world, he is sending her a clear, cruel message with his all-too-familiar look.

But what is this thing Gayatribai is doing? She is staring right back. If the man has steel in his eyes, she has iron in her jaw. Her arms are crossed across her chest. Her feet are planted firmly on the ground. The vermilion is gone from her hair, but her brow seems to be making a statement all its own.

Katya tugs at Kabir's hand and, once again ducking away from camera crews, she walks over to Gayatribai. The woman looks at them and her expression changes. Her face is wide open. She throws a quick look at the people around them and then pulls Katya and Kabir aside.

'That man,' she says. 'Not Mr Sachin Patekar, but the man next to him.'

'Yes?' Katya says, straining her neck to look at a shorter man, standing a few paces behind the camera-hogging chief agriculture officer.

'He . . .' Gayatribai's voice trails away.

'Oh my God,' Kabir says. His fingers grow tight around Katya's hand. 'Isn't he . . . the man from the godown?' Kabir says. Katya feels her heart tighten in her chest. She starts to shake.

Katya springs forward, towards the man Kabir and Gayatribai are looking at. In the next instant, her thoughts halt her. Also stopping her are both Kabir and Gayatribai's hands. They pull her back.

'No,' the woman says. 'I still don't want to make this matter open. Never. Not for any purpose. My daughter is here, after just one day of being married. My husband . . . is still in embers . . . and there is work to be done. All this will bring too much noise. It will drown out the slogans rising here. I don't need that type of revenge.'

In this moment, Katya needs to beat back this rising sense of helplessness. This is a moment in which a clear thought can settle in her head, if only she quells the despair.

And it does. 'The whole world doesn't need to know,' she says quietly. 'Only the enemy does. The enemy needs to make a statement right now, in front of the cameras.'

She tells Gayatribai about her small plan. The woman's brow deepens for a moment. Looking from Katya to Kabir, Gayatribai slowly nods. Both women know there is a small chance their plan will go awry. Both women feel it won't.

Katya turns to Kabir. 'If I move into that mêlée, the cameras will swoop into a close-up. If it's you, they won't pay any attention.'

'Because I am the colour of mud?' Kabir says, laughing softly.

'Yes, my love. Because you are the colour of mud.'

They watch as the boy bounds over to Mr Sachin Patekar. To the television crews, it looks as if a local boy, with dirty knees and ratty hair, is distracting the government official. The cameras take a break.

The man looks startled. He looks over at Gayatribai and Katya. The steel fades into a frown.

Kabir snaps his fingers and beckons at the man to lean down so Kabir can whisper into his ear. Contempt and curiosity mix in the man's expression. As he listens, all masks fall . . . and, just as the women had expected, his face is pure panic.

It's as if they can read his thoughts. No, he doesn't want the television crews to be told that his right-hand man, standing alongside him, is a rapist. Even if the government officials could stamp out those allegations within a week, that week would bear heavy upon him. These press reporters . . . they are unpredictable. And his bosses . . . they have been watching his office closely for a while. The police would have to investigate. And who knows where else a simple rape investigation may lead?

He looks over at the clutch of women standing across from him. Of course, he doesn't see that they have no plan to actually carry out their threat. Of course, he doesn't know that if he challenges them, they will deny everything and dismiss it as a fourteen-year-old boy's wild and irresponsible imagination.

What the man sees is the group of women who stood up in the fields and chanted. What he sees is a vile woman from the Western world, who claims to be a witness to the rape and who would know how to spin this. What he sees is women who seem to be unfettered by feelings of shame—how could they have told this boy about something as shameful as rape? If women lose the fear of shame, what might they do next? What he sees is a farmer staring right back at him with a reckless gaze. *She has nothing to lose!*

Kabir tugs at the man's hand. He thrusts his chin towards the television crews, a gesture he has learned in these past weeks. 'Hello, hello,' the man says to the reporters. The cameras turn back towards him. The man clears his throat.

'Hello, I would like to make a correction. Certain factualities have been raised to my attention. It appears that Bajirao . . . Mr Bajirao Andhale, the farmer who committed suicide, qualifies for all forty criteria for compensation for his death. The money shall be paid into the bank account of . . . will be paid in full . . . to his widow, farmer Gayatribai Andhale.'

'When?' a reporter shouts.

Katya feels like going over and hugging the young male reporter who has asked the question. Yes, she will continue to teach young reporters in her classes how to ask the right question at the right time.

'These things are taking some time,' the man says, clearing his throat. 'But . . . we government officers have our ways of putting some things on a priority basis. We will make the payment tomorrow morning.'

The other man from his office has recovered from his shock. He now tries to murmur to Mr Sachin Patekar.

'You shut up!' Mr Sachin Patekar says to him. The man springs back, his eyes wide with fright.

The cameras take this in. More questions rise up in a flurry. Mr Sachin Patekar answers one or two. Gradually, when the camera crews have wandered away, he turns around. Patekar walks up to where Gayatribai and Katya are standing with Kabir.

Gayatribai crosses her arms on her chest again, but Katya can hear her breath grow short. Katya's mind starts to race. What is she to do if Patekar threatens to reveal what Gayatribai wants to keep private?

Mr Sachin Patekar brings the palms of his hands together.

He stops a couple of feet away from Gayatribai. He clears his throat and says, 'Tai . . . I . . . I had no idea. I didn't know I was keeping serpents in my care. What that man did . . . I have only heard rumours about these things. I did not know these things were true. I did not know that these men were soiling the pride of Maharashtra. Please . . . forgive me. I do not like what the farmers are doing by jumping into suicide. But I cannot bear what these serpents are doing to the ladies. Please tell my sisters I will move heaven and earth to make it stop.'

Just like that, Mr Sachin Patekar turns around and shuffles his feet away. He spits on the ground. Away from the television cameras and with no fanfare at all, Mr Sachin Patekar has left two women from different worlds stunned.

22

Immigrant Song

TWENTY-TWO MILES north of Dhanpur, the hospital waiting room has an espresso machine quite like the one Katya has seen in the dean's office in Seattle. Around the machine are recent issues of *Time*, *Vogue* and *Cosmopolitan*. On top of the four end-tables made of teak inlaid with ivory are crystal plates laden with cashew biscuits. A tall scented candle fills the room with the aroma of geraniums, and the dim lighting spotlights paintings of Swiss landscapes. A 48-inch plasma-screen television is set to CNN, but the volume is turned down to a low hum.

No one in the waiting room seems to want to help themselves to the cashew biscuits. They trust the doctors here, not the snacks. A young man from Boise, Idaho, waits for his mother to come out of hip replacement surgery. An elderly woman from Baton Rouge, Louisiana, shares photographs of her grandchildren. She is here for her husband's colon cancer surgery. The next time they are here for any treatment, she says, she will bring the grandchildren along, so they could go to the rides at the water park nearby.

'Did you say a *water park*?' Kabir says. 'In this district? Near Dhanpur?'

'Yes, dear, haven't you been? You must get your mother to take you,' the woman says, smiling cheerily at Katya.

'Where do they get the water?' Kabir says, to no one in particular. The people in the room look at him, wondering why a teenage boy would be interested in that detail.

Katya is seated across from an Indian man who keeps glancing over at Kabir and her. Katya has done a fine job so far of not meeting his eye as she leafs through magazines and speaks in whispers to Kabir every now and then. But the old lady's comment directed at her makes her look up, and she absently catches the man's eye now.

He speaks immediately. 'Mother, or father?'

Katya frowns.

The man continues, 'Who is admitted here? What procedure? You live in America, right?' He jabs his chin in the direction of Kabir, as if to explain how he has discerned Katya lives in America. 'Brought a parent here?'

Katya shakes her head. 'No. We're here for a friend.'

'What procedure?'

'Lung cancer surgery.'

'Smoking?'

'Passive.'

'Ah, the worst kind. No fun.'

After a pause, during which Katya and Kabir exchange a quick glance, the man speaks again, 'Staying at one of the villas here?'

'Villas?' Katya says, testily.

'You don't know about the villas? The ones with the twenty-four-hour maid service? Who was your tour operator?'

Kabir steps in. 'We're staying at the village of Dhanpur. We're here with our friend, Gayatribai. You must have heard of her. She's an activist.'

Katya thus has enough time to slip deeper into her reading, or, really, her peering at the words in front of her, so she wouldn't have to talk to the medical tourists around her. In a way, she is grateful to them, at least for Gayatribai's case. It is because of them that this place has high standards and five-star comforts. Among the fine medical staff that draws patients from across the world is the kind surgeon who offered to do Gayatribai's surgery at a hefty discount. He has read her story in the local papers. He says Gayatribai has the kind of voice that needs to be raised, loud and clear. He would snip the cancer right out of those hearty lungs.

Kabir is still talking to the obnoxious man. Katya has no way to nudge her boy to be quiet, not without it seeming quite directly impolite. The man has asked Kabir what he means by referring to a local Marathi village woman as an 'activist'. Typical. But Kabir doesn't seem exasperated by this. He is telling the man about some of the things Gayatribai has done and will probably do when she is well again. The man is listening with a bemused look. Then, he asks Kabir, 'And you are going to leave her alone here to do it, haanh? You're off to America? How can you be sure anything will happen? Nothing will change here, you know.'

Katya glances sharply at the man. It strikes her at that very moment that his words were not very different from her own, from that day at the village pump, when she had tried to get Kabir with her on the next plane out of here.

Kabir is saying nothing. He sits back in his seat and stares at the floor. Katya doesn't need him to turn his face up to her. She knows there are tears in his eyes and he won't look up until he has fought them back.

Gayatribai's room is air-conditioned, and is darkened with curtains in a deep green. As they enter, she blinks at Kabir and Katya and tries to get out of bed. Katya rushes to her.

Kabir offers to wait outside until Gayatribai feels more comfortable.

'I want to talk to you,' Gayatribai whispers to Katya. Something in the woman's voice tells Katya this can't wait.

'Okay, but please don't strain your voice,' Katya says, sitting down by Gayatribai in the hospital bed.

'Katyabai, do you think I will be able to fight this fight?'

She knows Gayatribai isn't talking about the cancer. 'Yes,' Katya says without hesitation. 'But you needn't do it if you don't want to.'

Gayatribai seems to slip into thought. 'It will take years. Many more people will kill themselves. How will I keep working for them to stay alive? Sometimes I feel I am only a weak woman. Bajirao was strong.'

'What?' Katya says, straightening Gayatribai's blanket. 'You were always the stronger one.' She regrets her words instantly. Gayatribai's face shrinks into thought, like a weed turning dry under the sun.

'I . . .' Gayatribai says. 'I hadn't thought of it like that. We were both weak and strong in different times.'

Katya shakes her head and tears begin to well in her eyes. Why had she said that? Why had she tried to sow seeds of comparison in Gayatribai's mind? Was Katya angry at Bajirao for getting away from the clutch of her hand? For giving her the biggest failure of her life? Didn't Katya's own words to Bajirao have something to do with his descent into despair? Whatever her anger, why did she do this now to Gayatribai? What had Katya brought to this world but words, all the wrong words?

She must join her hands and plead, 'Mala maaf karaa.' Please forgive me.

Gayatribai comes back out of her thoughts. She now looks curious. She attempts a smile. She shakes her head back at Katya.

'Katyabai, please don't shame me by asking my forgiveness. I am not angry. I am grateful. I did not get a chance but I wanted to thank you for something.'

'For what?' Katya says, weakly.

'For saving my husband's life.'

Katya blinks at her. What is the woman talking about? Is she still under the influence of anaesthesia and pain medication?

'That day at the protest rally,' Gayatribai says, 'at night, when I was tending to his wounds, Bajirao told me. He heard your shouts at the protest rally. He says he could have been shot. If he hadn't put that stick down when you reminded him of Meera and me, the police could have shot him. You saved his life.'

Katya shakes her head, incredulous. 'Stop. Gayatribai, please stop. I couldn't save him. In the end . . . I couldn't save his life. I couldn't get things under control. It wasn't just the currents of the river. I think I couldn't save him because I hadn't bothered to find out what he wanted.'

'And what if he'd wanted death?' Gayatribai says.

'What?'

'Maybe I didn't realize it when I asked you to save his life. Maybe he wanted death. Maybe we had had too many years of our will being broken. Maybe it was finally too much. He must have stared too long at the cracks in our land. Sometimes, suicide is not a choice, but I think my husband chose not to live the way he was living.'

Katya looks long and hard into Gayatribai's face. The woman holds Katya's gaze steady. Katya understands just a part of what this woman, this farmer, is saying. Like the rest of the world, maybe Katya, too, had arrived too late to this story. When a quarter of a million farmers have already committed suicide, how could you lay your hands on just one more and say, 'You. You shall live . . .'?

Yet how could Gayatribai say this about her one man, her single story? Was she just trying to comfort Katya? It was maddening, all this unconditional acceptance of what was!

Gayatribai speaks after the women have sat there in a long silence. 'Katyabai, I want to say something. Shall I say it?'

Katya nods.

Gayatribai hesitates for a moment and says, 'Tumala kai pai-je?' What do you want?

Gayatribai reaches out and touches Katya's forehead and rubs a dry thumb against it, ironing away the creases there. Katya pushes her head into Gayatribai's touch. The woman now holds Katya's hand and brings it up before her face. She glances at the ring on Katya's finger. Katya is startled to see it there. She hasn't taken it off since Meera's wedding. She has longed every moment for Alec, but she hasn't called him.

'Tumcha marad?' Gayatribai says. Your husband? Katya thinks she sees Gayatribai's eyes light up beyond reason for a moment.

Katya shakes her head. She scrambles for a word she knows rests somewhere in her memory. 'Mangetar,' she says. Fiancé. And she sinks into thought again.

Gayatribai clicks her tongue. She says, in words that Katya has to race to keep up with, 'Katyabai . . . stop letting your thoughts torture you. Yes, my husband may have left me. But you . . . why do you sit thirsty by a river? Why does your face not bloom with moisture? Why do you run from the love of your man? You already know now that you can roam the world at will. I thank you and your son for walking with me so I could see that I can do it too. But now, you must take your boy and go home. Go back to the man who sits by your river.'

This is when she knows. This moment, when she knows what exactly she must do, has arrived in its full shape now, but it has been around in all those minutes falling upon days. It actually happened in that single minute when Katya missed a certain phone call made from a cell phone on a railway platform in Mumbai. The wisdom of that moment, lost in the panic of the days thereafter, now fills Katya with a throbbing clarity.

'Gayatribai,' she says, looking the woman squarely in her spectacular face. 'I don't care what you say, the truth is that I could not save your husband. But . . . I am giving you my son.'

She nods at the woman's astounded look. 'He's your son now,' she says. 'He will live here, with you, under the guardianship of his father.'

As she answers Gayatribai's questions and eases her concerns about whether the village will be good enough for the boy, Katya feels awash with peace.

She says, 'He belongs here, on the bench outside your home, not on the brick outside mine. He loves it here, where kids and cows and strangers, all come home.'

◦═◦

Outside, in the waiting room, Kabir falls upon her when she tells him. He hugs her and searches her face to see if it is clear of all doubt. He sees it is. He quickly builds a plan to live in two worlds hereafter. He would spend the next few years of his life working with Gayatribai and her 'crop circle of farmers' in the villages of Vidarbha. He would work with his Baba and find new ways to link the farmers to the government and the world beyond. He would go to the local school. Baba would make sure he stayed on track with his education.

Kabir grins, turns up the volume on his iPod and suddenly sings into his mother's face:

286

So now you'd better stop and rebuild all your ruins,
For peace and trust can win the day
Despite of all your losing.

Katya puts her hands on his mouth.

'Stop it, stop! You'll wake all the patients in the hospital,' she says, glancing at the nurse in the reception area. She pushes Kabir towards Gayatribai's room. 'Go meet that farmer and ask her if you can work as her intern,' she says.

༄

At Nagpur railway station, her hand is weak in its grip on the rung that keeps her on the train to Mumbai. Kabir and Ammar are making sure she has a comfortable seat. All these quotidian arrangements, as if they could dull the pain of parting from the one human being whom she has held as her own.

'You okay, Mom?' Kabir asks her as they wait for Ammar to fetch her clean drinking water for the journey. Ammar has a spring in his step. Of course. He now has his son by his side. And he has Katya's solidarity. Perhaps a friendship would grow from this some day? Katya can sense it will. It began with Ammar's sincere promise to her, to stay away from his 'practices of detachment' and to watch over their boy like the gentlest of hawks.

Katya leans over to Kabir and puts her chin on his head so he won't see her face. 'Well, my knee still hurts, my elbows are bruised and my heart is hurting from everything, but I am doing surprisingly well.' Her chin dips down and up with Kabir's nod. The hair on his head is a coarse magic carpet upon which her thoughts come to rest.

༄

In the summer of the following year, Katya stands up on stage once again, this time in a tiny independent bookstore in the University district of Seattle, among people who are already familiar with some of the pages of her latest book, *Bajirao's Choice: Life and Death on India's Cotton Farms*, which she has co-authored with Gayatri Andhale. The applause is slim because the subject of the book is severe. The book tour is leaving for Mumbai and Dhanpur, where farming activists from across the world will gather to build a foundation to promote sustainable irrigation projects and fair trade indigenous seed exchange. This time, Dr Katyayini Misra will travel with her partner, Alec Rauland.

Katya looks over at Alec now. She has that sensation she has grown to love, of sinking slowly, mindlessly, unthinkingly into that space where she best rests her head—that expanse of chest between Alec's east shoulder and his west, a stretch of skin and bone and muscle and heartbeat that she knows to be 'home'.

Katya's phone rings, but this time, it's not on 'silent'. They have all been waiting for this call. Kabir and Ammar have dialled up a Skype connection so that Katya's co-author, Gayatri Andhale, can answer any questions from the audience that Katya is not an expert on. But Gayatribai hasn't arrived yet. As two worlds wait across technologies, languages and cultures, Katya takes a moment to feast her eyes on the young man who stands in the shadows waiting for Gayatribai's arrival.

Kabir. Older, stronger, almost proficient in Marathi. He is looking back at her, his eyes dancing.

Six months ago, he had come back for a quick visit, to meet his mother and Alec, yes, but also to meet people from Seattle, American activists against genetically modified seeds and expatriate Indians, who had led a signature campaign on his blog and wanted to know how they could contribute to the struggle next. This teenager brought them pictures and stories and papers from all over Vidarbha. We don't need money yet, he said, translating from a letter from Gayatribai. We need pressure on the government, for subsidies. Stand in solidarity. Don't throw money at the problem. People had pledged their support for the long haul, but they had also insisted on setting up a fund, for whenever the money was needed. The proceeds from Katya and Gayatribai's book, too, would go to this fund.

All the while, Katya could only watch her boy, who now spoke in the voice of a man, and calm that deep inner voice of her own that told her to keep him here, at home, because he would never be safe in those places that had brought him harm. Then she watched as his dark head disappeared down the line of people going through Security Check at SEATAC Airport.

A messenger arrives and whispers in Ammar's ear. Gayatribai will be unable to join them. She has just received news of a death in the family. It's one of her sons-in-law. 'How did he die?', a reporter asks.

Acknowledgements

I am grateful to the people of Pandharkawada for sharing their stories with me and to Kishore Tiwari for taking me to them and for all the good work he does with the farmers' crisis. My work has also been deeply influenced by the fine journalism of P. Sainath, Dionne Bunsha, and Jaideep Hardikar. I am thankful to Seattle University for funding my research and to Hedgebrook Writers' Retreat for awarding me a residency so I could work in life-changing solitude.

Thanks are due to the astute readers of my evolving drafts —William Kupinse, Dionne Bunsha, Pamela Herbst, Tatyana Mishel, Timothy Killian, Jaideep Hardikar, Cleo Allen, Geeta Bhagat, Jennifer Fricas, Chandni Jha, Cyan James, and, especially, David Green. I am also indebted to the sharp minds of my editors Meru Gokhale and Archana Shankar at Random House India. Many friends and supporters have put their time, gifts, food and love in my corner as I wrote. Among them were Adam and Sofia Herbst. A loving thanks is due to my parents, for noticing that I liked to put word upon word, and to Chandni Jha, a sister everyone should have, for telling me to trust my characters and thereby trust myself. Finally, I reserve my deepest gratitude for my son Sahir, for so many reasons, but most of all for conferring upon his mother the title of 'idiot savant'. It's the sweetest thing anyone has ever said to me.

A Note on the Type

Minion is a digital typeface designed by Robert Slimbach in 1990 for Adobe Systems. The name comes from the traditional naming system for type sizes, in which minion is between nonpareil and brevier. It is inspired by classical typefaces of the late Renaissance, a period of elegant and highly readable type designs.